Absolutely Not in Love

Romantic Comedy by Jenny Proctor

How to Kiss a Hawthorne Brother Series
How to Kiss Your Best Friend
How to Kiss Your Grumpy Boss
How to Kiss Your Enemy
How to Kiss a Movie Star

Oakley Island Romcoms
Eloise and the Grump Next Door
Merritt and Her Childhood Crush

Some Kind of Love Series
Love Redesigned
Love Unexpected
Love Off-Limits
Love in Bloom

JENNY PROCTOR

For Josh

Felix is pretty much a dream guy,
and he was absolutely inspired by you.

CHAPTER ONE
Gracie

HOCKEY HAS A VERY distinct smell. Or at least, hockey gear.

I would recognize the stench anywhere, but *why* am I smelling it in my apartment building?

I drop my bag onto the landing at the top of the stairs and survey the short hallway that leads to my front door.

There isn't a square inch of available walking space. The *entire* hallway is covered with hockey gear.

Skates, pads, hockey sticks. Helmets. Bags overflowing with jerseys.

What *is* all this stuff? And *why* does it smell so terrible?

My neighbor plays for the Appies, Harvest Hollow's minor league hockey team, but the last time I checked, he didn't bring his gear home. I've definitely never seen it in the hallway. Besides, there's enough gear here to outfit an entire team.

The more pressing concern: there's no way I can get to my apartment—at least not carrying my cello.

With a *very* annoyed sigh, I reach for the closest hockey stick and use it to bang on Felix's wall. His apartment is the first of two on the same side of the hallway, mine being the second, but there's so much stuff piled up, I can't even get to *his* door so I can knock like a civilized human. But there's nothing about this particular situation that feels civilized, so I'm okay with the compromise.

"Felix!" I yell, hopefully loud enough for him to hear me. I bang a few more times for good measure.

Is there truly *no* getting away from hockey in my life? It's not enough that my brother played through our *entire* childhood, sucking up all our parents' time and attention with his games and practices and never-ending weekend tournaments? Now I have to wade through a landfill of used hockey gear just to get to my front door?

Does the universe have no compassion?

Felix's door slides open and he appears, one hand braced against the door jamb, concern filling his expression. "Gracie? What's wrong? Are you okay? I heard you yell."

A bead of water drips off of Felix's hair and lands on his chest—his *very bare* chest—then continues its journey south.

My eyes track the movement, sliding down Felix's toned, athletic body until I realize—*oh good grief.* The man isn't wearing more than a pair of black boxer briefs.

I swallow, taking in the dips and curves of his muscular frame. My eye snags on the shadow of what I *think* is a tattoo on the inside of Felix's left bicep. I swallow against the sudden dryness in my throat. It's not that I haven't noticed that Felix is handsome. He's a six-foot-four professional athlete. There's no *missing* anything about him, no matter how quiet he is. But I've known he was a hockey player from day one. That's all the motivation I've needed to avoid truly looking.

Me and hockey? It's never been a good combination. See: aforementioned hockey-filled childhood.

But my eyeballs seem to have an agenda all their own, hijacking my brain for a solid fifteen seconds while I stare.

But no. *No! No staring, brain!*

I give my head a little shake and finally lift my eyes to the ceiling.

"Geez, Felix, you could have put on some pants," I finally say.

He looks down and winces, then jumps behind his door. "Sorry. I'm sorry!" he says from just inside his apartment. "I was getting dressed when you banged, and then I just...*ran*. I thought you were hurt."

My heart stretches the tiniest bit. Something about his concern feels sweet. And the fact that he didn't *intentionally* answer his door half-clothed makes him seem much less...I don't know, arrogant? Though Felix has never really struck me as arrogant. Not like his one teammate—Eli, I think?—who has turned knocking on my door to ask me out into a frequently repeated joke. Well, a joke to him. To me, it's just annoying.

I breathe out a sigh. "Not hurt. Just stranded. What *is* all this stuff?"

"Give me a second," he calls, his voice distant as he moves farther into his apartment.

A minute later, he's back, wearing a pair of joggers and a plain white T-shirt, already dotted with water from his still-damp hair. "It's old gear the team brought over," he says. "I'm taking it over to the youth hockey league tomorrow." He picks up two enormous bags and hauls them into his apartment, making them look entirely too light. He lifts a bundle of hockey sticks, holding them under one arm, then grabs a helmet that rolled over to my door. "I'm sorry. I thought I had enough time to shower and get all this inside before you got home."

I inch my cello case forward as he clears the gear away. "It's fine," I say, though my tone sounds prickly and sharp.

His gaze narrows. "You sure?"

"Positive. You possibly triggered a little post-hockey-childhood traumatic stress, but I'll get over it."

"You played hockey?" he says, his eyebrows lifting.

"Ha! No. Definitely not. But my brother played. And trust me—he spent enough time on the ice for both of us." I lean my cello against the wall and lift a bag, shifting it closer to Felix's door.

"So *he's* the reason you hate hockey players so much."

An image of Gavin, my first real boyfriend and the only one who ever played hockey, flits through my brain. If any one person is to blame for turning me off to hockey players, it's him. But my opposition runs much deeper than just one poorly behaved idiot high schooler. "I don't *hate* hockey players. I just hate hockey. There's a difference."

Felix moves the last bit of gear away from my door, clearing the way for me to carry my cello down the hall. "Want me to get that for you?" he asks as he steps out of the way.

I shake my head as I swing my cello onto my back. "It's fine. I've had a lot of practice." I unlock my door but pause and turn back around before sliding it open and going inside. This close to Felix's door, I can hear whatever music he's playing inside. "Is that Tchaikovsky?"

He nods and runs a hand through his hair. "*Variations on a Rococo Theme.*"

I nod. "Yeah. I know it." I performed it as a soloist with my college orchestra senior year.

This isn't the first time Felix has mentioned classical music, but it's always been in a general way. A passing compliment on something he's heard me practicing through the wall or a question about what the symphony is playing next. But I thought he was just being nice.

This feels different. He's actually *listening* to classical music? *For fun?*

He folds his arms over his chest and leans his shoulder against the wall beside his door, his feet crossed at the ankles. "So, hating hockey. Is that why you haven't agreed to go out with Eli?"

I roll my eyes. "I don't want to go out with Eli because he's too cocky for his own good, though the hockey doesn't help. It's a pretty firm policy for me."

"You don't date hockey players?" There's a hint of something in his voice that almost sounds like disappointment, and I half-wonder if I'm imagining it. Maybe he's just disappointed for Eli's sake?

"Nope," I say, pushing the thought aside. Either way, it doesn't matter. "I spent enough time in a hockey rink the first eighteen years of my life to last a lifetime."

"Watching your brother," Felix says, and I nod.

More like *resenting* my brother while I pretended to watch. But that's more family drama than I care to discuss with my neighbor.

"I'm glad to learn this about you," Felix says. "Everything makes so much more sense now."

I slide my door open and put my cello inside, then mirror his posture, leaning my shoulder against the wall. "What does that mean? What makes more sense?"

He shrugs. "How hard you work to avoid me. Or how much you frown and roll your eyes whenever my teammates come over."

"Your teammates are *loud*," I say. "Loud and cocky and...big."

He smirks. "I'll give you loud and cocky, but big?"

"Humongous," I say. "And..." I struggle to find the right word, but then it pops into my head and makes so much sense, I can't believe I've never used it before. "*Wild*."

Felix smiles, revealing a dimple I've never seen before. "Wild?"

I purse my lips, not liking that he finds this so amusing. "I know hockey players, Felix. I grew up surrounded by them, and they're definitely *wild*. What else would make someone strap knives to their feet and skate around on rock-hard ice knowing full well they're going to get pummeled over and over again? It's insane."

In my experience, that same wildness crosses over into every aspect of hockey players' lives—something Cheater Mc-Cheaterpants Gavin proved loud and clear—and it's not a wildness I want in *my* life.

Felix holds my gaze for a long moment, then he ducks his head the slightest bit. "I guess you've got us all figured out," he says.

The fervor evident in my words only moments before evaporates in a second. The tone of Felix's words—he sounds hurt. And I'm definitely not imagining it this time.

Before I can truly process or apologize, he steps back into his apartment. "Sorry again about earlier," he says. He slides his door halfway closed. "Good night, Gracie." Then his door closes and locks, and I'm alone in the hallway.

Huh. Alone and feeling like that conversation did *not* end how it should have.

I move into my apartment and drop onto the couch feeling out of sorts. It's Friday, so I'm tired anyway. But now I'm tired *and* grouchy and wishing I could rewind the last five minutes of conversation and do them over again.

It's not like I didn't mean what I said. I have zero desire to have a relationship with a hockey player. But hockey is Felix's *profession.* I could have been nicer about it.

I groan and kick off my shoes, then curl up on my couch. I could honestly just go to sleep right here and not wake up until tomorrow morning.

In my dictionary, tired has two definitions. There's *regular* tired. The kind of tired I feel after I go on a run or finish a really strenuous symphony rehearsal.

Then there's *teacher* tired.

This tired doesn't compare to anything else on the planet. Because it isn't just my muscles or my mind that are worn out. It's my muscles...and my brain and my emotions and my nerves. Not to mention my ego.

Middle schoolers are sweet most of the time, but when they aren't? They are literal demon spawn.

Miss Mitchell, are you a size bigger than you were last year?

Miss Mitchell, why don't you have a boyfriend?

Do you think you'll EVER get married?

Did you forget to fix your hair this morning?

Have you been wearing that ALL DAY?

Most weekends—at least weekends that aren't symphony weekends—all I want to do is crawl into my pajamas, order enough take-out to last me three days, watch mindless television, and forget I have to go back to work on Monday morning.

It's fine. *I'm fine.* I love my job. Teaching orchestra at Harvest Hollow Middle was my actual dream job when I was in college. I won't begrudge it now. But it does make me appreciate weekends and summers.

I pull a blanket off the back of the couch and spread it over me, debating how hungry I am. Popcorn and Coke Zero hungry? Or for real actual dinner hungry? I'm definitely not cooking, so if I'm eating real food, it's gonna be something delivered to my doorstep.

My purse is on the floor beside the coffee table, so I stick out my foot, tugging it closer so I can grab my phone. These are the lengths I will go to to *not* move my body any more than absolutely necessary.

Phone in hand, I check my bank account balance, groaning when I see a number in the very low three digits. It's not like I'm surprised. I'm a teacher with a side gig as a musician. No one does either job if they have expectations of wealth or grandeur. All of my bills are paid for the month, so I'm not truly at risk of running out of money before my paycheck hits next week. But I still can't justify splurging for takeout.

I sigh and pull myself off my couch and head toward the freezer, suddenly wondering what Felix is doing for dinner.

Which is ridiculous. I've rarely given my neighbor more than a passing thought.

I've also never seen him in his underwear.

But *still*. Abdominal muscles notwithstanding, Felix is just as much of a hockey player now as he was yesterday, so there should be *no* thoughts, passing or otherwise, dedicated to him.

I pull a pizza out of the freezer and preheat the oven, leaning against the counter while I wait. I missed a call from my brother while I was talking to Felix, so I call him back, knowing he'll try at least ten more times tonight if I don't.

"Gracie!" he says when he answers the phone. "How's my favorite little sister?"

"She's tired and grumpy and she's also your *only* little sister. How are you?"

"Fantastic. I just scored sweet seats for the Appies game next week. Just above the glass, so we'll be close enough to feel the speed of the game, but high enough for Maddox to see everything. He's gonna love it."

I pull the pizza out of the cardboard box and peel off the plastic. "Sounds thrilling."

"You're still coming to his party, right?"

I shake my head at Josh's enthusiasm. His son's tenth birthday is still a month away, and he's already asked me no less than five times if I'm going to make it to the party.

"Josh. It's on my calendar. I'm not going to miss the party."

"I know, I know. But he's turning *ten,* Gracie. Double digits! It's a big deal."

It still feels crazy to me that Maddox is almost ten years old. Almost as crazy as it is that Josh took to fatherhood so easily. He was nineteen when he found out his girlfriend of two years was pregnant. And even though it derailed his plans to play pro hockey—he played half a season in college and was headed that direction—he didn't think twice about dropping out of college and moving back to Harvest Hollow. He and Jadah got married, he started an apprenticeship with Jadah's father, a local electrician Josh still works for, and dedicated himself to being "the father his baby deserved." Those were *his* words when he was nineteen, and he's lived by them every day since.

"Has Maddox given any more thought to the cello?" I ask. I've been trying to convince my nephew to play—he'll be at Harvest Hollow Middle next year, and I'd love to have him in class—but so far, he's been about as enthusiastic as I am about hockey.

"Nah. He says he's okay learning an instrument, but he wants it to be something cool like the drums," Josh says.

"So you're saying I *shouldn't* give him my old cello as a birthday present."

"I'm not saying you *can't,*" Josh says. "I'm just saying...he might not like it."

"Fine," I say as I slide the pizza into the oven. "I give up. No more cello talk. What should I get him instead?"

"He's on a huge Felix Jamison kick right now," Josh says. "Maybe pick up one of his jerseys?"

I jerk when he mentions Felix's name, and my hand bangs against the top of the oven, burning my knuckle.

"Ouch!" I say, followed by a couple of expletives that make me hope Josh doesn't have me on speakerphone. Though, with the way he's talking about Maddox's birthday present, it's unlikely my nephew is within hearing range.

"You okay?" Josh asks. "What did you do?"

"I just burned my hand. I'm okay." I turn on the sink and run cold water over my knuckles. "So, a jersey?" I ask, feigning ignorance. "An Appies jersey?"

"Yeah. Jamison. He's the goaltender, and that's the position Maddox wants to play, so he's totally obsessed right now. He's got his poster on his wall and everything."

I close my eyes. *Of course* my nephew has my neighbor's poster on his wall.

And *of course,* if my brother knew that I share a living room wall with the one hockey player his son is obsessed with, he would lose his mind and insist he come over and meet Felix, and then he would try and be Felix's best friend, and it would probably work because Josh is *everyone's* best friend, and then he would be over ALL THE TIME talking about hockey.

And then my perfect apartment, with its high ceilings and enormous windows and exposed ductwork that feels modern and cool and exactly like the kind of place a musician should live would become *overrun* with even *more* hockey energy than it already has, and this time it would be personal because it would be *my brother.*

It's so easy to imagine it happening.

But this is my oasis. I can't let Josh into my oasis.

I turn off the water and dry my hand. It's red, but it doesn't look like it'll blister. "What kind of books is Maddox reading? Maybe I'll get him some books."

"Yeah? That'd be cool," Josh says. "I'll ask Jadah. She knows more about books than I do."

"K. Just tell her to text me. And I can ask the librarian at the school what she recommends too."

"Hey, speaking of Jadah, she's teaching tomorrow morning, and she's making me go with her. Want to come? Please don't make me hot yoga by myself."

I roll my eyes. "You're such a wimp."

"I'm not a wimp. I'm going, aren't I? I just don't like to suffer in solitude."

I pull a Coke Zero out of the fridge, pressing the cold can against the burned spot on my knuckle. "What time is she teaching? If you say anything before nine a.m., I'm out. It's the weekend. I'm not getting up before school hours on the weekend."

He's silent for a beat before he says, "It's at six-thirty. But I promise I'll buy you breakfast after. Maddox is staying with Mom and Dad tonight, so we can go by and pick him up after class, then he can come eat with us. You can talk to him about books yourself."

I groan. Josh knows exactly what to say to make me cave. Breakfast with just him I'd skip in a minute. But breakfast with

Maddox? Even if it means stopping by Mom and Dad's, which isn't nearly as much fun for me as it is for Josh, I'm a sucker for my nephew, and Josh knows it.

"Ugh. Fine. But it better not be fast food breakfast. And not Waffle House, either. I want something good."

"Deal. I'll pick you up at 6:15."

"I can just meet you there if that's easier."

"Nah. I'll be driving past your scary apartment anyway. But don't make me come up for you. I don't want to get mugged on my way in."

I roll my eyes. "It's *not* scary. I'm perfectly safe here." Not that I have any intention of ever letting Josh come inside. He might run into Felix, and that's not a risk I'm willing to take.

"If you say so. But you have to admit the boarded-up windows on the first floor make the place look like a crime scene."

I've wondered myself what's on the ground floor of the building where I've been living for the past six months. There's an enormous door at the foot of the stairs, but it's locked and heavy, and Josh is right about all the exterior windows. They've been boarded up since I moved in.

I keep meaning to ask the landlord—removing the boards would at least help with curb appeal—but I keep forgetting. Probably because once I'm *inside* my apartment, everything is perfect and I stop caring what the outside looks like.

"I promise there has been zero crime since I moved in."

I don't mention the enormous hockey player who sleeps in the apartment next door, but a flash of Felix's concerned expression when he barreled into the hallway still crosses my mind. Something tells me he *would* come to my rescue should I happen to need one.

Hockey player or not, he just seems like that kind of guy.

Not that I care *what* kind of guy Felix is. I don't. I also don't care about how good he looked. All that smooth, toned skin. The dimple in his cheek. The tattoo I definitely *don't* wish I could see up close. The fact that he named a Tchaikovsky piece like it was no big deal.

Nope. I don't care one. single. bit.

CHAPTER TWO
Felix

"Hey, Felix," Eli calls from across the locker room. "You up for dinner?" With practice over, the locker room has mostly cleared out by now, though that's typical. I tend to take my time showering. I don't mind hanging out with the guys, so I'm not avoiding them on purpose. But let's just say I don't mind the quiet, either.

Eli and our newest team member, Logan, who just dropped down from the NHL to work through some bad press after an altercation with a fan, are the only two guys still around. Eli's company is tolerable enough, and I like Logan, but dinner?

I pull on my hoodie, buying myself a few extra seconds to deliberate. I already had dinner with a few teammates once this week. That feels like a pretty solid effort.

It's a careful balance.

If I yield to my first impulse, I'll go home to my empty apartment, eat in silence, then spend the night reading and relaxing on my own.

But I'm self-aware enough—read: I've been to enough therapy—to realize that if I ever want to have *more* in my life, I won't find it living like a recluse. So I go out with my teammates. Have dinner with friends. Make a conscious effort to interact with my community.

And I'm not doing half bad.

I've been with the Appies going on two years, and my teammates feel like friends as much as they do fellow players. And Harvest Hollow has grown on me. I have favorite restaurants, a preferred place to grab coffee. I even know people who aren't on my hockey team, which is saying something, considering how much we travel.

This might not seem significant for the average person, but for me, every ounce of normal I claim is noteworthy. My social anxiety has been a looming threat for me since I was a kid. It's only therapy that has given me the ability to function normally; as long as I keep my world small, intentional, I can function without anyone else even knowing it's an issue.

But it's always in the back of my mind. I've developed a sort of internal barometer that's constantly measuring, weighing, asking the question. How am I *really* doing?

If I let myself go home instead of saying yes to dinner with Eli, am I only letting myself hide? Or have I earned a night in?

I think of my neighbor and the run-in we had last week. I've been hoping to see her again, preferably while I'm wearing more than just my underwear.

A wave of embarrassment washes over me at the memory. I'd just showered and was in the process of getting dressed when she yelled from the hallway. A shot of adrenaline fired through me at the sound, and I didn't even think. I just ran.

Not that I minded when her eyes roved over me. Gracie has never given me a second glance. I'd rather not date a woman who only wants me for my body, but if seeing me shirtless makes her notice me when she never has before? I'll take it. I work hard enough to stay in shape. Might as well reap the benefits, however they come.

A desire to see Gracie feels like a pretty solid reason to head home. Even my therapist wouldn't argue if it meant the possibility of me dating someone.

"Nah, not tonight," I say, finally answering Eli. "I'm, uh, meeting Ivy." Not exactly a lie. Ivy is what I call my library. It's my favorite part of my apartment. It deserves a name.

Logan scoffs, and I look over to meet his eye. He's the only guy on the team who knows who Ivy really is. Or *what* Ivy really is, I guess. He's also the only one who knows anything about my anxiety. Which is weird, since he's the newest member of the team. We connected pretty fast, though. Plus, he's dating Parker, the team's social media manager. The nature of her job required me to be honest with her about what I can and can't handle when it comes to team promo stuff, so telling Logan felt like a natural extension of that.

"Seriously, when are we gonna meet this woman?" Eli asks.

"Yeah, Felix," Logan echoes. "When are we going to meet her?"

I drop down onto the bench and pull on my shoes. "Ivy likes her privacy."

Logan rolls his eyes, then claps Eli on the back, saying something to him that I can't hear. Eli nods and heads out the door, and Logan moves toward me.

"Seriously?" he says, dropping onto the bench beside me. "You have to meet *Ivy*?"

I lift my hands. "I swear it isn't personal."

"You don't owe me any explanations, man. You can spend your time however you want." Logan pauses. "Just...you okay?" His expression is serious, like he's *really* asking and would sit here as long as it took for me to give him a real answer.

"I'm good," I say, meeting his gaze head-on. "Just want to get home."

Logan doesn't say anything, but I can tell by his expression that he wants more of an explanation.

I sigh and run a hand across my beard. "I'm just...hoping I'll run into my neighbor." Now that I've said it out loud, I realize how stupid it sounds, and wish I could call back the words.

I only have one neighbor, and Logan has met her, so he knows exactly who I'm talking about. "The neighbor who doesn't like hockey players?" he says, raising his eyebrows.

"She doesn't like *hockey*," I clarify. "That's not the same thing."

"Right," Logan says dryly. "Totally different."

"She did tell me she doesn't *date* hockey players though," I add a little sheepishly. "So, maybe it *is* the same thing."

Logan chuckles. "*Why* are we having this conversation again?"

Good question. All I know is I get more excited about the prospect of running into Gracie than I do anyone else I've met in Harvest Hollow. And I could listen to her practicing her cello all night long. The first time I heard cello music drifting through our shared living room wall, I thought it was a recording. I didn't realize it was *her* until she started and stopped a few times, going over the same measure multiple times. I ended up moving one of the armchairs in my living room up against the wall so I could sit and read and still be close enough to hear her.

"I don't know, man," I say. "I'm a glutton for punishment, I guess."

I stand and grab my bag.

"You know, maybe your *neighbor* needs to meet Ivy." He grabs his bag from his locker a few paces away, then gives me a pointed look. "I saw her at Book Smart the other night. At least I think it was her. If she's into books, your library might make her forget you play hockey."

"Book Smart?" I ask, and he nods.

"The bookstore on Maple Street. You've never been there? Dude, come on. You? I thought it'd be your favorite place."

We head toward the door together. "Call it self-preservation. I'm out of shelf space."

"Yeah. And your apartment is so cramped, there's definitely no room for a new shelf."

My lips twitch. The guys like to tease me about my spacious apartment—minor league hockey players aren't exactly rolling in extra cash—but they'd never let me live it down if they knew the actual truth.

I can afford my apartment because I own the entire building.

I bought it a year ago using money from my grandmother's trust fund. My original plan was to have my apartment fill the entire top floor, but Gracie's apartment was already outfitted as living space, and I decided it might be nice to have a little rental income coming in to help with property taxes. Originally, the building was home to Sheffield Family Publishing. They printed elementary school textbooks, early readers, that sort of thing. Pretty sure the managing editor lived in what's now Gracie's apartment, right up until the company went under in the early 2000s. My apartment is much larger than hers, occupying the whole of the space that held the actual printing presses. I kept the original flooring in the living room, and you can still see ink stains marring the wide, wooden planks.

I get how it sounds. People hear *trust fund* and think I must be loaded. Or worse—they meet my father and make the same assumption. But the trust fund my grandmother left me is paltry compared to the kind of money my father makes. He's in real estate development in Chicago, where I grew up, and owns what feels like half the city. Had I gone into business with him, my name would be on the deeds of a lot more than just one building, and my bank account balance would have a lot more numbers before the decimal point.

I also wouldn't be playing hockey. So. There's that.

Despite my father's disappointment over every single professional choice I've ever made, I'm happy where I am. A minor league hockey salary is not impressive, but I invested what was left of my trust fund after I bought the building, and I earn enough interest to live comfortably if not extravagantly. Plus, I have future business plans for the first floor of the warehouse. It's on hold until the off-season, but I'm still excited about it.

"I could probably add a few extra shelves in the guest bedroom," I say. "You really think Gracie likes books?"

Logan holds up his hands. "All I know is I saw her in a bookstore. Want me to ask Parker if she knows her? If Gracie grew up around here, she might." Even though Logan and Parker's relationship is relatively new, they both grew up in Harvest Hollow, and they've known each other for years—since they were kids.

"You don't have to do that. Or...you could, I guess," I say. "But only if it comes up."

"It's not a big deal. I'll just ask her. Do you know her last name? And what else do you know about her?"

I groan, wondering if I'm going to regret this. "Not much. Her name is Gracie Mitchell. She teaches orchestra at Harvest Hollow Middle. She plays the cello. And she hates hockey," I add, almost as an afterthought.

"Got it," Logan says, already typing something into his phone. "I'll let you know what she says." He slips his phone into his pocket just as we reach the parking lot. The outside air is crisp and cool and officially feels like fall. Not the fake fall that often happens in the South when summer disappears for three days, then comes back with a vengeance. But actual, for real fall. The kind that isn't going anywhere.

My hoodie is warm, but I'm still wishing for something a little warmer.

"Any idea *why* she hates hockey?" Logan asks.

"I only know that her brother played," I say. "She made it seem like her family spent a lot of time supporting him."

Logan scratches his chin. "You said her last name is Mitchell?" His brow furrows, then he stops at the edge of the parking lot. "Wait. I think I know her brother. Josh Mitchell. He was a great wing. *Man*, I haven't thought about him in

years. I wonder what happened to him. I thought for sure he'd
play college, maybe even go pro."

"Yeah? He was that good?"

"In high school he was, but that doesn't always mean anything. But I'll for sure ask Parker. She'll probably know."

We part ways in the parking lot, and I drive home via Maple
Street so I can check out the bookstore. I don't go inside, but
it looks like the kind of place I'd enjoy hanging out, so I make a
mental note to return some weekend when I've got extra time
to kill. Now that the season's officially starting, I won't have
many of those, but I'll take what I can get.

Gracie's Honda is already parked in her spot when I pull in
my Audi beside it. It's ridiculous how happy this makes me.
I was *fine* before last weekend. But now that I've admitted
the possibility of actually liking her, it's like my brain kicked
into fifth gear and turned me into a sweating, nervous mid-
dle-schooler.

What do I even plan to do? Knock on her door just to say
hi? Unless she happens to be coming out when I'm going in, I
probably won't even see her.

I consider my options as I lock my car and head toward the
warehouse door, stopping on the sidewalk outside to check my
mail.

I could...make dinner and knock on her door, offering her
the extra. Or I could ask to borrow an egg or a cup of milk
or something. Maybe I could play my music too loud, hoping
she'll come over to ask me to turn it down?

I open my mailbox and pull out several days' worth of mail.
Since there are only two of us who live here, we use traditional

black mailboxes, lined up side by side just to the right of the heavy warehouse door.

I riffle through the stack of letters, and—*yes.*

Our mailman is my new favorite person. I've got two pieces of Gracie's mail. It would only be neighborly to return them to her in person.

I take the stairs two at a time, my heart already pounding.

I can do this. It isn't a big deal. I have her mail. She needs her mail. That's all this is.

The excitement rushing through me almost feels foreign for how long it's been since I've felt something similar. I've dated a little since moving to Harvest Hollow. But I've never had a relationship last longer than a few dates. My semi-awkwardness makes it tough. Hockey makes it tougher. With the way we travel during the season, it's hard to see anyone seriously, and I'm not really into the casual hookups a lot of the other guys look for when we're on the road.

It's not lost on me that I'm only days away from our first pre-season home game. We'll have a week of training after that, then a weekend tournament in Atlanta before we're back in Harvest Hollow for our official season opener. After that, I'll be on the road as much as I'm home.

But if I use that as a reason not to try with a woman, I'll *never try.* Not until I stop playing hockey, and that feels too lonely and depressing to consider.

A few guys on the team maintain relationships, and some of them are even married. If I want this, I have to just go for it.

I drop my bag onto the floor outside my door and take two more steps to Gracie's. I lift my fist, knocking quickly before wiping my palm on the leg of my joggers. It's only then that I realize I'm still holding all *my* mail along with hers, so I turn and toss mine toward my bag. Instead of landing in one place, the mail scatters like confetti in the wind, landing all over the narrow hallway outside our apartments.

I swear under my breath, then turn to pick it up, dropping Gracie's mail in the process.

I'm half-crouched, butt facing Gracie's door, when she slides it open.

"Felix?" she says.

"Hey," I say, quickly standing up and dropping the letters I was gathering. I spin to face her. "I have your mail."

I don't, actually, have her mail. Or *any* mail. All of it is still on the floor.

She looks around the hallway, a question in her eyes. "You do?"

"Yeah, it's—sorry. I dropped it all. But there are a couple of things here that are yours." I crouch down and start gathering up the mail—*again*—and try not to think about how much of an idiot I am. "Right. Here we go. Gracie Mitchell." I hold out the letters. "These two are yours."

She takes the letters, slowly looking over them before she looks back at me, her eyebrows raised. "Wow. An advertisement from a local orthodontist and a new credit card offer. I don't know what I would have done without these," she says, humor in her tone.

Heat floods my cheeks. "Right. I mean, sure. I knew it was junk mail. But it had your name on it. It felt wrong to just throw it away. I'm pretty sure that would be a felony anyway."

She leans against the door frame and taps the letters into her palm, studying me closely, a smile playing around her lips.

It's only then that I truly take in what she's wearing. She's dressed all in black. Fitted pants with a tuxedo stripe down the leg, a sheer black top over a black tank top, and heels. Her dark hair is loose around her shoulders, and her brown eyes look bigger than usual. Maybe because she's wearing more makeup? She looks amazing. Like, *take my breath away* amazing.

"You know," she says, and I force myself to focus on her words. "When I get your mail, I just stick it in your mailbox."

I swallow. "Right. Yeah. I can do that next time." I take a step backward toward my apartment.

"Thank you though," she says. "I appreciate you bringing it by."

I manage a nod, but really I just want to escape so I can lament my poor social choices in private. Still, I can't keep myself from asking, "Are you going somewhere?" The question comes out sounding almost like a judgment, so I quickly add, "I only ask because you look really nice. Not that you don't always look nice. You do. But tonight, with all the black. You—good."

I close my eyes and wince. *You good?* I might as well beat my chest and grunt like a caveman.

She looks down at her clothes. "Oh. Thanks. I have a gig tonight."

"Ah. Now all the black makes sense. With the symphony? What are you playing?" I've been meaning to look up the Harvest Hollow Symphony. See when their performances are.

And not just because of Gracie. It's something I wanted to do even before I knew she played the cello.

"Not the symphony tonight," she says. "It's just a quartet. We're the background music at some sort of business bureau dinner thing happening downtown."

"How does a gig like that rate compared to the symphony?"

She purses her lips to the side. "Nowhere near as good as the symphony, though it does pay better. But not as bad as a wedding."

"What's wrong with weddings?"

She shoots me a droll look. "Have you ever noticed the cello part in Pachebel's Canon?"

I love that she's talking to me like this—opening up a little. "I'm guessing it's not very exciting?"

Her lips lift into a wry smile. "It's the same eight notes played over and over again."

"I see your point," I say.

We stand there a few more seconds until the awkwardness is almost too much to handle. *Why* is it so awkward? Is it me? Or is it just that she doesn't want to be talking to me?

"Okay, well, I should get going," she says. She reaches just inside her door and grabs a coat, slipping it on before wrapping a mustard yellow scarf around her neck. The color brings out the gold flecks in her dark brown eyes.

"Right. Of course. Don't let me keep you." I fish out my keys and unlock my apartment, then scoop up my bag.

Gracie comes out of her apartment, cello slung over her back. She turns and locks her door, then walks past me, a hesitant smile on her face.

"Good luck tonight," I say.

She nods, her expression still wary, like she doesn't know what to make of me. When she reaches the top step, she spins. "Oh, actually, there's something I've been meaning to ask you."

I immediately perk up. "Sure."

"I was just wondering if you have a way to contact our landlord directly. There's a thing happening with my stove, and I've tried to email the agent I worked with when I signed my lease, but she isn't responding."

I frown. There's something wrong with her stove? The agent *should* be responding and relaying all of Gracie's concerns to me. Trouble is, I can't exactly say that to Gracie because she doesn't know that her landlord is actually *me*.

It was something the leasing agent I worked with recommended—that I keep it on the down-low that I'm the one who owns the building. She said having tenants who know their landlord lives right next door is an easy way to have people bothering you all the time, complaining about things, making demands. It made sense at the time, but now that I know Gracie a little better, it seems like an unreasonable precaution. She's been totally chill, hasn't complained about a single thing in her apartment.

Until now. But if there's something wrong with her stove, that isn't a complaint. That's a legitimate need, and I should address it.

"Um, yeah," I answer. "I think I have his number somewhere. Or maybe his email? I'll see if I can find it for you."

She nods. "Thanks. It's not urgent or anything, but maybe the next time I see you, you can give it to me?"

I nod. "Sure. Sounds good."

I watch as she disappears down the stairs, then I slowly retreat into my apartment.

I mean, it could have gone *worse*. I've never been particularly great at talking to women, even with all the practicing my therapist has made me do. And I've definitely had conversations far more horrible than that one. And it's nice that now I have a reason to talk to her again. Because when I give her the landlord's number, I'm going to have to tell her it's *mine*.

But that's not going to make her interested in me. And I *really* don't think she's interested.

I stand at my counter, hands propped on my hips, and chuckle.

It's funny. Finding out I'm a hockey player usually has the *opposite* effect on women.

Unfortunately, the fact that it doesn't impact Gracie at all only makes me like her more.

CHAPTER THREE
Gracie

"OH, I'M SO GLAD I'm not the only one who is late," my stand partner, Joyce, says as I set my instrument on the floor of the green room and take off my coat. Joyce's cello case is open in front of her, so she's a few minutes ahead of me, but she's still rosining her bow, so it's *only* a few.

Our symphony conductor has a zero-tolerance policy for tardiness, especially on performance nights, so the strain on Joyce's face is justified. By the sound of things, the rest of the orchestra is already on stage warming up.

"Traffic was so much worse than I expected," I say. "I swear, there must be a million tourists in town to look at the fall leaves."

Harvest Hollow is nestled in the Appalachian mountains between Asheville and Knoxville and has become somewhat of a destination for leaf-lookers in the fall. It's great for the economy, so I can't complain. And odds are good that a lot of the people in the audience tonight are the same people who are clogging up the roads. But the audience hardly matters if I lose my seat in the orchestra for missing our first fall performance.

I hurriedly open my case and pull out my cello.

"Can you blame them for coming? The colors are amazing this year," Joyce says. "But there are probably people in town for the hockey game, too."

I look up. "There's a hockey game tonight?" That would explain why Felix was wearing a suit—looking too good for words—when I saw him leaving earlier.

"Tomorrow," Joyce says. "At least according to my husband."

I suddenly wonder where Felix was going all dressed up if not to one of his games. A date, maybe? That thought makes me frown, so I shove it away. What do I care if Felix dates? I hope he dates. I hope he dates all the hockey-loving women in the whole wide world.

"It's supposed to be a big game," Joyce continues. "They have a guy on the team now who was some sort of NHL hotshot, and when they played their first preseason game last week, he tore up the ice. He's from here, too, I guess, so now people are going crazy about seeing him play."

"People are always crazy about Appies hockey in this town."

Last weekend at breakfast, Josh went on and on about the new star on the team—Logan Barnes. Pretty sure that's the same guy who stayed with Felix for a little while. I remember him specifically because he was always incredibly polite whenever he saw me. Chill and nice, without being even a little bit flirty, which was a nice change from the hockey guys who usually show up at Felix's place.

Earlier this week, five or six of them came barreling up the stairs to bang on Felix's door. Logan brought up the rear, looking a little sheepish, apologizing for his teammates' antics even as Eli slid up to me—I'd just gotten home from re-hearsal—and asked if he could buy me dinner. *Again.*

Eli's actually pretty cute—all of Felix's friends look like they were stamped out at some sort of hotness factory—but he wouldn't be my type even if he didn't play hockey. And honestly, they all pale in comparison to Felix.

Not that I think Felix is impressive.

I'm just saying, objectively, if I'm only talking about the physical, Felix is...I don't have words for what Felix is. Which is troubling. He's been on my mind a lot more lately, some-thing I'm afraid has everything to do with him charging out of his apartment, still damp from his shower, to make sure I was okay. The expanse of the bare, broad chest was *not* insignificant, but weirdly, the thing that keeps coming back to me is the look that was on his face. He looked genuinely, sincerely concerned, then totally chagrined when he realized how much he'd inconvenienced me.

I shove the thoughts aside—I have much more important things to think about than my off-limits neighbor—and fol-low after Joyce, who has already made her way onto the stage.

The house lights are still up, and it's nice to see the per-formance hall full. There is *a lot* of gray hair, something that always makes me a little sad—why don't young people ever want to hear the symphony play?—but an audience is an audience, and I'm happy we have one.

I'll never get tired of the sound of an orchestra warming up, the cacophony of so many instruments tossing random notes into the air. It sounds like anticipation—like potential.

I breathe out a happy sigh as the rest of my thoughts and worries fall away, and I revel in the peace that fills me every time I play.

Moments later, the lights dim, and a hush falls over the room, the musicians quieting their instruments and the crowd silencing their chatter. The orchestra stands as our conductor makes her way onto the stage, and the audience fills the room with applause.

And then we play.

We're doing three pieces tonight, including Dvořák's "New World Symphony," which has always been one of my favorites.

I lose myself in the music just like I always do. I *am* grateful for the audience, but I don't think about them when I'm playing. It's just me, the music, the dips and swells of emotion. People argue classical music is boring, but if they truly listened, they'd hear the stories, the heartache, the celebration.

In the moment of silence right at the end of a piece, when I've just lifted my bow off the strings and the vibrations are still echoing through my body, that's when I feel the most wholly like myself.

Applause fills the auditorium as the conductor bows, and the same satisfaction that comes after every performance pushes through me. But tonight, there's an unexpected hollowness around the edges of my emotion that leaves me feeling slightly off-kilter. Maybe it's the expression on Joyce's face when her husband waves from his seat in the second row. Or the way the first chair violist moves to the back of the violin section to help his wife, who has a broken foot, get off the stage.

I *do* love playing in the symphony. And for the past few years, it's been enough. But it suddenly occurs to me that it might be nice if there were someone here to enjoy it with me—someone who was here *for me*.

Joyce touches my shoulder. "Great concert, Gracie. It's always a pleasure playing next to you."

I smile. "Same. Goodnight, Joyce."

She makes her way off stage, but I linger a little longer. I offer my students extra credit for coming to one of my concerts, and I tell them to come up and wave at me so I can see they're here. I never want to disappear too quickly just in case.

I look out into the auditorium, smiling when I see one of my students, Annabelle, standing with her mom, halfway down the aisle closest to me. She waves and smiles, and I wave back. She's a cellist like me, an eighth grader, and one of my students who probably has the potential to play professionally one day.

As Annabelle moves toward me down the aisle, someone else catches my eye. But it isn't another student.

It's *Felix*, wearing the suit I saw him in earlier and looking good enough to eat.

My heart pounds in my ears, and my breath catches in my throat.

So that's why he was all dressed up.

Our eyes meet, and he lifts his head in acknowledgment.

A flush creeps up my neck.

What is he even doing here? Surely he didn't just come for *me*. But he's alone. Who goes to symphony concerts alone?

I don't have time to think about it because Annabelle has finally reached me, her smile wide and her arms open for a hug.

I take the stairs at the edge of the stage and greet her, doing my best to give her my full attention as she chatters on about the concert, but I can't ignore the handsome giant still hovering at the back of the auditorium.

He's still there, which means he has to be waiting for me. It's the only thing that makes sense. But why?

He *has* been making more of an effort to talk to me lately. That whole thing with the mail last week was totally weird, and I've run into him in the hallway or on the stairs much more frequently the past few days—so frequently, I've half-wondered if he's making it happen on purpose.

Also frequently enough that I've started to look forward to it, which is the last thing I should be feeling.

I cannot, under any circumstances, develop a crush on my hockey-playing neighbor.

"Are you first chair, Miss Mitchell?" Annabelle asks, looking up at me with wide eyes.

"I'm not. But you know what? The woman who is first chair was my cello teacher back when I was your age. Can you believe that?"

Out of the corner of my eye, I see an older gentleman approach Felix.

Felix shakes his hand, then ducks his head and nods. He briefly glances my way before taking the man's symphony program, pulling a pen out of his pocket, and signing the back of it.

A hockey fan at a symphony concert. Now I've seen everything.

"Do you think I'll play like that with *you* someday?" Annabelle asks.

I smile, seeing so much of myself in Annabelle's eagerness. "I'd put money on it, Annabelle. I'll see you in class on Monday, okay?"

She nods and says goodbye, and I thank her mom for making the effort to get her here. Even with the discounted student tickets, it's still a big deal, and I'm always appreciative when parents make it happen.

When the two of them have finally walked away, I look to the back of the auditorium.

Felix is gone.

My heart sinks, which is a very, *very* bad sign.

I may not want to have a crush on my hockey-playing neighbor, but if the way my thoughts are still spiraling is any indication, I definitely do.

Honestly, it just makes me mad. I worked so freaking hard to put up the walls I needed to stay happy and healthy. That means no hockey.

Still, once my cello is packed up and I'm making my way across the lobby of the performance hall, I can't help but scan the crowd, looking for Felix's tall, dark form. There's no way I'd miss him in this sea of gray hair and polyester, but he's nowhere to be found.

"Gracie!" a voice calls from somewhere behind me.

I spin around, all thoughts of Felix leaving my mind at the sight of my college roommate hurrying toward me.

"Summer!" I hurry to close the distance between us and pull her into a hug. "What are you doing here?!"

She squeezes me tightly, despite the enormous cello strapped to my back. "I came to see you. To surprise you!"

"You were here? For the concert?" Summer only lives a few counties over in Silver Creek, but she's an attorney—an assistant to the DA—with aspirations of world domination. Between her work life and my teaching schedule, we don't get to see each other nearly as often as we'd like.

She smiles wide. "You know I'm a sucker for Dvořák. Excellent job, by the way. The cellos sounded great. Are you any closer to bumping Joyce out of first chair?"

"Joyce will be first chair until she retires," I say. "But she's welcome to it. I don't want the pressure."

"Miss Mitchell!" a voice calls from a few feet away.

I look up to see another one of my students. "Hi, Sophie!" I say as I smile and wave. She runs over and gives me a hug. "Thank you for coming!" I look up and make eye contact with her dad, who waves in acknowledgement. "Thanks for bringing her!" I call out as Sophie runs back to him.

"Look at you," Summer says. "Miss Mitchell and all her little orchestra groupies."

"Shut up," I say. "They're my students."

"They love you."

I shrug. "They're good kids. How long are you in town? Can you stay? Can we get food?"

"I can stay until Sunday if you'll have me," she says, looping her arm through mine. "Would it be a terrible imposition for me to stay with you? I promise you can say no, and I'll grab a hotel room."

I wave away her concern. "Don't even think about a hotel. I don't have a guest room, but I do have a very comfortable couch."

"I'll take it," Summer says. "I'd sleep in your bathtub if it meant a little more time with you."

We head toward the parking lot still arm in arm, my heart so full, I almost completely forget about Felix until I see his black Audi waiting to turn out of the parking lot. The windows are tinted, so if I didn't recognize his car, I wouldn't know it was him, but I've been parking next to him for six months. I'd know that car anywhere. I even recognize his license plate number.

"Hey, you okay?" Summer asks, following my gaze. "Is that someone you know?"

"Oh, no. I thought I recognized someone, but I...did we talk about food yet? Are you hungry? I'm hungry."

Summer eyes me curiously, her eyes darting back to Felix's car as it finally turns onto the main road and disappears out of sight. "I'm hungry," she finally says. "But don't think I'm letting this go. You're telling me who was driving that black Audi while we eat."

I scowl, and she lifts an eyebrow. "I bet people hate going up against you in court," I say.

She smirks. "A reputation I cherish, thank you." She pulls out her keys. "Come on. Let me drive to dinner, then we can circle back and grab your car."

We wind up at DeLucca's, a tiny Italian place downtown that serves the best garlic knots I've ever had. We settle into a corner booth, where Summer immediately orders a bottle of wine and two baskets of garlic knots at my recommendation. The wine is more expensive than anything I would ever splurge on by myself, so even though I've never been a big drinker, I happily let the waiter fill my glass.

I take a sip, eyeing Summer across the table. "Are we celebrating something tonight?" I nod toward the bottle.

She grins. "A tiny promotion? It isn't a huge deal, but I'm possibly the youngest person in the office ever to be promoted so fast, so...maybe that's worth celebrating?"

"Shut up," I say. "That's amazing! Of course that's worth celebrating."

Summer launches into the work dynamics that led to her promotion, thankfully forgetting about Felix's black Audi. Once that topic is exhausted, she starts in about her older sister's upcoming wedding, which gets us almost all the way through the garlic knots and halfway through our main course. Summer's sister, Audrey, who is a wildlife biologist over in Silver Creek, just had a whirlwind romance with Flint Hawthorne—one of the biggest movie stars in Hollywood. Summer has kept me updated via text, but hearing her talk through the details in person feels way too trippy. The whole thing sounds like it came straight out of a romance novel or some over-the-top movie.

"Seriously though," Summer says. "You would flip if you saw the guest list. It's supposed to just be their closest friends and family, but like, Flint Hawthorne's closest friends are all A-list actors. Harry Styles is on the list. Harry *freaking* Styles."

"And you're sure you can't get me an invite?" I might listen to classical more than any other kind of music, but I was a diehard One Direction fan when I was a kid. So much so that I figured out cello covers of their biggest hits and uploaded videos of me playing them to YouTube, where I absolutely tagged every single member of the band. I'd take them down—the braces and One Direction T-shirt aren't doing me any favors—but I'm actually kind of proud of the music.

"Girl, I would if I could," Summer says. "But you know Audrey. If it were up to her, it would *only* be family. She's got the guest list on lockdown."

I've only met Audrey a few times, but I've heard enough about her through Summer that this doesn't surprise me at all. "I'm happy for her," I say. "And you, too. You better send me lots of pictures."

I refill my wine glass, letting myself relax. Summer has clearly forgotten all about Felix and his fancy Audi. I offer her the bottle, but she declines. "I'm done for the night," she says. "But you have more, because we're going to talk about you now, and I think you might need it."

I pause mid-sip. Well, *crap*. I should have known better. "Do we have to? I promise there is nothing worth talking about."

Summer lifts an eyebrow. "Your life is that boring, huh?"

"Totally boring," I say. "Same old, same old."

Summer leans forward, her elbows propped on the table. "How's your dating life?" she asks.

"Nonexistent."

"Are you on any dating apps?"

I scoff. "Are *you* on any dating apps?"

"Several," she says, without breaking my gaze. "And I've got a date almost every weekend."

"That's fine for you," I say. "But that doesn't sound like very much fun to me."

"I'm not talking about casual hookups," Summer says, though I know her well enough that I don't need the clarification. She's a social person who loves to be around people, but she's never been one to sleep around. "I'm talking real first dates."

"Only first dates?" I ask.

"Until I find the right guy," she says, with a confidence that says she's positive she will.

I take a gulp of wine, my skin prickling under Summer's intense stare. Summer is my closest friend and I trust that she'll love me no matter what, but when she puts me in the hot seat like this, it's impossible not to squirm.

"Don't knock them if you aren't willing to try them," Summer says. "What's your opposition?"

"I just don't understand why people can't meet the old-fashioned way anymore," I say. "Browsing in a bookstore or picking out oranges at the grocery store. Why does it always have to start on the internet?"

"Because it's hard to meet people when everyone is so glued to their phones," Summer says matter-of-factly. "Unless you want to spend every weekend trolling bars, and the older I get, the worse that sounds. At least on a dating app, I can filter out the ones who have no potential without wasting a good outfit or money on drinks I don't want or need."

"Okay. Fair point" I say. "I still don't want to do it."

"Fine," Summer says, holding up her hands. "Suit yourself. But I'm just saying, it would probably be a lot easier to find your angsty musician if you were willing to try it." She smiles, and I sense her interrogation finally losing steam.

Her comment about an *angsty musician* is a throwback to the type of guy I dated in college. Tall, waify, achingly broody. The exact opposite of Gavin and every other hockey player I've ever known—something I definitely did on purpose.

The violinist I dated the longest, Anton, was an aspiring conductor who had angular cheekbones, jet-black hair, and a permanent five-o'clock shadow. He was aloof and gorgeous and mysterious—and a terrible boyfriend.

But *man,* could he play the violin.

"Any new hunks in the Harvest Hollow Symphony?" Summer asks.

"Not even one. There's a new trombonist who keeps telling everyone—loudly—how single he is, but he also keeps emptying his spit valve on people's shoes, so he's a definite no."

"Sounds disgusting," Summer says.

"Trust me. It is."

"What about at the school?" she asks. "Any hot single teachers?"

I drain the last of my wine. "Not one. I mean, the gym teacher isn't bad to look at. He's asked me out a few times, but I've never seen him in anything but gym clothes, even when I've run into him when we *aren't* at school."

"Hmm. Yeah. I'd pass on that, too."

I fidget with my napkin, wondering if I should even bring Felix up. If anything, it might keep Summer from setting me up with an online dating profile, something she will absolutely do before the weekend is over if I don't give her a reason not to.

"I do have this neighbor," I finally say.

Summer's expression brightens, like a puppy that's just been offered its favorite treat. "Yeeeessss. Do tell."

"There's nothing *to* tell," I say. "I mean, he's nice to look at, but he isn't my type at all. He's a hockey player, and you know how I feel about hockey players."

Her eyes go wide. "Define hockey player. Like, are we talking about a weekend beer league?"

I shake my head. "He's a pro. In the minor leagues, but yeah. Still pro. He plays for the Appies."

"Wow. Impressive." She grabs her phone off the table. "What's his name?"

I hesitate, knowing exactly how Summer is going to react when she sees Felix's picture. I probably should have considered his searchability before bringing him up.

Summer levels me with a stare. "The longer you *don't* say his name, the more it's going to make me think you already have a thing for him."

I scoff. "You're terrible."

"Name, Gracie."

I fold my arms across my chest. "Felix Jamison."

She types into her phone, then stares at the screen while I fidget in my seat.

"Ohh, he's the goalie," she says. "Tough gig."

I was not surprised when I first discovered that Felix is the goalie. Goalies are often the quiet, more thoughtful types, at least from what I remember about Josh's teams. And that tracks with what I've observed of my neighbor.

Summer scrolls for another second. "Holy hotness, Gracie." She flips her phone around so I can see the picture she's pulled up. It's one of Felix crossing the parking lot outside the stadium, wearing the requisite suit the players all wear as they arrive for games. I don't know how long it's been a tradition, but even Josh wore a suit to games when he was playing for the youth league. In the photo, Felix is running his fingers through his long, dark hair, his expression sultry.

The suit is different from the one he was wearing tonight—it's a lighter shade of gray—but the purple striped tie is the same. I sigh. "That's...not a terrible picture."

"Are you crazy?" Summer says. "The man is gorgeous. I actually think he kind of *is* your type. He's definitely got the dark, broody thing going on. Just with a lot more muscle."

"You should see him in person," I say. "He's enormous."

"Hmmm. Sounds delicious." She scoots her chair a little closer. "Okay. Tell me everything."

I shrug and fold my arms across my chest. "There's nothing to tell."

"Nope. You wouldn't have mentioned him if there was nothing to tell."

I groan. I know Summer's persistence will get the truth out of me eventually, but also, I maybe kind of *do* want to talk about it. Maybe another person pointing out how *wrong* Felix is for me will help me kill this crush once and for all.

I pause long enough for our waiter to clear away our dinner plates and drop off the cannoli Summer ordered. I try not to think about the growing size of the check we'll be splitting. This kind of a splurge is definitely out of the ordinary for me, but it's not like I see Summer every weekend. If there's ever a reason to justify spending a little extra money, it's Summer.

"Felix, Gracie," Summer says, gesturing with her fork. "Let me hear it."

I quickly summarize the last few interactions I've had with Felix. The underwear encounter. The thing with the mail. The increased frequency with which we've been running into each other in the hall. "Then there's other stuff too," I say. "Like, my brother just randomly called me last weekend and told me Felix is Maddox's favorite player. And while I was at the grocery store the other day, I saw Felix in the parking lot, loading this old lady's groceries into her car like he was an actual bagboy. Suddenly, it feels like he's everywhere. Coming up in conversations even when I'm not running into him."

"Maybe the universe is trying to tell you something," Summer says.

"And then there's the fact that he..." I pause, knowing if I finish this sentence, Summer will know *exactly* who was leaving the symphony concert in a black Audi.

"The fact that he what?" Summer asks.

I pour myself another glass of wine and take a slow slip. "He was at my symphony concert tonight," I finally say.

"I knew it!" Summer says, her expression triumphant. "I *knew* there was someone important driving that car."

"I just don't know what he's trying to do," I say. "I've told him I don't date hockey players. Why would he come to my concert if he knows I'm not interested?"

Summer taps her lip. "Good point. So, was *everyone* at the concert tonight only there to see you?"

"Summer. You were there, and you saw the crowd. There might have been ten people in attendance who were less than sixty-five years old. And I've *never* seen him there before."

"Okay, so he *was* there to see you. Doesn't that make his attendance even more amazing?"

"It isn't. It's...*annoying*," I bite out. "Because probably he was only there to try to change my mind about dating hockey players. I bet he has this all planned out. The mail and the sexiness and the smelling so good when he's in the hallway. He's trying to wear me down. Which, maybe it's just me, but that feels really arrogant. *That* feels like a hockey player." My head suddenly feels swimmy, addled by too much wine, but I feel good about the point I've just made. A hockey player *would* be cocky enough to persist—to refuse to take *no* for an answer.

Summer slides the cannoli we've been sharing toward her, and takes a big bite, her expression saying she doesn't think I deserve to have any. "Honestly," she says, once she finally swallows, "the mental gymnastics you're performing to justify your position right now are pretty astounding." She uses a fork to scrape up the last of the chocolate chip mascarpone. "Why are you being so stubborn about this? This guy could be great, and you don't even want to give him a chance." She holds up her phone, still showing the picture of Felix crossing the parking lot. "Look at him, Gracie. You're telling me *this man* might be genuinely interested in you, and you aren't interested back?"

"Really?" I ask. "That's how shallow we are now? We only talk about how a man looks?"

"Of course we don't," Summer argues. "But it's an okay place to start. And based on what you've told me, Felix Jamison also seems like a nice guy."

I drop back into the booth, the motion making my brain clang around inside my skull. At least, that's what it feels like is happening. I glance at my wine glass, which is empty again, and suddenly I can't remember if I've had two glasses or three. "Hockey players are all the same," I say with a huff. "You just have to trust me on that."

She purses her lips, judgment clear in her expression. It's one of the reasons I love Summer so much. She is fiercely loyal and supportive to a fault, but she won't hide her feelings to spare someone else's, especially if she senses any degree of injustice. "How does it make your brother feel to know you regard him so highly?"

"My brother is different," I shoot back. "He got out. Jadah saved him from himself when she got pregnant with Maddox."

Summer shakes her head. "You aren't being fair, Gracie. Josh is a good guy. He would have stayed a good guy even if he'd kept playing hockey. I think this is a lot more about Gavin, which is stupid because your high school boyfriend was an idiot boy, and you were only seventeen years old. This isn't the same scenario at all."

My jaw clenches at the thought of Gavin, the first and only hockey player I ever dated. He was Josh's age, a senior when I was a junior, and he was one of the most popular guys at school. I thought I was immune to the lure of popularity. I was the nerdy, bookish musician. I didn't care about pep rallies or homecoming or anything else regular high schoolers cared about. But then Gavin looked at me, he *saw me,* and suddenly, other people saw me too. The attention was intoxicating. *He* was intoxicating. And then a switch flipped, and I couldn't remember why I hated hockey so much.

For the next six months, I was actually excited about going to Josh's games. I even made a habit of stopping by the rink at the end of his practices just to see Gavin.

My family was floored. I'd been protesting going to the rink for any reason, games or practices, for *years.* And now I wanted to be there any time Josh was there.

There were all kinds of red flags. Josh later told me he never really liked Gavin and he particularly hated the way he talked in the locker room, but for once, the giant hockey-shaped barrier between me and my brother was gone. He liked that I no longer complained about the sport he lived for, so he ignored his misgivings in favor of the newfound harmony in our home.

Until Gavin stood me up on prom night.

Nothing like getting all dressed up and waiting for your boyfriend to pick you up only to find out he "forgot" about the dance and made other plans. Turns out those "other plans" had been waiting for him, all blond hair and long legs, after his hockey game that afternoon. His first groupie.

The next morning, Gavin posted a picture on his Instagram account of him in her bedroom, *in her bed.*

So that was awesome.

To this day, every time I hear something on the news about bad boy hockey players hooking up with random women in whatever city they're playing, I think of Gavin and recommit to my no-hockey rule.

"I get what you're saying," I say to Summer. "I do. But some things *are* the same. He's an Appie, Summer. That means he's traveling. It means in every single city, there are women who find out where the players are sleeping and proposition them *just* because they play hockey. It means he has the same wild ambition, the same death wish, they all have. Why is it so wrong for me to disqualify someone who has dedicated his life to a sport I don't like? Aren't we allowed to have deal breakers?"

She shrugs and tucks a strand of hair behind her ear. "My sister had a thousand misgivings about dating someone like Flint Hawthorne. Things she might have even called dealbreakers. And look at them now. He's the greatest thing that ever happened to her."

"And I'm happy for her," I say. "But that isn't what this is. It isn't the same."

She holds up her hands like she's finally ready to concede. "Okay. I won't say anything else about it. But I still think you're being stubborn. And it might mean missing out on something really great."

Maybe I *am* being stubborn. But Summer doesn't get it. She doesn't understand what hockey does to me. The sight of the sticks, the bags, the sound of the blades cutting the ice, it stirs up this feeling, this discomfort, that I can't quite shake.

Somehow, I just *know*. If I go down this road, I'll wind up getting hurt.

I fold my arms across my chest. "I'd rather take my chances with gym shorts Jim."

She presses her lips together. "The gym teacher at your school is actually named *Jim*?"

"James," I say. "But everyone calls him Jim."

And I really, *really* don't want to date him.

"You don't want to date him, honey," Summer says, echoing my feelings.

"You're right," I say. "I don't. But I don't want to date Felix either."

She eyes me. "Okay. If you're sure about that, then will you introduce him to me?"

I close my eyes and grip the edge of the table, thinking of the way my skin flushes with heat whenever Felix is near. The way his slightly spicy scent envelops me whenever we pass in the hallway, making my knees feel wobbly and weak.

But the thought of him dating Summer—that awakens something inside me that I can't even define. It's deep and primal and makes my jaw clench. If the table in front of me wasn't bolted to the floor, I could probably flip it over for all the angry energy coursing through me.

Oh no. I know exactly what this feeling is.

I pry my fingers off the table and force them into my lap, but it's too late. Summer is too good at reading my face not to see my jealousy for what it is.

"That's what I thought," she says with a smirk. "Even just *thinking* about me and Felix made you jealous. You like him, Gracie. Admit it."

"I don't," I insist. "I don't care if you meet him. I'll introduce you tonight. Then you'll see that he's no different from all the other cocky hockeys."

She stifles a snort. "Cocky hockeys?"

I frown, rethinking the words. They're close to what I meant, but they aren't quite right. "I had too much wine, didn't I?"

Summer nudges my water toward me, and I wrap my fingers around the cool glass, letting the sensation ground me in the moment.

"So by cocky hockey, what you mean is that Felix isn't *really* into you, he's just trying to get in your cello case?"

I raise my eyebrows. "My cello case?"

She smirks. "It sounded classier than getting in your *pants*."

"You're horrible."

"You're the one making the assumptions. I'm just rephrasing what you're already saying."

And she's doing it on purpose to make me see how silly I'm being, how much I'm relying on stereotypes. Which, *fine*. I am. Is that what she wants me to admit?

"I'm only a product of my experiences," I say. "And there's nothing wrong with that."

Summer pulls out her wallet and hands her credit card over to the waiter, her light brown waves shimmering as she smiles up at him.

"Wait, wait, we're splitting the check," I say, reaching for my wallet.

"We aren't," Summer says, waving the waiter away. "My treat tonight. My promotion came with a raise, and I ordered two different appetizers *and* dessert. That's double what you would have ordered."

I swallow my pride with a huff. "Fine. But this is the only time. We're splitting everything else for the rest of the weekend."

"Deal," Summer says.

I study my best friend, a wave of gratitude washing over me.

Maybe I *should* introduce her to Felix. She's gorgeous. Successful. Funny and easy to be around. She could distract him away from me.

Which is what I want, right? For him to leave me alone?

The same jealousy that reared up before fills me up, claws at me, making my throat feel tight and my stomach feel queasy.

I sigh and let my shoulders drop.

I am in so much more trouble than I thought.

CHAPTER FOUR
Felix

"I'M JUST SAYING, DARLING," Mom says, "he's the perfect person to ask if you have questions about renovating an old building. I don't know why you *wouldn't* ask him."

I can think of a lot of reasons why I wouldn't ask my father for his opinions, but as late as it is, I'm not in the mood to hash it out with Mom *now*. We've had a nice night. Great dinner, a great symphony concert. I don't want to ruin it by talking about Dad. Especially not when I've got a game tomorrow. I'd rather not do anything to mess with my headspace.

My mother leans over my kitchen table, eyes scanning over the four different plumbing estimates I've gotten regarding the *very* old pipes in my building. Well, in *half* my building.

I knew the pipes were old when I first renovated, but the plumber who did the original work claimed they still had years of life left and there was no reason to replace what was still fully functional. Only the pipes in my apartment are new; the ones that lead from the main water line into the building, and then everything in Gracie's apartment, are all still original.

That decision came back to bite me pretty quickly. The old pipes are copper, giving our water a terrible, bitter taste, so

I had to install a filter at the main line that cost more than replacing the plumbing would have. By the time I realized it, Gracie's apartment was already fully renovated and finished, so the filter was the easiest solution. But now, there are a couple of places on the first floor where the pipes look like they've corroded to the point of being soft, so I'm having to replace them anyway.

It isn't going to be cheap or convenient—especially since it will displace Gracie for a few days. She might have friends or family close by where she could stay, but I'll have to at least offer to put her up in an Airbnb. She could always stay at my place—I have a guest room she's welcome to—but I have a feeling she wouldn't be comfortable with that particular arrangement. If she doesn't date hockey players, I doubt she'd want to live with one either.

A familiar pang of disappointment shoots through me at the thought. Logically, it makes sense for me to move on from Gracie, drop the idea of taking her out, of getting to know her. But so far, I can't seem to shake it.

Either way, I'm kicking myself for not consulting with more than one plumber before I had the original work done. I was probably a little *too* focused on handling the project by myself.

Or, more specifically, handling it *without* my father's help.

"I seem to remember Derreck talking about pipes in the old Franklin building," Mom says. She taps her finger against her lip. "The one near Willis Tower. You know how hands-on your father is. I think he'll know what to tell you."

"Yeah, maybe you're right," I say, gathering up the estimates. I hadn't meant to have this conversation at all, but Mom saw them on the table and asked what they were.

"You know he just wants you to be happy, Felix," she says, clearly reading my mood more than she's listening to my actual words.

"I know, Mom. I'll talk to him. I will."

Maybe. Eventually.

She rolls her eyes and moves into the living room, mumbling something that sounds an awful lot like *stubborn boy* as she goes. She reaches my bookshelves, pausing her steps as one hand slides over the titles.

If we can avoid talking about Dad, Mom and I could talk about books all night long. That's the good thing about Mom. She has feelings about the relationship I have—or mostly *don't* have—with my father, and she never stops trying to push us back together. But even when I refuse her efforts, she doesn't let it ruin *her* relationship with me. She still comes to see me play even though Dad won't. She still finds ways to make sure I know she cares.

"Have you read this one yet?" she asks, pulling the latest Andrew Sean Greer title off the shelf. "I've been meaning to grab it, but I haven't had the time."

"It's my favorite of his," I say, heading toward the living room. "You're welcome to borrow it if you don't finish it while you're here."

I generally don't mind loaning out books, though I've been known to grumble if people don't return them. But I never mind sharing my collection with Mom. My mother is even more meticulous about her book collection than I am. If she borrows a book and likes it, she'll almost definitely order me a new copy from her local bookstore, have them ship it to me, and keep the borrowed copy for herself. Unless she sees that I've made notes in the margins, then she'll mail it back to me with her own notes written next to mine.

We might not see eye to eye about Dad, but we *always* have books.

"Vivie did a lovely job with this place," Mom says. She's at the window now, standing next to the potted money tree my older sister picked out. She isn't an interior designer by trade—she's much too busy being the very rich wife of my father's very well-paid CFO—but she has a good eye, and she was thrilled when I called her and told her she could treat my apartment like her blank canvas. I ended up having more opinions than I thought I would—enough that the place feels like mine, like home—but I couldn't have done near this well on my own.

"How is Vivie?" I ask as I follow Mom to the living room.

"Oh, you know Vivie," she says with a dismissive wave of her hand. "Perfect, as always. Did you know she and Henry are trying for a baby?"

"Yeah, she mentioned it last time we talked." With way too much detail, but I don't bring that up to Mom. My sister is a chronic over-sharer, which is hilarious to me but has always been incredibly irritating to Mom.

Before I can say anything else or mention how much I love the idea of becoming an uncle, a knock sounds on my apartment door, and I backtrack, heading toward the kitchen.

I glance at my watch, my gut tightening as I near the door. It's almost ten p.m. which means it's probably one of my teammates—no one else would show up at my place so late—but I'm not particularly in the mood to hang out with the guys while my mom is around.

Not that she would be anything but gracious.

Mom has always been supportive of my career, but it's only because she's supportive of *me*. It's definitely *not* because she has any particular affinity for the sport or even thought it was the wisest course of action when I signed on to play in the AHL. The majors probably would have been slightly easier to swallow, but minor league hockey? I know she didn't understand. Maybe still doesn't.

Which is why it's such a big deal that she's here. The whole point of her coming to visit is so she can watch me play in our first official game of the season. It should be a great game. Last week's pre-season matchup was awesome, and it got us all fired up.

But good game or not, Mom is still married to my father. And his opinions about hockey are about as nuanced as his opinions about me *not* going into business with him.

That is to say—*not nuanced at all.*

If there's any chance Friday-night antics with my team might reflect poorly on me and then get back to Dad, I'd rather avoid them, no matter how supportive my mother claims to be.

Fortunately, it isn't an Appie on the other side of my door. It's the exact opposite.

"Gracie," I say, not even trying to hide my surprise. My skin prickles with awareness as my heart ticks faster in my chest. "Hi."

I glance over my shoulder at Mom, who has looked up from her book, her eyebrows raised. I've mentioned that I have a neighbor generally, but I've never called Gracie by name. I definitely haven't mentioned that Gracie is talented and beautiful and basically everything I've ever desired in a woman.

It's hard to guess how Mom would play meeting Gracie. She isn't the matchmaking type, but I can easily imagine her raising an eyebrow. Then, as soon as we're alone, following up with a lecture about condoms and safe sex and the importance of accepting responsibility should I ever get a woman pregnant. She's always been more practical than she has been emotional about things like relationships.

"Hi," Gracie says. Her cello is strapped to her back, and her cheeks are flushed. "Hello."

My eyes lift, distracted by movement over Gracie's shoulder, and another woman with dark brown hair crests the top of the stairs.

Gracie follows my gaze, motioning the woman forward. "This is my best friend, Summer. *She* wanted to meet you," she says pointedly.

"Oh. Okay, cool," I say, though the look on Summer's face says this isn't entirely the truth. "Um, are you a hockey fan?"

She smiles politely. "Not really. Just keeping an eye on Gracie. Since you're her only neighbor, I thought it important to get a read on you." She levels me with a serious look.

I hold her gaze, recognizing immediately that this is more than just a friendly greeting. It feels like some sort of test. I have no idea what it's for or why, but if it has anything to do with Gracie, I definitely want to pass.

"Summer is a defense attorney," Gracie says, and suddenly her friend's scrutiny makes a little more sense.

I extend my hand. "It's nice to meet you, Summer. Any friend of Gracie's is a friend of mine."

Gracie wobbles on her feet the slightest bit, and she grabs the door frame to steady herself. "She came all the way from Silver Creek to see my symphony concert tonight," she says. "Wasn't that so nice of her?" There's a looseness to Gracie's demeanor that I've never noticed before, and I wonder if she's had something to drink.

My eyes dart to Summer, who is standing just behind Gracie, and she makes a motion with her hands, miming taking a drink, then holds up her finger and thumb a few inches apart from each other, confirming that Gracie has at least had enough that Summer feels like she needs to warn me.

I'm torn between wanting to smile because Gracie looks pretty cute with her flushed cheeks and wide eyes, and pulling her into my apartment, settling her on my couch, and making her drink a bottle of water and eat a few crackers so tomorrow morning is as painless as possible.

Pretty sure Gracie wouldn't go for option two, so I push my hands into my pockets and hope Summer will take care of her when I can't.

I clear my throat. "Um, yeah. That *was* very nice of her. It was a great concert."

"It *was*," Gracie says. "Something you know because you were there." She leans a little closer and taps her finger into my chest. "Why did I see you there, Felix?"

Her tone drops when she says my name, and a bolt of heat shoots through me. I shouldn't love the way my name sounds on her lips.

"I *was* there," I say slowly. "Excellent job."

She frowns. "Thank you. But that doesn't answer my question. *Why* were you there? And why did you bring me my mail, and why do you always look so sexy and stuff?"

Behind Gracie, Summer covers her mouth with her hand, but her laughter is clear in her eyes.

I press my lips together. "And stuff?"

She waves a hand up and down, motioning to my body. "Don't pretend like you don't realize you have all *that* going on."

Huh. So she's been checking me out. I like the idea of this way too much, and I fight to push down my smirk.

Gracie breathes out a huff, wobbling the slightest bit on her heels. She's wearing the same black pants she had on when I saw her last week when she was on her way to play a gig with her quartet.

"I just want you to be honest with me," she says. "Are you trying to impress me? To change my mind about hockey players?" She shoots a look over her shoulder at Summer, who has a hand pressed to her mouth like she's trying to stifle a laugh. "Because it's not. going. to. work." Gracie emphasizes these last words with four more finger pokes into my chest.

I can't resist flexing against the last poke, and she draws her finger back, her brows furrowed as she looks at her finger, then back at my chest. "*Ugh.* Your stupid muscles."

I finally allow myself the smirk I've been fighting. "What did you think you'd find?" I ask, lowering my tone so there's no way my mother will hear. "You've seen me in my underwear, after all." It's out of character for me to be so forward, but this is the first time Gracie has ever admitted to noticing *anything* about me, and it's making me bolder, *flirtier,* than usual.

Behind Gracie, Summer gasps and starts to laugh.

Gracie scowls. "I did—that is—*no,*" she finally says. "That is *not* what happened."

"Pretty sure that's exactly what happened," I say, leaning against the open doorway. Energy courses through me, buzzing just under my skin. I've never been particularly good at talking to women, but this feels fun and natural, maybe even easy.

"But only because you came parading outside with no pants," Gracie hisses. "Not because anything was—because we were—*doing anything.*"

"Who said anything about that? All I said was that you've *seen* me. And you have."

She huffs again and crosses her arms over her chest. "You're being difficult on purpose."

"Felix?" Mom calls from the living room. "Who's at the door? If it's someone you know, you should invite them in. It's rude to make someone talk to you from the hallway."

It's a very Emily Jamison thing to say, but I barely take notice because in front of me, the color is leaching out of Gracie's face. Her eyes dart around, landing on the pair of heels Mom discarded just inside the front door.

"Oh. You—*you're on a date,*" Gracie says softly. She swears and takes a step backward, wobbling again, this time enough that I reach out a hand to steady her. She's still carrying her cello on her back, and I'd hate to see her go down, taking her very expensive instrument with her.

She steps out of my grasp and my fingers only graze her shoulder, but Summer is right there, looping an arm around Gracie's waist. "Okay. Time for you to say goodnight."

"He wasn't trying to impress me at all," Gracie says to Summer, like she's already forgotten I'm standing here. "He's on a date!" she whisper yells. "He took *a date* to my concert."

My brain fires off a dozen different thoughts in the two seconds it takes Summer to start leading Gracie away.

Why would it matter even if I *was* on a date when Gracie has made it clear she has no interest in dating hockey players?

Why does she seem so flustered, so *bothered* by the idea?

Why am I so happy about the possibility of her being bothered?

The truth is, I did hope she would see me at her concert, that it might mean something to her that I was there. The fact that my mother was in town and I knew she'd enjoy hearing Dvořák's "New World Symphony" was a nice bonus, but even if Mom wasn't visiting, I probably still would have gone.

Either way, the last thing I want is for Gracie to disappear into her apartment thinking I'm with another woman.

"Gracie, wait," I say.

She stops and turns, her cheeks an almost violent shade of pink.

"I'm not on a date," I say. "I *wasn't* on a date."

She eyes the heels sitting inches away from my feet.

With perfect timing, my mom steps into the doorway, her curiosity clearly too much for her to ignore any longer. "What's going on?" she says, and I drop an arm around her shoulders.

"Gracie, I'd like you to meet my mother, Emily Jamison," I say. "Mom, this is my neighbor, Gracie Mitchell. She's a cellist in the Harvest Hollow Symphony. And this is her friend, Summer."

Gracie only stares, her eyes wide, until Summer nudges her in the side and Gracie shoots out her hand. "Your mother," she says. She swallows and licks her lips. "Mrs. Jamison. It's so nice to meet you."

"And you, dear," Mom says as she shakes their hands. I have no idea if Mom has been able to hear our conversation, but her impeccable poise will keep her from saying anything either way. Mom's a class act, impossible to ruffle in even the most awkward situations.

She smiles warmly. "Your performance was lovely, Gracie. I've seen the Chicago Symphony dozens of times, and you all sounded just as good. Truly. Your conductor is a marvel."

Gracie nods. "She is. We're lucky to have her." Her eyes dart to me, embarrassment filling their depths, then she quickly looks back at my mom. "So you're just in town for a visit? From Chicago?"

"I am. For Felix's hockey game tomorrow. He says it's supposed to be quite the match-up."

"Right. The game," Gracie says. Her face contorts the slightest bit, and I bite back a laugh. She couldn't be more obvious if she tried.

"Are you all hockey fans?" Mom asks, her tone warm, her interest genuine.

"Huge fans," Summer says before Gracie can open her mouth. "Right, Gracie?"

Gracie forces a smile. "Oh, you know," she says through her grimace. "As much as the next classical musician."

If Mom notices Gracie's sarcasm, she doesn't note it. She only smiles, her expression warm and sincere. "Maybe I'll see you at the game tomorrow." Mom takes a step back and pats my shoulder. "I think I'll head to bed now, Felix, but don't say goodnight on my account. Invite your friends in. I'm sure I'll sleep like the dead after the day I've had. You won't keep me up."

"Oh no, we're actually going to bed too," Gracie says quickly. "So tired." She tugs Summer toward her apartment. "So, so tired."

"Geez, Gracie. You're going to knock me over," Summer says under her breath, though it's still loud enough for me to hear, and it immediately makes me smile.

"It was so nice to meet you, Mrs. Jamison," Gracie says. She unlocks her apartment and practically shoves Summer inside. "Good night!" she calls, and then she's gone too.

Mom is silent for a beat, her eyes still fixed on my open apartment door, her expression curious. "Well, she's odd," she finally says, and I bark out a laugh.

"Not usually. I think you might have intimidated her."

Mom eyes me knowingly. "Felix, dear, that young woman was not intimidated. She was *flustered*. And I think we both know why." She gives me a pointed look, then bends and scoops up her heels. "Are the two of you dating?"

I run a hand through my hair. "No. But I—" Do I want to say more? I'm not necessarily opposed to talking to Mom about women. I'm just not sure I want to do it right now. Before I can decide how to finish my sentence, Mom finishes my sentence for me.

"But you wish you were?"

I breathe out a sigh. "Something like that. But she isn't really into hockey."

Mom turns and heads across the living room. "Then it's a good thing you're more than a hockey player."

Her words resonate deep in my gut. I *am* more. And if there's ever been a time to remind Gracie of that, it's right now.

As soon as Mom is safely ensconced in my guest bedroom, I hurry through my still-open front door, fueled by adrenaline and a recklessness that feels foreign and exhilarating and nauseating all at the same time. I move to Gracie's door, lift my fist, and give it three swift knocks.

She opens it almost immediately, but she doesn't say hello. Just stares, her big brown eyes wide and luminous.

"What do you want?" she asks.

I brace both hands above the door jamb and lean close, close enough to catch the scent of her hair and see the freckles dotting her cheeks. "I just wanted to make a couple of things clear."

She lifts her brows, her lips parting as she leans forward the slightest bit.

"Number one," I say. "I would have gone to the symphony concert tonight regardless of whether you were playing. It's something my mom and I like to do together."

Color climbs up her cheeks, like she's embarrassed she even considered I was there for her. But she has nothing to be embarrassed about.

"That doesn't mean I didn't think about seeing you." I lick my lips and lean even closer. "That doesn't mean my eyes weren't on you the entire night."

Gracie sucks in a breath, but she still doesn't say anything.

I drop one hand from the door jamb and slip it around her waist, my fingers pressing lightly against her back as I whisper, "You might as well have been the only one on stage, Gracie."

She closes her eyes, and I see the flutter of her pulse in the hollow of her throat.

"As for changing your mind about hockey players," I continue, "and this is point number two, my mother raised me to be a gentleman, so if you tell me you don't want to date a hockey player, I won't push you."

Gracie tucks her dark hair behind her ear, and I resist the urge to slide the silky strands through my fingers.

"I appreciate that," she says softly.

"But just for the record, I would *love* for you to change your mind. And if you ever do, I hope I'm the first one you think of."

Her lips quirk up to the side as she arches toward me, her back shifting under my palm.

It's all I can do not to pull her closer, to feel the press of her body against mine.

"Not Eli?" she says, humor lacing her tone.

My jaw clenches at the thought, my words coming out raspy and rough. "Definitely not Eli." I slide my hand from her waist, grazing her elbow as I pull it back, my fingers brushing over the soft silk of her black blouse. I hold her gaze for a long moment. "Good night, Gracie."

I'm just inside my apartment door when I finally hear her whisper, "Good night."

It isn't much.

But it's something.

And with Gracie, I'm quickly learning I'll take anything I can get.

CHAPTER FIVE
Gracie

"YOU ABSOLUTELY HAVE TO go out with him," Summer says from behind me.

I lean against my front door, my back pressed flat, my elbow still tingling with the lingering heat of Felix's touch.

"Seriously, Gracie. He looked at you like he wants to *eat* you." Summer steps up right in front of me, snapping her fingers in front of my face. "Yo. You in there? Speak, or I'm going to get Felix so he can come over and kiss you out of your trance."

I roll my eyes and shove her hands away. "I'm not in a trance. I'm fine."

"Are you sure? Because the kissing thing sounds like it could be really fun."

I pull off my heels and toss them toward my bedroom door. "I'm not going to kiss Felix."

"You are going to go out with him though. Please tell me you are."

I spin to face her, hands on my hips, but I'm too wobbly to hold the pose before I collapse against the wall behind me. My brain is muddled and cloudy, totally consumed with how it felt when he leaned in close, his scent wrapping around me like some sort of pheromone-infused cozy blanket.

Or maybe it's just the wine. *Please just be the wine.*

(I don't want to admit it, but it's not the wine.)

"This doesn't change anything," I say, pushing off the wall and heading toward the living room couch.

"You're right," Summer says, following behind me. "He was sexy before, and now he's still sexy. Plus, it's really cute that he went to the concert with his mom. I also love that he put the ball in your court. Or, in this case, maybe the puck on your ice? Is that how it works? I know nothing about hockey."

"Close enough." I drop onto the couch and tuck my feet under me. My water bottle is sitting on the table beside me, and I reach for it, making myself take several long sips.

Summer sits down beside me. "Did you see how soft his hair looked just then?" She flops back onto the cushions. "Seriously. I had no idea I was into long hair and beards, but he looks like a dark-haired Thor. And those shoulders. Geez, he filled your entire doorway. He's got to be what, six-three? Six-four?"

"I told you, didn't I?" I say, turning my head to look at her. "Goalies are usually pretty big guys. His hair isn't long enough to be Thor though. It doesn't even touch his shoulders."

"Same vibe though. Those are definitely not the fine-boned hands of a musician."

Nope. There's nothing fine-boned or delicate about Felix. He's more like a very solid, very sexy oak tree. Though, there's a certain grace to the way he moves that belies his size. That's probably the goalie in him. He seems very intentional—very connected to his body.

Summer pulls a blanket off the back of the couch and tugs it over her. "Tell me more," she says. "What else does his goalie status tell us?" She frowns. "Wait, does it annoy you that I'm asking? Wanting you to talk about hockey?"

It's an unfortunate conundrum that the sport I've sworn out of my life forever is actually the one I know the most about. After so many years watching my brother play, I can talk the talk as well as the most diehard fan.

"It's okay," I say. "But if my eyes start to roll back in my head, turn on one of Bach's cello suites until I seem like myself again."

Suddenly, music is playing through the living room wall I share with Felix, and Summer sits up a little taller. "You mean *those* cello suites?" She stands and walks to the wall where she leans her ear close. "Umm, that's totally Bach."

Summer's parents are both musicians, retired professors from the music department at UNC-Asheville, so she knows her classical music almost as well as I do. It's one of the things we bonded over our freshman year of college.

I groan and pull a pillow over my face. "He's doing this on purpose."

She turns and props her hands on her hips. "I'd be pushing my luck if I said I wanted to go to a hockey game tomorrow, right?"

I drop the pillow and scowl.

"Okay, okay." She holds up her hands in surrender. "Just checking."

"Why would you want to go to a game anyway? If you keep this up, I might start to think you're interested in him."

"In Felix? Nah. That man *only* has eyes for you." She drops back onto the couch. "I'm mostly just curious. The Appies are all over social media right now, and the buzz is big. Might be fun to see what all the hype is about."

"The hype is the product of a social media genius who knows how to capture an audience," I say. "It isn't even about the hockey. At least not entirely. They've turned the Appies into their own vibe."

"And you know so much about this because?" Summer asks pointedly.

I roll my eyes. "I live in Harvest Hollow. Whenever I'm on TikTok, their stuff comes up. It's only based on proximity, not actual interest."

"Uh-huh, sure," Summer says, her voice thick with sarcasm. "That's exactly what the TikTok algorithm is based on. Location." She pokes around on her phone for another minute or two. "Soooo, does your location-based, totally accidental and only occasional TikTok viewing mean you have or have not seen the montage of sexy Appies in suits arriving for game day?" She holds out her phone so I can see.

I've definitely seen it. And watched the three seconds of screen time dedicated to Felix at least a dozen times. "Can't remember," I say noncommittally.

"Right. Which means you probably aren't even a little bit curious about all the female fans who will be throwing themselves against the plexiglass tomorrow, hoping to catch Felix's eye."

"Women do not throw themselves against the plexiglass," I say with a feigned indifference I hope Summer buys. Better that than owning up to the surge of jealousy that exploded in my chest the second she mentioned other women. It's bad enough she saw my jealousy at dinner.

All of it is ridiculous.

I will *not* be jealous of Summer, and I will *not* be jealous of hockey fans who are interested in a man who doesn't mean anything to me.

"You would know better than I would," Summer says. "I'm just saying there are some crazy fans on Tiktok, and some of these videos look like they're about Felix *specifically*." She looks up from her phone. "Is there a goalie fetish? Is that a thing?"

"If there is, I don't know anything about it," I say.

A beat of silence stretches between us while I wrestle with my inexplicable jealousy, broken only by the soft strains of Bach floating through the living room wall. The truth is, there probably are women throwing themselves at the plexiglass at Appies games. But I'm guessing that's probably true for all professional sports. There's something appealing about the energy and effort and dedication required for that level of elite athleticism.

And goalies do have their own brand of sexy. At least, I thought they did when I was a teenager, even if I was loath to admit it out loud. "When I was growing up, I was always impressed by the kids who were willing to play goalie," I finally say. "Josh never wanted to. Said it was too much pressure—especially because the younger the team, the weaker their defensive skills are, so goalies are often the only thing between a win or a loss. But the goalies always seemed like they had this quiet confidence."

"I mean, I've only been around him for a minute or two, but that *definitely* sounds like your neighbor," Summer says.

Based on tonight's interaction, Summer's observation rings true. Felix has seemed nervous a few times before, but tonight, when he leaned into my apartment and told me he hopes I change my mind about hockey players, *that* was the confidence I might expect to see in a goalie. And it was *dead sexy*.

On the other side of the wall, the music shifts into the second of Bach's six cello suites. It isn't as well known as the first, but it's still one of my favorites to play. I suddenly wonder if he's ever heard me playing it, if maybe his music selection for this evening was intentional.

"I played this for my All-State Orchestra audition my junior year," I say softly, pointing toward the wall.

"That was the year you met my mom, right?" Summer asks. "When she did the cello workshop?"

I nod. "It was also the year Josh's hockey team went to the playoffs."

Summer frowns. "Based on the tone of your voice, this story doesn't have a happy ending."

"Nope. You still want to hear it?"

She bites her lip, then nods. "Tell me. I think you *need* to tell me, and that makes me want to listen."

I take a deep breath. "So, All-State was up in Boone every year, and the district used an activity bus to get us all there on Friday afternoon. Between the two high schools, there were thirty of us who made it through auditions and were selected for the orchestra. Once there, we rehearsed all weekend, spent two nights in a hotel, then rehearsed Sunday morning until our concert that afternoon. Of course, our families were invited to the concert, so the understanding was that after our performance, we could ride home with our parents."

Summer leans forward and tucks her arms around her knees, pulling them to her chest, her gaze trained on me. "Your family didn't come, did they?"

"They were at Josh's regional playoff game in Asheville. He was a senior, and if they'd lost, it would have been his last game on the team. That was the reason they gave me. I'd have lots of performances, but they couldn't miss what might be Josh's *last game.* Which I maybe understood, I guess. But..." I shake my head, hating that years later, I can still conjure up the loneliness that trailed me that weekend. "All I know is that I rode the activity bus back to Harvest Hollow alone," I say. "Thirty kids from two high schools, and I was the only one with no one there. It was just me and two teachers. I'm not sure I've ever felt so lonely."

"Gracie, it's not cool they did that to you," Summer says. "It's not. Your stuff was important, too."

I let Summer's words wash over me, and for once, I recognize the truth of them. For a long time, I thought maybe I was the problem. But Summer's right. It wasn't cool. All the times they made me feel less than, like my things weren't as important simply because they didn't understand them—that wasn't good parenting.

But there isn't anything I can do about it now. As far as I see it, I can let my frustration and bitterness completely ruin the relationship I have with my parents, or I can accept it for what it is, set healthy boundaries where I need them, and move on.

For the most part, it's working. I'm even finding ways to focus on the positive and recognize that, in their own way, my parents *did* try.

They paid for my lessons. They bought my first cello. They paid for half of my education when I got a music degree.

That's not nothing.

But I will always be a mystery to my parents. No one else in my family likes classical music. No one else plays an instrument or listens to anything but Spotify's curated list of recent hits. I was so different from my brother, it's no wonder they had no idea what to make of me.

When they thought I wasn't listening, my parents joked about how I must have been swapped at birth. Somewhere out there, two classical musicians were wondering how they wound up with a daughter who dreamed of hockey skates and slept in Appies jerseys every night.

Still, I can't expect them to become different people any more than they can expect me to become the world's greatest hockey fan.

I will always choose the symphony, and they will always choose wearing matching jerseys and watching the Stanley Cup over plates of pigs in a blanket and chips and queso.

But this life that I'm building for myself can be different. It can be what *I* make it.

"It's okay, right?" I ask, shifting my attention back to Summer. The earlier buzz of the wine has worn off, making me sleepy and a little melancholy. I sniff against an unexpected wave of emotion. "It's okay if I just want to move on from that part of my life, right? I'm sure Felix is a nice guy. But there are so many reasons why it would be complicated. I don't want complicated."

Summer studies me for a long moment. "It's totally okay," she says. "A part of me wants to tell you that you shouldn't let your past keep you from an incredibly hot guy who seems interested, especially because the guy in question seems like more than just a pretty face. But I also trust you. If you say he's not the man for you, then he's not the man for you. And I won't mention him again."

I push down a surprising pulse of sadness as I consider her words. But that's dumb. I shouldn't be sad because Felix Jamison is not the man for me.

He simply can't be.

The next morning, I drag Summer to hot yoga, then we come back long enough to shower and change before we head to the farmer's market so Summer can enjoy the magic of Harvest Hollow in the fall. She grew up in the mountains too, so she's used to the gorgeous colors, the reds and yellows blanketing the hillsides and adding pops of color to every front yard. But Harvest Hollow has a particular love for the few months when summer cools into winter. Everything is pumpkin spice and apples and hay bales and scarecrows and warm cider stirred with cinnamon sticks, and I love every bit of it.

"Honestly," Summer says as we stroll through the market, apple cider donuts in hand, "I used to think that places like this only exist in the movies. But here we are." She stops and picks up an apple from an overflowing bushel basket, lifting it to her nose.

"They grow apples where you live, too."

"Oh, I know. But this farmer's market? It would be the perfect location for a romcom meet cute." She spins around to face me. "A farmer and a florist, maybe. Or a baker!" She takes a bite of her donut. "A baker and a bookshop owner."

"Our local bookshop owner just hit it off with a fireman. Does that feel romcom enough for you?"

She gasps. "Please tell me he rescued her from a fire."

I frown. "He *did,* and it was terrifying because it wasn't just a movie, it was her actual real life."

"Geez, you're right. So sorry. She's okay, right? And she got love out of the deal?"

I smile, thinking of my friend, Emmy, who runs Book Smart over on Maple Street, and her new boyfriend, Owen. "She totally did. It was cute to watch it all unfold..." My words trail off when Summer stops walking, her eyes locked on something just over my shoulder.

I turn, tracing her gaze to a booth set up at the edge of the parking lot. It looks like the local radio station is broadcasting live, and several Appies hockey players are sitting at a table at the front of the booth, signing autographs and handing out team merchandise.

Can I seriously *never* escape this freaking hockey team?

Summer grips my arm. "Do you see that guy? The one at the end?"

"End of what?" I ask, still not clear who she's staring at. Maybe because the second I saw the Appies logo hanging above the booth, I immediately started looking for Felix.

"The guy on the end with the man bun," Summer says. "I feel like I know him. Could I have met him somewhere before?"

"Are you talking about one of the hockey players?"

Summer nods, biting her lip, and I'm finally able to pick out the guy in question. I've never seen him before, but Summer is transfixed. "You could probably look him up on the team's website," I suggest. "Maybe see if his name knocks something loose in your brain?"

"Ohh, good idea," she says, pulling out her phone.

While she searches, my eyes scan the players one more time. I recognize Eli, the guy who has knocked on my door one too many times asking me if I'm ready to have dinner with him yet, but Felix is nowhere to be found—something that sends relief and disappointment pumping through me in equal measure.

The relief, I understand. The disappointment is just silly. What would I even do if I *did* see him? Go up and ask him for his autograph?

"Huh," Summer says, still looking at her phone. "His name is Nathan Sanders, and he's from Portland, Maine, so probably I *don't* know him. Weird."

"Maybe he just has a familiar face?" I nudge her shoulder. "Or maybe he has a face you like, and you just *want* to meet him?"

She barks out a laugh. "What? That's not—why would he feel familiar? That would be weird."

"Maybe it's your heart that recognizes him."

Summer rolls her eyes. "Please tell me you're joking."

"This could be *your* meet cute. The hardened assistant DA and the brutish pro hockey player who's really just a giant softie and knows exactly how to crack through her shell."

She pauses. "I would actually read that book. But I'm anything but hardened." She reaches over and grabs my arm. "Oh, hey, isn't that your brother?" She points toward the line stretching out from the radio station's booth.

I smile. "And my nephew." I loop my arm through Summer's. "Come on. I'll introduce you to Maddox—*oh geez.*" My words cut off, and I change directions, turning sharply to the right and diving behind a stack of hay bales.

Summer freezes, her eyes wide. "Gracie?"

I shush her quickly and motion her over. When she's finally crouching beside me, I breathe out an enormous exhale and let my shoulders relax. "Felix is over there. I didn't see him before, but he must have switched seats with one of the other guys because he's there. He's sitting *right there.*"

"Okay. And we're scared to see him again because...why?"

I huff out a frustrated breath. "Because...I don't want things to be awkward."

She levels me with a stern look. "Gracie. You're going to see him eventually anyway. Besides, he told you he wouldn't pressure you. It's only going to be awkward if you make it that way."

She moves like she's going to stand up, and I tug her back down. She lands with an oof, dropping to her butt beside me.

"It's not just the dating thing," I say. "Felix is Maddox's favorite player. And I'd rather Josh *not* know that all this time, I've been living next door to an Appie, especially Maddox's *favorite* Appie, without telling him."

"Will you not *ever* tell him?" Summer asks, eyeing me skeptically.

"Eventually? Probably?" I say. "But is it so bad that I want to keep Josh and all his hockey enthusiasm out of my personal life? If he knew Felix was my neighbor, he would literally be at my house every day."

"A valid concern," Summer says. She lets out a little snort. "Can you imagine what your family would think if you actually *did* date Felix? Oh, man. They would be so thrilled."

Annoyingly thrilled, I think. I won't lie and say it doesn't play some role in my resistance to Felix's charms. Showing up at a family dinner with Felix as my date? My parents would treat me like the prodigal daughter who finally found her way back to the hockey-enthused fold. I'm willing to own that my pride on this point might be slightly childish. But after so many years, I can't stand the thought of giving my parents that kind of satisfaction.

I shift onto my knees and lift up just enough to see over the top of the hay bale.

Maddox is at the front of the line now, smiling wide as Felix signs a poster of the team, then passes it over to Eli for him to do the same thing.

Felix laughs at something Maddox says, his expression warm and genuine, then he holds up his hand, offering him a fist bump before shaking Josh's hand. The interaction only lasts a couple of seconds, but Maddox is completely glowing as he takes the poster from Eli.

I bite my lip, my eyes shifting back to Felix as he greets the next person in line. He smiles again, the late morning sunshine glinting off his dark brown hair, and my gut tightens.

Honestly, does he *have* to be so handsome? My resistance would be so much easier if he wasn't.

"Aunt Gracie?" I turn to see Maddox standing directly beside me. On my knees, we're basically eye-to-eye.

"Maddox!" I say. "What are you doing here?"

"Better question," Josh says. "Why are you hiding behind a hay bale?"

I scramble to my feet. "Who's hiding? I'm not hiding!" I dust the hay and dirt off my knees, making sure my back is to Felix. "I was just, uh, tying my shoe."

Maddox's eyes drop to my feet. "You're wearing boots," he says. "They don't have any ties."

I hold up my feet as Summer starts to chuckle beside me. "Oh hey. Look at that I guess I am." I gesture to Summer. "You remember Summer, right? My college roommate?"

Josh nods, his expression clearly saying he knows I was up to something even if I won't admit it. "Yeah. Good to see you, Summer."

"And this is my favorite nephew ever, Maddox," I say.

Maddox rolls his eyes. "I'm your *only* nephew."

I gesture to the poster in Maddox's hands, trusting that if anything will distract away from my weird behavior, it's hockey. "Is that the hockey team?"

Maddox holds up the poster, his smile wide. "Yeah. And a few of the players signed it for me." He points at Eli's signature, which looks like little more than a scribble. "This is Eli Hopkins. He's a right wing." His finger slides over to Felix's name, which is written in cursive neat enough to be its own font.

Felix's handwriting isn't at all what I would expect from a typical athlete, and yet, it somehow seems exactly on point for Felix.

"And this is Felix Jamison," Maddox says. "He's the goaltender, and he's my favorite. At the end of last season, he had the highest save percentage in the whole Atlantic Division."

"I think he'll be the best in the AHL this year," Josh adds. "Which, short term, that would be great for the Appies, but long term, it'll only increase the odds of us losing him to the NHL."

"Nah, I bet he'll be an Appie forever," Maddox says. "He said in an interview last week that Harvest Hollow is his favorite place to live."

"Amazing stats *and* a love for your hometown?" Summer says under her breath. "Impressive."

I'm more impressed with his handwriting, but okay, sure. His hockey stats are enough to raise my eyebrows. "He sounds pretty cool," I say, ruffling Maddox's hair. "Is that the first time you've met him?"

He nods, his shoulders lifting the slightest bit. "He gave me a fist bump." He looks back toward the hockey players, and I resist the urge to follow his gaze, to grab another glimpse of Felix's warm smile.

"Hey, you wanna go buy some apple butter with me?" I ask, reaching for Maddox's hand. "Maybe we can grab a jar for your mom, too."

He looks up at his dad, who shrugs. "Fine by me. We don't have anything else to do until the game."

Once we're far enough away that I can *stop* worrying about whether my neighbor will spot me with two of his biggest fans, I'm able to relax and actually *enjoy* wandering around the farmer's market, especially now that Maddox is with us.

He's a funny kid—the funniest, really—and I genuinely love hanging out with him. He takes to Summer right away, who answers his questions with the same level of dedication she gave to the civil procedures class that was nearly her undoing her first year of law school. She listens intently, then answers like Maddox truly matters—like his reasons for asking are as important as anything else.

My heart stretches the tiniest bit. My parents did a lot of things right, but they didn't always talk to me like my thoughts were important, especially since they were so frequently different from their own. Josh got lucky. He loves hockey as much as they do, so his opinions *always* mattered. But mine? Not so much.

When I have kids—if I *ever* have kids—I want to talk to them just like Summer is talking to Maddox. Like they matter.

Like whatever they love is the most important thing. Whether it's music or horseback riding or swimming or drawing.

Or hockey, I think, a weight settling into my stomach. I'm a Mitchell, after all. If my own family is any indication, where seventy-five percent of us are diehard fans, the odds are pretty good I might have at least one kid who loves the sport. Especially if I live in Harvest Hollow.

Hockey isn't really big in North Carolina generally, but the presence of the Appies in Harvest Hollow has gone a long way to creating a hockey-friendly culture, at least in our community. Add in the recent social media efforts Summer was talking about last night, and a hockey-friendly culture has morphed into a practically rabid fanbase.

The schools don't have teams, but the local youth league is thriving, with tons of businesses always willing to sponsor games and tournaments. It's nothing like you might find further north where kids can just play outside on frozen lakes, regardless of whether they have the money to join a league. But it's pretty much impossible to grow up here and *not* be exposed to hockey, at least on the most basic level.

Throw in my family? My genetics?

There's no way I'll be able to keep any future offspring from learning about the sport.

And I wouldn't want to. Not really. I would have died if my parents had tried to keep me from playing the cello. I was in the third grade when the high school orchestra visited my elementary school and played all the different instruments for us. A guy with shaggy blond hair and thick, black glasses played "Hedwig's Theme" from the Harry Potter movie soundtracks on the cello, and I was transfixed from the first familiar note all the way to the end. As soon as he finished, my hand shot up in the air, and when the teacher leading the demonstration called on me, I looked right at the cellist and said, "Can you play it again?"

It was two years after that when I finally started lessons—two years of begging and pleading and promising to save up my allowance money to pay for a cello myself—and it felt like coming home. Like my hands had been made for the singular purpose of holding that instrument.

I look up at Maddox, bouncing on his toes next to his dad.

I wouldn't tell that kid he couldn't play hockey to save my own life.

And I won't say it to my own kid, either.

I finally turn and let myself look back across the farmer's market at the radio station booth. My eye immediately snags on Felix's broad shoulders, his dark hair glinting in the sunlight. He's standing just outside the booth with a kid wearing an Appies jersey who is crouched in a goalie stance, his arms outstretched. Felix makes a couple of adjustments to his position, then nods and gives him a high five.

I have no idea how or why. And I don't know if it will last. But for the briefest moment, with thoughts of Felix and Maddox flitting through my brain, my animosity toward the sport I've spent half my life hating thaws the slightest bit.

It's always been all or nothing in my brain.

But maybe—*maybe*—it doesn't have to be.

CHAPTER SIX

Felix

THE ENERGY AND EXCITEMENT inside the Summit, the arena where the Appies both practice and play our home games, is palpable. The guys are all keyed up, buzzing around the locker room, taping sticks, putting on the last of our gear.

"We'll gather in five," Coach calls.

Across from me, Logan stands, helmet in hand. He seems stoic, his expression serious. We all want to win—there's no doubt about that—but Logan has the most on the line tonight. His performance at last week's preseason game was stellar, but that just means he'll be watched more closely tonight. I don't have a single doubt that he'll eventually be called back to the NHL, but I'm sure he's feeling the pressure just the same.

"Hey," I say, meeting his eye. "We've got this."

Logan only nods as he moves toward Coach, who is waiting at the opposite end of the locker room.

"Let's dooooo it," Eli says as he comes up beside me. He's practically pulsing with energy, but that's typical for Eli right before a game. I tend to be the opposite. I get quiet, focused.

Eli drops his hands on my shoulders, giving them a friendly shake. "How are you feeling, man?"

"In the zone."

Eli smiles and brushes his blond hair out of his eyes. "Like always." He pounds the top of my shoulder pads. "Hey, how's your neighbor?"

I pause, my gaze narrowing. "Gracie?"

"Yeah, man. I think I'm starting to wear her down. She'll be having dinner with me before the end of the month."

My jaw clenches, and I rub a hand across my beard. "I highly doubt that."

Eli's eyes widen, then he grins. "Oh, I see how it is. You're making a move yourself." He holds his hands up and backs up a few steps. "I can respect that."

I don't know if I'm making a move, exactly, but Gracie has been on my mind almost nonstop since last night. I was even distracted falling asleep because I couldn't stop thinking about whether she had enough water to drink before she went to bed to avoid feeling hungover this morning.

"Oh, by the way," Eli adds, "Alec wanted me to tell you he volunteered you for two more skills clinics with the youth league next month."

"Two?"

"Yeah, man. Captain's orders. One just for goalies, then a second one next month for the younger kids. He knew you'd say yes."

"Because you're a sucker," Van says as he walks by, tape and hockey stick in hand.

I wouldn't say I'm a *sucker*, but Eli's right about me saying yes. I usually do.

My therapist tells me my desire to please is slightly hyper-active—something that probably traces back to wanting to impress a perpetually unimpressed father.

Is it such a bad thing? That I'm always doing stuff to make other people's lives easier?

As far as I see it, there are worse ways to cope with family dysfunction.

When it comes to the hockey team, saying yes to things like youth skills clinics isn't required. But it does earn me brownie points with our social media manager. She's always doing pro-mo videos for TikTok, many of which require dancing, and I'd rather not be front and center for those.

Parker would never force me, or anyone else, into the spot-light, but it doesn't feel right to stay in the background while the rest of the guys do the chicken dance across the ice. In my mind, all the extra volunteering at least helps balance things out.

"You good with it?" Alec says as he passes me.

I nod, picking up my stick and following behind him. "You know I am."

Minutes later, the crowd roars as we take the ice. It feels good to be back in front of an audience, their enthusiasm making the room vibrate with energy. At first, I let myself listen—the swish of our skates as we warm up, the clatter of sticks, the cheering of the crowd as they pound on the glass.

But once I'm in the net and the puck drops, all background noise fades away. It's just me and the game and my determination to stop every single shot. My pregame mantra runs through my head and settles me into the zone.

I'm steady. I'm focused. No one controls me but me.

I make eye contact with Logan as he skates by to take his position, and he grins.

Then we're on.

The guys are good to me, playing killer defense, but by the end of the second period, the other team still hasn't scored, and I've got a near-record number of saves for one game. Logan is on fire tonight, the rest of the guys, too, and their energy makes it easy for me to keep up the pace for one more period.

The last shot I block, I catch with my glove, and it hits hard. I'll probably have a bruise, but when the game-ending buzzer sounds seconds later, I don't give my hand a second thought.

We won.

And it was a total shutout.

We're all cheering and celebrating the win when I see Logan a few yards away, looking into the stands, his eyes trained on Parker.

Nathan skates by and pats me on the back in a gesture of support, but I can't take my eyes off Logan's lovestruck face.

He looks like a man who knows what he wants—who *has* what he wants.

My eyes drift over the crowd—Mom is out there somewhere—but it doesn't feel the same.

I want something more.

Someone more.

The feeling stays with me the entire time I'm showering and getting dressed. The guys are all going out, and I'd generally join them—I'll easily give up a night with Ivy when we've got a win to celebrate—but with my mom in town, I bow out, even when Eli suggests I bring her with me.

"What are you worried about?" he asks. "You think your mom might fall in love with me?" He runs a hand over his hair, slicking it back like he's trying to be smooth. "I mean, let's be real. She probably will."

I roll my eyes and shove Eli away. "You guys have fun. I'll see you next week."

I find Mom waiting in the area of the Summit designated for family and friends of the players. She smiles wide as I approach, then reaches up and gives me a big hug. "It's been too long since I've seen you play," she says. "You were amazing."

"Thanks, Mom." She's wearing an Appies jersey she must have bought before the game, and it's swallowing her petite frame, but it feels good to have her support me like this. I can only guess how hard Mom had to fight against Dad to make this trip at all. I won't wish her away even if I would rather have a girlfriend wearing my jersey and watching me play.

An image of Gracie pops into my mind, and I find myself wondering what she'd look like wearing Appies team colors, a number thirty-one across her back. The thought triggers such an intense jolt of longing that I lift a hand to my chest, rubbing it across my heart like I can massage the feeling away.

I don't know Gracie well enough for her to cause that kind of reaction, but there's something bigger at play here. I want a relationship. I'm ready for one.

Mom pulls out her cell phone. "Here. I want to show you something." She scrolls through a few screens, then holds it up so I can see a text exchange she had with my father.

Emily: Game is over, and the Appies won in front of a sold-out crowd. So proud of Felix.

Derrick: How did Felix play?

Emily: He was perfect. Total shutout.

Derrick: Good.

I'm not sure what Dad means by *good.* If it hadn't been a shutout, would he have said something like *better luck next time* or *that's too bad?* But the hope in Mom's eyes says she wants this to make me happy. And it *is* nice that Dad asked.

"That's great, Mom. Really great."

"I promise he cares, Felix. He's proud of you."

I force a smile. "I know. I'm glad you were here tonight, Mom."

Beside me, another teammate, Ryan, greets his girlfriend, who practically bowls him over when she launches herself into his arms. Ryan barely got any playing time, but she's still here, kissing him like he just scored the final goal for a Stanley Cup win.

Mom follows my gaze. "I thought that neighbor of yours might come to watch you play."

If only. Even if Gracie does, eventually, agree to go out with me, I doubt she'll ever come to a hockey game, which, considering my present mood, has me reconsidering my newfound crush.

Will it matter if the person I'm with isn't here to support me at my games?

Any other day, I might have said no, but watching Ryan with his girlfriend and Logan, earlier, when he was looking at Parker, it's hard not to want what they have. I know for a fact Parker loves hockey almost as much as Logan does. She knows the game, knows how to skate, knows how to speak Logan's language.

But does every relationship have to be like that? Does mine?

The question stays with me through the rest of the weekend.

Hockey won't always be a part of my life, at least not like it is now. But even when I'm no longer playing, I'll still enjoy the sport. Watching it, talking about it. It's part of who I am.

Will it matter if the woman I'm with doesn't feel the same way?

I drive Mom to the airport in Knoxville on Sunday morning, promising to come to Chicago for Christmas, then head back to Harvest Hollow. I take the long way home, through Gatlinburg, then cut through Great Smoky Mountains National Park so I can enjoy the views. The mountains are a blaze of color, red and yellow and orange as far as the eye can see.

When I finally pull into my parking space at the warehouse, there's a text waiting on my phone.

Logan: Dude. You home? Can we stop by a sec?

We. That must mean Parker is with him.

Felix: Just got home. Come whenever. I'm not going anywhere.

It's less than ten minutes later when they knock.

"Hey," Logan says, carrying a giant box through the front door. Parker follows behind with a stack of books in her hands.

"Your text came at the perfect time," Logan says. "We were right around the corner getting lunch."

"Glad it worked out. Hi, boss," I say to Parker. "What's in the box?"

"Jerseys," Parker says. "For the youth clinics. There are six jerseys on top for the goalie clinic, and you need to get those back to me soon. The others are less time sensitive. Maybe just get them back to me before the end of the month?" She pauses and looks around my apartment, her hands propped on her hips. She's never been here, and it always makes me nervous when people from the team see my nicer-than-average place. Hopefully, Logan has already filled her in.

"How many of these things are you doing?" Logan says as he drops the box onto my kitchen table. "Didn't you do the last one too?"

I shrug. "I don't mind."

"He's a favorite with the youth coaches because he's so patient with the kids—more patient than just about anyone else." She eyes me, her expression pointed. "Still. You don't *have* to say yes, Felix. You already do so much more than most of the other players."

"He went to sign merch at the farmers market yesterday before the game," Logan says unhelpfully.

Parker narrows her eyes. "Felix, there were plenty of guys there. You didn't have to show up."

"I didn't mind." I move into my kitchen and pull out a couple of glasses, pouring water for Logan and Parker. I don't know that they need it, but it gives me something to do with my hands.

Am I seriously getting scolded for being *too* helpful?

When I spin back around, water glasses in hand, Parker has her arms folded across her chest and her lips pursed. If I didn't know Parker so well, I might cower under that gaze, but for all her intensity, she's got a good heart. She'll make her point, but she'll make it gently.

"Just say whatever it is, Parker. I can tell you want to." I hold out the water, and she takes both glasses, handing one to Logan.

She takes a long drink before setting her glass on the counter. "I know you don't do as much of the social media stuff as the other guys, but you're doing more than enough to make up for it. I promise there isn't some invisible score-sheet here. You know I won't push you to do stuff that's outside of your comfort zone."

I push my hands into my pockets. "I know that. I do."

She shrugs. "Then relax a little. You don't have anything to prove, Felix. You're an asset to this team, and you're doing enough."

Her words strike an uncomfortable chord deep in my gut. *You don't have anything to prove.*

I know I'm a solid hockey player. My stats are great, I'm responsible, reliable, and I don't get into any trouble. Two years ago, I was even offered a contract with the NHL. Ultimately, I turned it down because I would have been third goalie in line, which would have meant a lot more time riding the pine than I'm getting as an Appie and a lot more volatility in my career. Especially with my social anxiety, the idea of stability and less time in the spotlight, both things the Appies offered me, sounded a lot better.

I *know* all this, so why do Parker's words still ring true? Am I still trying to prove myself? Prove that I'm worth keeping around?

Logan motions toward my living room. "Maybe you need to spend a little more time with Ivy?"

Parker rolls her eyes knowingly. Clearly, Logan has told his new girlfriend *all* my secrets, even the undercover name I use for my book collection.

"Or...maybe you should spend some time with Gracie?" Parker says.

My eyes swivel to Logan. Does the man have no boundaries when it comes to this woman? "You told her?" I say.

He holds up his hands. "I told you I'd ask about her, and I did. It didn't take rocket science for Parker to guess you were asking because you're interested."

I run a hand through my hair. "I'm not even sure I *am* interested. She hates hockey. That feels like a pretty giant red flag."

Parker studies me closely. "Your tone says you like her though. Otherwise her not liking hockey wouldn't make you sound like I just kicked your puppy."

I drop onto a barstool and lean on my counter, suddenly wishing I *was* spending time with Ivy. In fact, that's exactly what I plan to do as soon as I'm alone. I've got a stack of new books from the library and a sudden craving for solitude.

"It doesn't matter if I like her," I say. "I don't think anything is going to happen."

Parker doesn't look all that convinced.

"Either way, I didn't know her," she says. "I think she must be older than me, but her brother did play hockey with my brother Brandon—and Logan, too. Josh Mitchell. Brandon says he played a year of hockey at Ohio State, but when he found out his girlfriend was pregnant, he dropped out of school and moved back home, married her, and started working with his father-in-law. He and Brandon still see each other every once in a while. He says Josh is a great guy, but he doesn't remember anything about his sister."

"The brother never played hockey again?" I ask.

Parker shakes her head. "I mean, he might still play for fun. But he's not doing anything serious. He's an electrician now."

I have to respect a man willing to step up and take responsibility like Gracie's brother did, especially when it means walking away from college hockey. Most guys don't go pro from college, even to the minor leagues, but it's the easiest way to get a shot. If Josh Mitchell was a decent player, it had to have been hard to walk away.

"Oh, before I forget," Parker says. She slides the stack of books toward me across the counter. "These are yours. Thanks for loaning them to me."

"No problem." I pick up the books and carry them toward the bookshelf. I slow as I reach the far end of the living room—the end closest to Gracie's apartment. Gracie is practicing, the sounds of her cello floating through the wall and wrapping around me like some kind of warm weighted blanket.

After our game yesterday, I was halfway convinced that Gracie *not* liking hockey was a dealbreaker.

The second I hear her playing, all that flies out the window. I listen to classical music all the time, but somehow, hearing *her* play it feels different. Like *more.*

I lean forward, one hand pressed against the bookshelf, and listen for another moment, the music filling the emptiness I've been carrying around since last night.

"Hey man, we're going to get out of your hair," Logan says from behind me.

I spin around, embarrassed to realize I'd briefly forgotten they were even here. "Sorry, I guess I'm a little distracted."

"We've got things to do anyway," Parker says. "But think about what I said, all right?"

I nod. "Thanks. I'll see you guys later."

As soon as they're gone, I drop into the chair nearest my wall and lean my head back.

As long as Gracie is playing, I plan on sitting right here to listen.

CHAPTER SEVEN
Felix

I JOLT AWAKE TO the sound of pounding on my front door. *Frantic* pounding. I have no idea how long I've been asleep in my living room chair, my book open and draped across my lap, but it's almost dark outside, so it's been a few hours, at least.

"Felix?" Gracie calls, and I scramble out of my chair, hurrying to the door.

I practically yank it open to find Gracie standing in the hallway, dripping wet.

I look her up and down, my eyes wide. "What is it? What happened?"

She brushes a strand of wet hair away from her face. "I have no idea," she says, her voice laced with panic. "I think a pipe might have burst? There's water everywhere, and you never gave me our landlord's number, and I have no idea how to make it stop."

"The water is still running? You didn't turn it off?"

She moves toward her front door, and I follow behind. "It's pouring out of my bedroom wall like a freaking fountain," she says. "How do I turn that off?"

This shifts me into overdrive, and I hurry past her, cursing the old pipes in the building as I race to her laundry room. Behind the water heater, there's a shutoff valve that will turn off the water to her entire apartment. The agent that showed her the place should have shown her where it is, but even if the agent *did,* something like that is an easy thing to forget when you're frantic.

Water squelches under my feet as I turn the knob, and the gushing sound coming from Gracie's bedroom finally slows, then stops.

Gracie exhales behind me. "How did you do that?"

I step out of the way so she can see the valve. "See the knob right there? With the blue handle? That turns off the water to your entire apartment. Useful if you ever have plumbing repairs—"

"Or an exploding pipe?" she says, cutting me off.

I nod. "That, too."

She walks past me to her bedroom, pausing in the doorway, hands propped on her hips. She's barefoot, wearing black leggings and a blue tank top, both of which are soaking wet and clinging to her like a second skin, revealing every single one of her curves.

I cast my eyes to the ceiling, not needing that particular distraction amid my first crisis as a landlord. Especially since Gracie still has no idea that the phone number I never gave her is *mine.*

I definitely meant to have the conversation with her, to give her my number and find out what's wrong with her stove, we just haven't had the chance. Or maybe I just haven't known how to bring it up. *Surprise! I own your apartment. Now about that stove...*

It's not like I was trying to keep it a secret. But generally, if I can avoid talking about my money, or my family's money, I will. And owning a newly renovated building, especially when my hockey salary is barely a livable wage, is an excellent way to advertise some level of hidden wealth.

I step to the bedroom door, stopping next to Gracie as I survey the damage. There's *a lot* of it. The exposed pipes and ductwork that I left in both apartments give the place a very modern, cool feel, but I wonder if, in this case, drywall might have minimized some of the mess. Gracie's bed is soaked, and there's at least an inch of water pooled on the floor. The dresser sitting just under the ruptured pipe has water dripping from every corner, and the open closet on the other side of the dresser looks like someone sprayed it down with a garden hose.

My brain is a jumble of emotions. Guilt that this happened in the first place. Worry that Gracie will never forgive me when she discovers I'm to blame. Not to mention the stress over what it's going to cost to handle the repairs.

"I think every article of clothing I own is wet," Gracie says, her voice small. She turns and looks up at me. "Tell me what to do here, Felix. I have *no idea* what to do."

I don't know what to do either. My first impulse is to scoop her into my arms, carry her away from this mess, and never look back. But that's neither practical nor logical.

I have to fix this. I have to make this right for her.

And even though I may not know where or how to start, I know someone who will.

He's the last person I want to call right now, but at this point, I'm not sure I have any other choice.

I pull out my phone to call my dad, but before I can hit send, Gracie shivers beside me.

I look over, immediately noticing the goosebumps all over her exposed shoulders and arms. She has to be getting cold wearing clothes that are soaking wet.

I pocket my phone.

At least this part of the problem, I can solve on my own.

"Okay, first things first," I say. "You need to get warm and dry."

She lifts her eyebrows. "In an apartment full of water, with no dry clothes?"

"Come to my place. You can shower. I'll lend you something to wear until we sort this out."

She looks me up and down, like the idea of wearing my clothes is laughable. But what other choice does she have? She wraps her arms around herself. "I should probably call the landlord first though, right?"

"Yeah, about that." I run a hand through my hair, nerves tightening my gut. "I actually *am* your landlord." I look up and meet her gaze. "I own the building."

"You?" she says, her brow furrowed. "But you're a hockey player."

"In the minor leagues, making a less-than-impressive salary," I say. "I'm not the only guy on the team with other stuff going on. Part-time jobs. Off-season side hustles. It's hard to make it work, otherwise." It's not the full truth. But I don't exactly want to launch into the details of my unusual financial situation right here, in the middle of her waterlogged apartment.

She lets out a little chuckle. "Sounds like the life of a musician." She shivers again, and I quickly unzip my hoodie, shrugging it off and draping it around her shoulders. "Felix, no," she says, trying to shrug out from under it. "I'll get it wet. I'm soaked."

"You're also shivering," I say. "Just take it. I insist."

She sniffs, then lifts her hands to grasp either side of the hoodie. Her fingers brush against mine, and they're icy cold.

Acting on instinct, I grab her hands, holding them inside mine, rubbing my palms over the backs of her hands to warm them up. I hate that my remodeling decisions landed her in this situation in the first place, but I'm not sorry to have an excuse to touch her. Or sorry that she isn't complaining or pulling away.

"We need to warm you up," I say.

"The water was really cold." She lets out a little laugh. "At first, I tried to stop it with my hands. Like I could somehow staunch the flow. It seems ridiculous now, but I just...panicked."

"Water was gushing from your bedroom wall. I think your panic was justified."

"When I realized there wasn't anything I could do to stop it, I did the only other thing I could think of," she says. "I ran to get *you*."

Heat spreads through my chest at her admission. I *like* that I'm the person she ran to for help. I mean, *yes*, I'm her only neighbor. But still. It has to mean something that she trusts me enough to have asked in the first place.

I lift her still-freezing hands and blow on them softly, and she lets out a tiny gasp.

"Does that help?" I ask, my voice low.

Her lips part as she gives the tiniest nod, her body arching toward me the slightest bit. "Thank you, Felix," she whispers.

If we stand here like this for more than a few more seconds, I'm going to wrap my arms around her, pull her against me, and use a lot more than my hands to warm her up. For once, it doesn't seem like she'd stop me, but I don't want to take advantage of the situation.

"So, what do we do first?" Gracie says, her voice almost a whisper.

I focus on her words, force my brain to answer logically.

"We shower," I say.

Gracie's eyes go wide, and she smiles, letting out a little laugh.

It's only then that I realize what I've said.

Apparently, the logical part of my brain is on vacation.

"Not *we*," I quickly correct. "That's not what I meant. I mean *you*. *You* shower." I drop her hands and press my palms against my face with a groan. "Can I try again?"

Gracie giggles and bites her lip. "I don't know. This is pretty entertaining."

"What I should have said is *you* can shower while I call my dad. He's a developer, and I'm sure he's handled something like this before. He'll be able to tell me the best path forward."

Gracie presses her lips together like she's suppressing a smile, then slowly nods. "Okay. A warm shower sounds nice. Thank you for offering."

"It's my fault this happened, and it's my responsibility to fix it. A shower is the least I can offer you. Once you're dry, we can figure out what's next."

"Can what's next involve me borrowing your dryer?"

"Definitely," I say.

Together, we walk back to her living room. The water is slowly making its way down the hallway, seeping into the floors, her area rug, the sneakers that are sitting by the chair next to the window.

I motion to her cello. It's out of its case and leaning against a cello stand in the corner. Water hasn't reached it yet, but I'd still feel better if we didn't leave it in the apartment. "We should take that with us, right? Even just the humidity from all this water probably isn't good for it."

"Definitely not," she says, rushing forward to pick it up.

I move in behind her and grab her case and the cello stand, then we head over to my apartment where my front door is still standing open.

Gracie takes two steps into the kitchen, then freezes, her eyes roving around the wide, open space. "Well, *this* doesn't feel fair," she says.

I grimace. "Yeah, so...your apartment was already outfitted as living space," I say a little sheepishly. "The building used to be a publishing house, and the managing editor lived at your place." I motion to my spacious living room. "The printing press lived in mine."

She takes a few more steps forward, her eyes moving from floor to ceiling, then back again. "I mean, it makes sense," she finally says. "Especially since you own the building. But in my head, your apartment was exactly like mine. Which, now that I think about it, doesn't make any sense because that would leave a lot of empty space filling up the rest of the building."

Her teeth chatter the slightest bit while she talks, which only makes me walk faster, but then I hesitate, debating whether to take her to my bathroom or the one off the guest bedroom.

My shower is bigger and nicer, so I cut through the kitchen instead of the living room and take her into my room. Nerves make my stomach clench, but this doesn't have to be a big deal. My bedroom is clean, my bed made. There's no reason to be nervous. Still, having Gracie in such a private space feels like an enormous deal.

I pull a couple of clean towels out from under the cabinet and set them on the counter.

"There's soap, shampoo, conditioner. Just help yourself to whatever you need," I say.

She nods and steps past me into the room. "So, um, should I be worried about the pipes in *your* apartment?"

I grimace. After what she's been through, it's a valid question. "Since this wasn't living space before I remodeled," I say, "all the plumbing, except the main line that runs directly into the apartment, is all new."

"Huh." She nods and smiles, her tone teasing. "How convenient that *you're* the one who got the new pipes."

I groan, happy, at least, that she's willing to joke about her completely demolished apartment. "The old pipes were the result of bad advice from a plumber and a dwindling renovation budget. Trust me, I'm not proud of my decision. Especially now."

"What is it people say? Hindsight is always twenty-twenty?" She tugs my hoodie a little tighter and wraps her arms around herself.

"I appreciate you being so gracious about it." I move to my bedroom door. "Is there anything else you need? I'll grab something for you to wear and leave it on the bed."

"If you don't mind going back to my apartment, there's a laundry basket on top of my washing machine. Pretty sure it's only towels and my hot yoga clothes, but I'm crossing my fingers there's also a pair of underwear."

I raise my eyebrows, my hand lifting to my beard. "Do you want me to...look for you?"

She rears back, suddenly looking mildly panicked. "For my underwear? Absolutely not. I mean, not that it would be a big deal. Everyone wears underwear. But who knows what state this particular pair might be in?"

She's rambling, her cheeks growing pinker by the second, and it's possibly the most adorable thing I've ever seen.

"Honestly, I'd like a little more control of the situation the first time a man sees my underwear," she goes on. Then she winces, and the light flush climbing her cheeks turns a fiery red. "Not that I'm suggesting *you* will see my underwear. Or that you even want to. Or..." She closes her eyes, lifting one hand to her brow. "You know what? Never mind. Maybe just grab the whole basket for me?"

It's only fair she has an embarrassing moment after I bumbled my way through accidentally suggesting we shower together, but I can be a gentleman and let her recover in solitude.

It'll do me some good because standing here talking about Gracie's underwear is *not* helping my present state of mind.

"Got it. I'll make sure it's here before you're out," I say. "Take your time though. Seriously. No rush."

Relief fills her expression as she steps backward into the bathroom. Before she shuts the door, she shrugs out of my hoodie and holds it out to me.

My eyes drop, noticing for the second time the way her clothes are clinging to her like a second skin. I force my gaze upward to the ceiling above Gracie's head. Her tank top is a pale shade of blue, and damp like it is, it's leaving *very little* to the imagination.

My fingers graze against hers as I take the hoodie, and I let my eyes drop to her face.

"Seriously, thank you," she says. "Pretty sure this is going above and beyond when it comes to your duties as landlord."

I hold her gaze. "I'm not doing this because it's my duty, Gracie."

Something flashes in her eyes that makes my heart dip and swoop, then she disappears into the bathroom, the door closing with a soft click.

I blow out a steadying breath, then move to my dresser where I riffle through my drawers, trying to find something, *anything* that won't swallow Gracie whole.

I finally settle on a Loyola University T-shirt and a pair of sweatpants she'll hopefully be able to cinch up at the waist to fit her. I grab an Appies hoodie, then toss it back in favor of a navy blue one with a logo for the Art Institute of Chicago instead. That seems like a much safer choice when it comes to Gracie.

I drop the clothes on the bed, then head across the hall and grab the laundry basket Gracie mentioned. I don't touch anything inside it—no way I want Gracie thinking I went pawing through her laundry after the conversation we just had—and leave it next to the other clothes I picked out for her.

The water is running inside the bathroom, and I try not to think about Gracie on the other side of that door, *in my shower.* Or about the fact that the next time I see her, she'll be wearing my clothes.

It's the sexiest thought I've had all day, but it doesn't last long.

Because now I have to finally do what Mom has been telling me to do for weeks.

I have to call my dad.

If anyone can kill my sexy Gracie thoughts, it's him.

CHAPTER EIGHT
Gracie

I AM *NOT* FREAKING out over taking a shower in Felix's perfectly perfect bathroom.

Okay, I'm *totally* freaking out.

But this shower is next level. Gorgeous tile and sleek chrome and two separate shower heads, one that hangs directly overhead and falls like rain.

Whatever shampoo and conditioner Felix uses is clearly something high-end. The labels look like they're in French, and the scent is subtle and manly and absolutely delicious. It's not a wonder he has such fantastic hair.

But it's his fancy-looking bar soap that surprises me the most. Because it doesn't smell manly at all. It smells like orange blossoms. For some reason, the fact that a six-foot-four elite athlete uses soap that smells like citrus and flowers makes me insanely happy, and I can't stop smiling.

Who is this man?

Also, *where* did he get these incredibly fluffy towels?

Don't get me started on his magazine-worthy apartment. Enormous windows, custom kitchen, not to mention the floor-to-ceiling bookshelves that fill the back half of Felix's living room. There's even a rolling ladder, which wouldn't be necessary in a regular house because Felix is so tall, he could easily reach a regular top shelf. But these shelves are *not* regular. They go halfway up to his apartment's very tall ceilings, and there isn't an inch of empty shelf space *anywhere.*

Because of course there isn't.

So *now,* Felix isn't just a man who listens to classical music and takes his mother to symphony concerts and fist bumps little kids when he's signing their hockey posters. He also has the most beautiful home library I've ever seen. Have I mentioned that he looks like he was carved out of marble?

I can pretend I'm only freaking out over the fancy apartment and the fancy stuff. But that would be a lie. I'm one hundred percent freaking out about *him.*

No big deal. No *freaking* big deal.

Wrapped in my very fluffy towel, I peek around his bathroom door to make sure his bedroom is empty. My laundry basket and a few other things are lying on the bed, and the bedroom door is closed, so I leave the bathroom and pad across the floor, the carpet soft and luxurious under my feet.

There has to be *something* about Felix that might make him less appealing.

He trusted questionable plumbing advice? Does that count as something?

As helpful as he's been, I can't even fault him for that. I have no doubt that whatever it's going to take to fix my apartment, Felix Jamison will do it.

I reach for my laundry basket first, fingers crossed that my guess was right and there really is dry underwear hidden somewhere among my hot yoga clothes. Luckily, my sports bra and underwear are right on top, and I'm happy to note they are at least a slightly-more-sexy-than-frumpy matching set.

A flush runs through me at the thought of Felix seeing them there, which is just *stupid*. It's laundry. There's nothing sexy about laundry.

I pull the bra on over my head and force myself to think about something else. *Anything* else. Like the softness of the duvet folded at the bottom of Felix's enormous king-size bed, or the framed artwork hanging on the walls.

The room is actually *decorated*. Like, in a classy, put-together way.

My apartment is adorable and fun and a reflection of my personality, but it isn't going to win any design awards.

This room is intentional and tasteful and calming—and *grown up*.

It suddenly occurs to me what is so different about Felix.

Dating guys in their twenties can go either way. Some of them—a few of them?—have their lives figured out.

Others are still sleeping on mattresses that rest directly on the floor and sitting in bean bag chairs left over from their college days.

But with an apartment like this, Felix is firmly, *solidly* in grown-up territory. He's also *loaded*—a fact that's still difficult for me to process.

I don't know exactly what minor-league hockey players make, but it's not enough to afford a place like this. He mentioned a lot of the guys have side hustles, which I believe. But my rent is not high enough to pay for this place, and I'm the only other tenant. He's got to have another source of income. Family money, maybe?

The only article of clothing in the laundry basket, aside from my underwear, is my pair of yoga shorts, but they're way too booty-ish for me to just wear them around, so I put them on as a base layer, then pull on the sweatpants Felix left for me. They are laughably huge, but they have a drawstring that I'm able to cinch tight. Once I roll the waistband a few times, they at least feel functional, if not flattering.

I hold up the Loyola University T-shirt and pull it to my nose. It smells so good—like clean laundry and something else uniquely Felix. The fabric is buttery soft, like it's been washed and worn a thousand times. When I pull it on, I almost shiver from the softness.

This is a perfect T-shirt. I want to think that opinion doesn't have anything to do with the actual *man* who loaned it to me, but the longer I'm in this apartment, the less certain I feel.

It's been a battle to keep myself from developing an interest in Felix even when we were only talking in the hallway. But now? Surrounded by his lovely things and basking in his generosity?

My defenses are waving a white flag of surrender and giving up the fight.

The shower warmed me up pretty well, but I am a woman who loves a good hoodie, so I can't help but pull on the soft, navy one Felix left. I wonder if it's intentional that nothing he left me to wear has anything to do with hockey. No jerseys. No sign of an Appies logo anywhere.

Based on how thoughtful he's been so far, it wouldn't surprise me if it was.

I toss my hair into a messy bun and frown at my complexion. Even Felix's perfect bathroom isn't stocked with makeup, which—that's a relief now that I think about it.

I've never seen women coming and going from Felix's apartment, but the thought of finding makeup in his bathroom sends an irrational wave of jealousy moving through me.

I don't like what that jealousy means. Or that I suddenly care about how basic my bare face and oversized clothes look.

Still, there's no way I'm wading through my water-logged apartment to my own bathroom, so this will have to be good enough.

Finally dressed, and feeling very much like a small child wearing a giant's clothes— wonderfully soft clothes that smell like absolute heaven—I make my way into the living room.

Felix is nowhere to be found, which means he's probably next door dealing with my apartment. I head that way, casting a fleeting look at his bookshelves. It doesn't seem fair to dawdle, but *oh,* to run my hands over those shelves.

Soon, I think. Even if I have to make up a reason to come over, I'll come back to visit these shelves *soon.*

I step into my living room and hear Felix's voice, but I can't see him. He must be around the corner in the hallway.

"Yeah, no I get that. You're right," he says, a slight edge to his tone. "I *did* know the pipes needed to be replaced." He breathes out a sigh. "But the plumber told me—" His words cut off quickly, like whoever he's speaking to isn't giving him much room to talk.

I bite my lip. Felix said he was going to call his dad, but it doesn't sound like he's enjoying the conversation.

"Yes, sir. I understand," Felix says. "I'll remember that for next time."

I don't want to eavesdrop, but if I move to where Felix can see me, I'll be standing in water. Instead, I turn and open my front door a few inches, trusting the sound of the heavy metal door sliding in its track will alert him to my presence.

Sure enough, Felix pops around the corner, eyebrows raised. His eyes run up and down my body, making my skin flush with heat. His lips lift into a small smile, and he holds up his finger, clearly telling me he'll just be a minute.

While I wait, my eyes drift around my apartment, suddenly making comparisons I've never thought to make before.

It felt like a *steal* when I signed my lease agreement. It's not overly flashy, but it has all new appliances—even if the stove has been acting up—new fixtures in the bathroom, and it's clean and full of natural light. On my limited salary, living *anywhere* by myself is an accomplishment, so this place felt like a dream come true. If my place were as big as his, I'd never be able to afford it. But it's still hard not to look around my small space and feel...I don't know. Inadequate, maybe?

I quickly dismiss the thought as silly. I'm not ashamed of what I do. I knew I wasn't setting myself up for wealth when I chose my profession, and I've always been fine with that. But in light of Felix's obvious wealth, I can't help but wonder what he thinks when it comes to my career and my very limited income.

"Sorry about that," he says as he steps into the living room, slipping his phone into his pocket. "How was the shower? Did you find everything you needed?"

"It was perfect. And thanks for the clothes, too."

His eyes rove over me appreciatively for a second time. "You make them look better than I do."

I roll my eyes, but my skin prickles with awareness. He can't truly be serious, but clearly, my body's sarcasm meter is completely broken. Either that or I just really like the way it feels to have Felix look at me with that soulful, steady gaze.

"So, um, what's the word on the apartment?" I ask. "What do we do?"

A flash of frustration moves across Felix's expression, but it only lasts a second before shifting into something much more neutral. "A disaster repair company is on its way over right now. They'll take care of removing the water and assessing the damage. Then I'll get the plumbing replaced, make any necessary repairs to the walls and floors, and replace any of your furniture that was ruined. Your mattress and your dresser, for sure. It'll be easier to judge what else we're up against once the water's gone."

"Well, but you won't have to do all that. I have renter's insurance. I'm sure it will cover the damage to my belongings."

He's shaking his head before I even finish my sentence. "I'm doing this, Gracie. You don't need to use your renter's insurance."

"That's why I *have* insurance," I protest.

"Not this time," he says, his voice firm and commanding. "You shouldn't have to wait as long as it will take for an insurance claim to come through. I'll get the repairs done, and I'll replace whatever is ruined. I don't want you to worry about anything."

I nod, catching my bottom lip between my teeth. Firm-and-commanding Felix is *very* sexy. "How long will it take?"

He runs a hand through his hair. "A week, maybe? Two weeks, tops." He frowns. "The bad news is your apartment will be under construction the whole time. You won't have any water, and workers will be in and out during the day."

"So I definitely won't be staying here." My stomach sinks at the thought. Two weeks with nowhere to live? I think about the handful of private students I teach in the afternoons and evenings a few nights a week. Nowhere to live also means nowhere to *teach*.

My mind quickly filters through my options. There's Josh's house. He doesn't have a guest room, but he does have a couch. But I can't imagine trying to teach with Maddox hanging around. And two weeks? I love my brother, but we would get on each other's nerves after two *days*.

There's always Mom and Dad's place. Their house is quiet enough that teaching wouldn't be a problem, but two weeks of pretending like we're happy to spend so much time together just feels uncomfortable.

Which leaves a hotel? An Airbnb?

"I realize how inconvenient this is, Gracie," Felix says. "I'm sorry. I'll make sure your rent is prorated for the month."

I nod. "Of course. I'm not worried about that."

He takes a step forward, his body language shifting as he pushes his hands into his pockets. "Also, I..." He holds his hands up. "I don't want to be presumptuous. And I'm more than happy to pay for a hotel if you aren't comfortable with the idea and you don't have anywhere else to stay. But...I *do* have a guest room." His gaze drops to the floor for a beat, his expression sheepish. "You're welcome to it," he says. "And you're welcome to use the living room for your lessons."

My lessons? He's even thinking about where I might teach my students?

A thrill of excitement—or is that fear?—pulses through me at the thought of staying with Felix. His library alone is enough to make me want to say yes. But two weeks living as Felix's roommate? Sharing the same space? Seeing each other every single day?

I look into Felix's light brown eyes, then take in his broad shoulders, the way his hair brushes against his collar. Attraction flares low in my belly, stronger than anything I've been trying to ignore the past few weeks.

If I really want to squelch any growing attraction, moving into his apartment, even just temporarily, is a terrible idea.

"It's too much," I say, my face heating as soon as I realize I've said the words out loud.

Fortunately, Felix takes them to mean he's *offering* too much, which is a lot better than what I really meant.

He's too much, and if we do this, I'm not sure I'll be able to resist him.

"It's not, Gracie," he says. "It's the least I can do. You're in this mess because of me." His jaw tightens the slightest bit, and a ghost of his earlier frustration passes over his face. "It would make me feel better if I could do this for you. Besides, I'll be on the road with the team next weekend. You'll have the place to yourself."

I'm going to say yes. It's stupid to pretend I'm not. It has to be better than staying with Josh or my parents, and it's the most logical choice since my students are used to coming here for lessons anyway.

But the biggest reason I'm saying yes doesn't have anything to do with logic or convenience.

I could tell myself it's all about the bookshelves and the fancy towels, but there's no denying it's really the man in front of me.

I'm saying yes because I like the idea of being closer to Felix. Maybe I just like *him*.

And I have no idea what to do about that.

CHAPTER NINE
Felix

FOR ALL THE CLOTHES she's wearing, I can no longer see a single one of Gracie's curves, but somehow she still makes my oversized sweats look sexy. Maybe because they're mine, and that creates an intimacy between us we've never experienced before.

All I know is I can't take my eyes off of her.

And now she's going to be sleeping in my guest room.

Maybe I'm not so mad at the old copper pipes after all.

For the next hour, Gracie moves through her apartment, gathering up anything she might need over the next week. Toiletries, her laptop and phone charger, her music stand and two enormous bins of cello music. We work together to carry it all over to my place, but we don't say much as we do. I can't tell if it's because I'm nervous or she's nervous, or if maybe she's just trying hard not to be pissed that so many of her personal belongings are soaked. I'm already making a mental inventory of all the things I'm going to replace for her.

On the upside, if I wanted a chance to get to know Gracie better, this is definitely a way to do it. I meant it when I said I respected her desire not to date hockey players, and I won't pressure her. That doesn't mean I'm not hoping that getting to know *me* will change her mind.

Most of her clothes are wet, so we use both of her laundry baskets and the two I have in my apartment to gather her waterlogged wardrobe and haul it over to my laundry room.

With so much standing water, the disaster repair guys, who showed up right after Gracie got out of the shower, immediately cut the power to the apartment, so our next move is to clean out her fridge and freezer, which is a smaller task than I expected.

"This is embarrassingly sad," Gracie says as she hands me the entire contents of her freezer, which only consists of two frozen pizzas and a box of macarons.

"You don't cook much?" I ask her.

"Not as much as I would like." She reaches into her refrigerator and pulls out a dozen eggs, setting them on the island behind her. "I cook more over the summer, but during the school year, by the time I get home at the end of the day, then teach lessons and sometimes even have rehearsal, I just want to eat whatever's easiest. Sadly, that means it normally comes out of a to-go container or a box."

Next to the eggs, she sets a container of blueberries, some vanilla yogurt, half a gallon of almond milk, and some roast beef deli meat. There are a few condiments in the door, but after checking expiration dates, she tosses those directly into the trash.

"That's it?" I say. "Nothing else?"

She shrugs. "I was due for a trip to the store."

A sudden—and probably ridiculous—desire to feed Gracie pops into my mind. She's a grown woman. She doesn't need me to feed her. But I can't shake the vision of her coming home after a long day at school, kicking off her shoes, and coming into my kitchen where I'm already making her dinner, Bach's cello suites playing in the background.

I imagine her slipping her arms around me, pressing her face into my chest, and a sharp longing pierces me from the inside out.

I had no idea I had this kind of fantasy, this yearning for domestic bliss, but it's real and potent and I'm not sure I'll be able to get past it if I don't at least try to make it happen. And now I've been presented with a golden opportunity. Gracie *will* be coming home to my apartment at the end of the day. I don't want to seem creepy or overeager, but feeding her wouldn't be that big a deal, would it?

I clear my throat, forcing my gaze back to Gracie, who has shifted her attention to her pantry. She pulls out a box of cereal and adds it to the pile on the counter, then pulls out a can of Pringles, popping off the lid and pulling out a healthy stack of chips.

She shoves two of them in her mouth at once, her eyes closing as she chews. "Oh my gosh. I think I forgot how hungry I was."

I would not have guessed that Gracie shoving chips in her mouth would be sexy, but when her tongue darts out to lick some salt off her lip, attraction flares in my gut.

We've been talking over and around the sound of the industrial-sized shop vacs the disaster guys are using to suck the water out of Gracie's bedroom, but with timing that couldn't be better if it was scripted, the vacuums shut off *just* in time for Gracie to hear my stomach grumble.

She grins. "Looks like we both missed dinner." She holds out the can but snatches it back before I can grab one. "Except, wait. Are you even allowed to eat these? Don't pro athletes have to follow a really strict diet?"

I wrap my fingers around her wrist, and pull her hand to my mouth, stealing the chip she's holding in her fingers.

Her mouth pops open in surprise, and I smirk. "I can eat a chip or two. But come on. I can do better than Pringles."

I pick up a stack of food from the counter and head to the door. Gracie quickly follows behind, stepping over the hose that's stretched down the stairs and out the main door.

"Are you telling me you cook, Felix?" she says, her tone teasing. "Is that what's happening here?"

I *do* cook, and I have every intention of making dinner for Gracie while she's staying with me. But I'll need time to plan for that. Right now, at almost nine p.m., takeout feels a lot easier.

"Would it surprise you if I *do* cook?" I ask as I add her food to my refrigerator.

"Probably not. But it might make me start searching your closets for hidden skeletons or dirty little secrets. There has to be *something* wrong with you, Felix."

I turn around and flash her a smile. "Something besides the hockey?"

A touch of color warms her cheeks as she scoffs. "Obviously."

"I *do* like to cook," I say. "But I was thinking takeout would be easier for tonight. Are you good with sushi?"

"Love it," she says. "That sounds amazing, actually."

I reach for my phone. "Perfect. I'll order us something."

And that's how we wind up sitting on the floor in my living room, sushi covering the giant trunk I use as a coffee table, eating and talking like it's no big deal that we're together, sharing a meal like this.

It takes me a few minutes to relax, to stop stressing over the fact that Gracie Mitchell is in my apartment. That tonight, she'll sleep here, and the night after that, and the night after that, too.

I have to stop thinking about it. I have to pretend like this is just a normal date. No—not even a date. This is just...a conversation that happens to include dinner. With my neighbor who isn't at all interested in dating me.

Still, as we talk about music and books and so many other things we have in common, I can't fully suppress the hope that this is the start of something great.

After we finish eating, Gracie tells me the story of how she fell in love with the cello over the Harry Potter theme. Then I tell her about my grandmother and how she's the one who taught me how to love classical music.

"Is this your grandmother on your mother's side?" Gracie asks.

"On my father's side." I settle back against the couch, my legs extended in front of me, my ankles crossed. "She was this really petite woman, probably not an inch over five feet tall, but she was tough as nails, too. And it's a good thing because she lived her life surrounded by really powerful men."

"So that's where you get your height," Gracie says, a wry smile spreading across her face.

I chuckle. "She used to make the same joke. Told me I'd better remember that all the best parts of me came from her."

Gracie leans forward the slightest bit, like she's really interested in what I'm saying. "I can tell by your tone that you guys were close."

"Yeah. We were. She also just...looked out for me. More than anyone else. I don't know, maybe she sensed I needed it."

"In what way?" Gracie leans her elbow against the couch and props her head in her hands, her focus solely on me. This level of scrutiny might make me uncomfortable in a different situation, but something about Gracie's manner puts me at ease. So much so that I don't even hesitate to answer her question. Something tells me Gracie won't judge me for it.

"When I was a kid, I struggled with pretty intense social anxiety," I say. "I still functioned, for the most part, and it's gotten easier to manage as I've gotten older, though a lot of hours of therapy helped, too. But before the therapy, before I even really understood what was happening when I would clam up and have panic attacks, Grandma gave me all these tricks to calm myself down." I shrug. "Classical music was one of them."

Gracie's expression softens, reassuring me that I made the right call in sharing. "It did that for me too. It still does."

"Grandma played the violin," I continue. "Never professionally, just around the house, whenever I begged her to play for me. But she was incredible. Looking back, I know I must have been biased, but I think she was talented enough that she *could* have played professionally had she been given the chance."

Gracie frowns. "She never tried? Why not?"

I grimace and run a hand through my hair. "I'll tell you why, but just know I'm fully aware that what I'm about to say is going to make me sound like a pretentious snob."

"Consider me warned," she says through an easy smile.

I breathe out a sigh. "She couldn't play in the symphony because my grandfather believed it was beneath her."

At this, Gracie's smile flips into a frown. "I'm not sure I understand. Because she was so talented?"

I shake my head, hating the inevitable turn in conversation this revelation will cause. "Because she was so rich."

"Ohhhh." Gracie's eyes light with understanding. "So she was the kind of person who would *fund* the symphony. Not someone who would play in it."

"Exactly."

It's not lost on me that I just told a working musician that my family—at least my grandfather—would consider her career beneath him. I can only hope she doesn't think I feel the same way.

"What does this grandfather think about your hockey playing?" she asks. "I'm guessing if a working-class job like playing in the symphony is beneath him, minor league sports are too?"

"Very good guess. He died a few years back. But he had plenty of time to let me know how disappointed he was with my career choice before he passed. And my father has picked up the torch with equal enthusiasm."

She frowns. "I'm sorry he did that. And that your dad is doing it now."

I run a hand over my face. "It's fine. I've mostly made peace with it. And I still have a good relationship with my mom."

"Yeah, she seemed nice," Gracie says. She's quiet for a beat before she adds, "I know a little something about what it feels like to disappoint a parent."

That sounds like a loaded statement, and I'm about to ask Gracie to explain if only just to shift the conversation off of my own strained family relationships, but she asks another question before I can.

"You said your dad is a real estate developer? Is that what your grandfather did too? I'm maybe starting to understand how you own this entire building."

She doesn't *really* understand.

If she were to google Derrick Jamison, she'd find a glossy website with links to his real estate portfolio—the largest in Chicago—a venture capitalist firm for which my father is the managing director, and the Jamison Foundation, the nonprofit organization my grandmother started and my mother now runs that shuttles millions of dollars a year to underserved arts programs in communities and public schools across the nation.

Dad isn't exactly Bill Gates wealthy, but he's close.

Close enough that when I dropped my mother off at the airport this morning, it was a private jet owned by my father's company she was boarding.

Needless to say, *this* building wouldn't even be on his radar.

"Okay, your face is telling a serious story right now," Gracie says, her hand motioning up and down in front of me. "What's with the tense jaw and the frowning eyes?"

The lightness in her tone reminds me to relax—no one *here* is judging me—and I manage a smile. "Frowning eyes?"

She nods. "Absolutely. They're very expressive. As soon as I mentioned your father, they turned sad."

"How about now?" I ask, glaring at her with an exaggerated frown.

She laughs. "Now you look like the beast from *Beauty and the Beast*. Which, come to think of it, you *do* have the right bookshelves."

"The beast? Really?" I joke. "You find me that unattractive?"

"Just that one expression!" she quickly says. "And most women think the beast is sexier anyway." She rolls her eyes and nudges my thigh with the back of her hand. "Look at you fishing for compliments. You aren't blind, Felix. You *know* you aren't unattractive."

"Maybe. But knowing I'm attractive *generally* and knowing *you* find me attractive are not the same thing."

She freezes, her gaze locked on mine for a long moment before she clears her throat and looks away. "We were talking about your father, right? Let's keep doing that."

I blow out a breath, my brain cataloging everything about the last fifteen seconds. There was a fire in Gracie's eyes, something that makes me think she really *does* find me attractive, and I add it to the list of tiny things keeping my hope alive.

It's a little desperate, maybe, but I'll tell her anything she wants to know about my father if it will keep her here, talking to me like this. "Because my eyes are sad when we talk about him," I finally say, and the playful mood between us sobers.

Gracie must sense it too because she bites her lip like she's nervous. "I mean, I also heard you talking to him earlier—right after I got out of the shower. That might have helped me draw some conclusions."

She tugs down the sleeves of her hoodie—my hoodie—then tucks her legs under her, pulling a pillow off the couch behind us and settling it in her lap. It occurs to me that it's been long enough, the first dryer load of her clothes is probably dry. She could change into something else if she wanted to, but I don't remind her. I like her wearing my things.

"You don't have to talk about it if you don't want to," Gracie says with a small shrug. "But I'm happy to listen if you do."

The depth of my father's pockets and how that has complicated the last decade of my life isn't something I ever like to discuss. I've gotten used to women who are interested in me only because I play hockey—apparently, a new trend in romantic fiction has turned hockey players into every woman's dream—but billionaire romance was a thing even before hockey romance was. I've enjoyed moving away from the influence of my father's wealth and out of a city where women heard my last name and immediately assumed *money*.

But that's not who I am. And I'd rather Gracie hear that from me than google my family and draw her own conclusions based on what she finds on the internet.

I pull out my phone and open my internet browser, where I navigate to my father's website. I hold out the phone, and Gracie takes it without question.

"This is my father's website," I say. "You can click around a little if you want."

She nods, then clicks and scrolls for a minute or two before she sets the phone down on the floor between us.

It's probably dumb we're still sitting on the floor—our meal is long over, so we ought to just move up to the couch—but somehow, sitting on the floor like this keeps the conversation casual, which is helpful considering the seriousness of our current topic.

"Okay," Gracie says. "So you're saying your dad is low-key important and has a little bit of extra spending money."

I chuckle. "Yeah, something like that." I look around my apartment. "He wouldn't have bothered with a building like this in a town like Harvest Hollow. And he doesn't think I should have bothered either."

"But you bought it anyway," Gracie says.

I nod. "I did."

"And you decided to play hockey instead of going into the family business?"

"Good guess."

"Good for you," Gracie says, a fire blazing in her eyes.

"When my grandmother passed away—"

"This is the grandmother who was the violinist?" Gracie asks, and I nod.

"When she passed away, she left me enough to buy this place and renovate it, and then invest a little extra. Eli manages the portfolios of a few guys on the team, and he's been a great help in figuring out where to invest. It's nothing compared to what my father has, but I'm living on my terms, and that's important to me."

"Wait, Eli—as in the guy who bounds into your apartment like a golden retriever puppy and has asked me out a million times?"

I grin. "Don't let him fool you. He's got a lot of brains behind that smile."

Gracie shifts, stretching her back, and I realize, *again,* that we're still sitting on the floor. "Here," I say, quickly standing. I offer her both hands. "Let's sit on the couch."

She slips her fingers into mine, and I tug her to her feet. When she's fully upright, she's standing incredibly close—close enough for me to feel the warmth of her, to feel the brush of her exhale across my collarbone. I loosen my grip on her hands—she could easily pull away if she wanted to—but I don't let go.

Slowly, she lifts her eyes to mine.

It has to mean something that she isn't pulling away, that her hands are still cocooned in mine, her fingers pressed into my palms.

An idea pops into my head. Well, several ideas, but only one that would be a good idea *right now.*

"Hey, can I show you something?" I ask.

She nods, and I finally let her go, a surge of excitement moving through me. I don't know why I didn't think of it earlier. If there's anyone who will enjoy what's hidden inside the oversized trunk that functions as my coffee table, it's Gracie.

"Let me clean this up," I say. "Then I'll show you."

She nods. "Okay."

I make fast work of clearing away our dinner mess, hauling it all to the kitchen and throwing it away.

While I'm in the kitchen, I see Gracie cross into the laundry room where she must be emptying the dryer and adding yet another load of her wet clothes.

I beat her back to the living room, and I sit down on the couch to wait. When she returns, she's taken off my sweatshirt, revealing the Loyola U T-shirt underneath. She has the hem cinched up and tied in a knot, accentuating her small waist and the generous swell of her hips.

I swallow against the growing lump in my throat.

She's so incredibly beautiful, even like this. In sweats, with no makeup, her hair pulled up in a simple bun.

"Ready?"

When she nods, I reach for the trunk, unclasping the brass locks, then lift the heavy lid.

"This is *also* something I inherited from my grandmother," I say.

Gracie sits down beside me and gasps.

Inside the trunk are more than three hundred records—many of them renowned classical recordings that qualify as true collector's items.

Gracie reaches in and pulls out a copy of Handel's *Water Music*, recorded by the Berlin Philharmonic. She hands it to me, then pulls out another, this one a complete set of recordings done by the Academy of Ancient Music in London of Mozart's *The Symphonies*. Behind that one, she finds Bach's

Unaccompanied Cello Suites performed by cellist, Janos Starker.

She holds this one carefully. "Can we listen to this one?" she says, her voice almost reverent.

"Absolutely." I take the record from her and walk to the ancient turntable that also belonged to my grandmother. It was the gold standard in her day, and as far as I'm concerned, it still sounds better than anything I could buy now. Maybe that's nostalgia talking. I don't care either way. Especially when the music starts, and Gracie takes a long, slow breath, her eyes closed.

"That tone," she says. "Nobody can get the richness out of a cello like Janos Starker did."

I'd maybe argue that *she* does, but I'm willing to own my biases on that front.

Gracie jumps from the couch and moves into the open space just in front of the bookshelves. "Come here," she says as she sits down on the floor. She stretches out full length, lying on her back, and lifts her arms over her head. She pats the floor next to her. "Join me?"

She doesn't have to ask me twice, even if I did just move us from the floor to the couch, and now we're back on the floor again.

I stretch out beside her, mimicking her pose, right down to my arms stretching out over my head.

"This is how I used to listen when I was a kid," she says, her eyes closed again. "I told myself it was the best way to *feel* the music instead of just hearing it."

We listen for a few more minutes, the music washing over us, before she says, "It works, right?"

I smile. "It totally does. I wonder why."

"No distractions, maybe," she says, her voice soft. "Why does music sound so much better from a record? Has music streaming ruined all of us, you think?"

"Grandma used to say the same thing. Not about music streaming—it was barely a thing when she died—but about the radio and cassette tapes. Even CDs. Nothing sounds like this."

"Your grandmother sounds like an amazing woman."

"You would have loved her," I say.

As soon as the words are out of my mouth, I wish I could call them back. They feel...too intimate, maybe? Too familiar?

They also feel *true*.

Gracie doesn't seem bothered by them, so I force myself to breathe, to let the music calm me just like it always did when I was a kid.

Beside me, Gracie shifts, and I open my eyes to see her on her side, propped up on her elbow and looking at me.

"Do you play an instrument?" she asks.

I can't help the grimace that immediately stretches across my face.

Gracie giggles, lifting a hand to cover her lips. "Oh no. That bad?"

"I was truly terrible," I say. "Grandma tried for almost three years to teach me to play. But I was hopeless. Eventually, she took me by the shoulders, looked right in my eyes, and said

'Felix, you'll always appreciate good music. That's going to have to be enough for you.'"

"I've had a few students like that," Gracie says. "It just never clicks. Did it make you sad at all?"

I shake my head. "Nah. I was pretty self-aware for a twelve-year-old. I heard how terrible I sounded, especially since I had her to play for me. The gap between what I could do and what she could do seemed insurmountable. I was mostly just relieved when she told me I could stop. Up until then, I'd worried I would disappoint her."

"I love that she let you stop," Gracie says. "I have some parents who just keep insisting, even when their kids are obviously unhappy and never getting any better. I have this one kid who wants to play the flute so badly, and her parents just keep pushing the cello. I don't get it. Just let the kid play the flute, you know? Or do whatever else she loves."

"Unless she wants to play hockey," I say, in what I hope is a teasing tone.

Gracie rolls her eyes. "You really must think I'm some kind of hockey-hating monster."

"Definitely not a monster," I say. "But you told me yourself you hate hockey."

"I did," she says, worrying her bottom lip. "But that doesn't mean other people can't love it. My nephew just started playing, and I don't have any problems loving my nephew."

"Got it. So the hockey ban doesn't apply across the board, only to men you date."

For a moment, the apartment is completely silent, the record shifting from one cello suite to the next, and a heaviness settles over our conversation.

Things were going so well. Why did I have to go and mention hockey? She clearly doesn't want to talk about it, and neither do I. I don't like thinking about the fact that my job—something I love—makes her so unhappy.

Gracie licks her lips, her eyes darting around the apartment before they finally settle back on me, though she still hasn't met my eye. She's more staring at my chin.

"Correct," she finally says, but there's a flicker of doubt in her tone that keeps the spark of hope in my chest alive. I pull my arms down and prop myself up on my elbow, mirroring her pose.

Slowly, she lifts her gaze to mine. A thousand emotions are playing across her face—lingering traces of pain and sadness, confusion, doubt. But there's something else there, too. Something that looks more like possibility, like an echo of the hope flickering inside me.

"Still haven't changed your mind, huh?" I say, my pulse suddenly pounding.

She lets out a little chuckle. "The amazing vinyl collection has me annoyingly close." Without breaking our gaze, she lifts her hand to my arm, sliding her fingers just under the hem of my T-shirt. "You have a tattoo," she says, sliding the fabric up an inch or so.

My breath catches in my throat, goosebumps skittering across my skin at her touch. She has to notice, but there's no

way I'm stopping her exploration. She can touch me anywhere she wants.

I lift my arm, shifting it outward so she can see the tattoo
that crosses the inside of my left bicep.

When the entire thing is exposed, Gracie lets out a little
gasp. "Is this music?" She shifts onto her knees, taking my
arm in both hands to study the section of musical score
that's inked on my skin.

"It's the first five measures of—"

"Wait, wait, don't tell me," she says. She studies the
notes, humming softly to herself. She's a professional musician. I know it shouldn't surprise me that she's probably
going to figure out the piece just by looking at it. But *damn*
if it's not sexy to think about her doing just that.

"It's Bach," she says, finally lifting her eyes to mine. She's
cradling my bicep, which is perfectly fine with me. "A violin
sonata. The first one, I think?" She looks back at the music,
then nods. "It *is* the first one."

I nod. It *is* sexy. So incredibly sexy. "It was my grandmother's favorite piece of music," I say.

Her expression softens for the briefest second, but then
she's rolling her eyes and falling back on her heels, her
hands falling away from my arm. "Seriously, are you even
for real?"

"What's that supposed to mean?"

"It means you're both a ridiculously hot hockey stud *and*
a music nerd. How is that even possible?"

I sit up, maneuvering my long limbs as best I can until I'm
sitting across from her, my legs extended out to the side. "Did

you just call me a *stud*?" I ask, my tone teasing. "Is that a word people still even use?"

"I also called you a music *nerd*. Did you miss that part?"

"That's a badge I'll wear proudly. I'd rather go back and focus on Gracie Mitchell thinking I'm *ridiculously hot*."

"Let's forget I ever said it and talk some more about your tattoo." She lifts her hand to my arm, her fingers brushing over the tattoo one more time. "I love that you honored your grandmother in this way," she says. "It's amazing."

I close my eyes as her hand slides downward, her fingers tracing a slow line down my arm, over my elbow, my forearm, my wrist. When she reaches my palm, she twines her fingers with mine.

Behind us, the last notes of the final cello suite sound, and a faint whirring noise fills the room as the needle catches over and over on the inside track of the record.

I'll listen to the noise all night as long as this moment doesn't end.

I rub my thumb over the back of Gracie's hand, loving the silken feel of her skin.

I don't know what's happening, but I know I want it more than I've wanted anything before. I've been feeling ready for a relationship lately, but this is more than that. Gracie is the embodiment of everything I want. She's brilliant. She's talented. She's beautiful. And I really want to make this work.

Then the dryer buzzes through the open laundry room door, and Gracie startles.

She jumps, pulling her hand out of mine, and the tension between us pops and fizzles. "My clothes!" Gracie says, a little too loudly. She scrambles to her feet. "I should get those."

She hurries across the room and disappears into the laundry room. When she comes back out, she's holding a heaping laundry basket.

I still haven't moved from where she left me on the floor.

"You know what? I'm feeling pretty tired," she says, her voice a little too high, a little too hurried. "And you know, now that I've got all these clothes to fold, I think I should just go to bed."

I quickly stand up, but she's all but running to the guest bedroom door. There's no way I can stop her now.

"Thank you for dinner," she says. "And for talking. And for letting me stay here."

I push my hands into my pockets. "Of course. I'm happy to help."

She nods. Swallows. Licks her lips, her eyes looking everywhere but at me.

"You're a good friend, Felix," she finally says, her voice so soft I almost don't hear her.

Then the bedroom door closes with a painful, resounding *click*.

It's almost as loud as the word *friend* echoing in my head.

CHAPTER TEN
Felix

"THAT'S IT? THAT'S ALL that happened? She just...went to bed?" Logan asks. He readies a shot and sends the puck flying toward me across the ice. I block it, then shift to the right to block another coming in from Eli, before sliding right again to block a third shot from Logan.

I'm too slow though, and this one gets past me into the net.

Logan grins. "What's the matter, Jamison? You feeling a little distracted?"

I skate behind the net and gather the pucks we're using for a three-shot shooting drill and send them back to Eli and Logan.

"Not distracted. Let's do it again," I say. I resume my position in front of the net, eyes darting between the two of them. They won't tell me who's shooting first. "The Gracie thing *is* weird though, right? Things were so good, then she just...freaked and ran away."

Eli backs up, then takes the puck wide, coming in from the side, a grin on his face. My eyes are on him, but I catch Logan's movement in my periphery and drop to my knees just in time to catch his first shot. I twist and catch Eli's shot in my glove, then dive sideways to get Logan's second shot.

I'll never be contending with three pucks at once during a game, but this drill still keeps my reflexes sharp. It's also a good way to clear my head and help me think through stuff.

"Nice," Eli says as I stand and slide the pucks back to him. He hits one to Logan, keeping two for himself. "And I don't think the Gracie thing *is* weird. She's already told you she doesn't date hockey players. You're making her rethink her stance, so props to you, man. But of course she's freaking out. It's a paradigm shift."

"Did you just use the word paradigm?" I say.

"It's the word of the day," Eli answers. "I have an app."

Logan chuckles. "He makes a valid point, with or without his fancy word app."

"So what do I do?"

My teammates share a look, some kind of wordless exchange happening that I can't make out from where I'm standing. Eli skates toward me, and I brace myself for his shot, but he's moving too slowly, almost casual-like. He stops a few yards away. "You give up, man."

I relax my stance. "I give up?"

He fires off a shot that flies past me directly into the net. Before I can regroup, Logan circles the net and chips the puck over my shoulder, then Eli shoots again. I dive forward, but I'm not fast enough and the third shot gets through too.

Eli and Logan stop in front of me, matching smirks on their faces.

"That wasn't funny," I say.

Logan shrugs. "It was a little funny. Eli, did *you* think it was funny?"

"Definitely funny."

We can't talk about Gracie anymore, because Coach Davis calls us over to end practice and make sure we haven't forgotten the schedule for the rest of the week, including our very early departure time first thing Wednesday morning for a run of three games we're playing in between here and New York.

That means I only have tonight and tomorrow night with Gracie to see if—*oh man*. Is that how bad this is? I'm considering my days, my weeks, in terms of time *with* Gracie and time without her?

All I know is when she touched me last night, her fingers grazing over my skin, something inside me clicked and settled—like I'd finally found something I didn't know I was looking for, but now I can't imagine life without it.

I felt *whole*, as cheesy as that sounds. Whole and *alive*.

Like her touch woke up a part of me that was dormant, and now everything is brighter, sharper, more intense. Which is so cheesy I can't even stand myself, but I genuinely feel like I was living in black and white until Gracie touched me and flooded everything with color.

"Are you good with that, Felix?" Coach Davis asks.

I freeze. I have *completely* missed everything Coach has been saying.

Logan chuckles beside me, then says under his breath, "New kid. Third string goalie. He's your roommate in New York."

"Definitely good with that," I say, nodding toward Coach.

He lifts a brow. "Should I put Barnes in a room nearby so he can make sure you get to games on time?"

If I didn't know Coach Davis so well, the jab might have been intimidating, but if he had an actual problem with me, he isn't the kind of coach who would call me out publicly.

"That won't be necessary, Coach," I say.

Coach Davis's eyes flash, then he says, "Does someone want to fill me in on why our usually unflappable goalie is day-dreaming today?"

A few of the guys laugh, looking back at me, but no one answers Coach's question.

"Okay," Coach says. "I see how it is. Y'all are making me think I asked the wrong question. How about this one? Felix, what's her name?"

To this, the team breaks out in a series of cheers and catcalls, those standing closest to me reaching over and pounding me on the back.

Coach Davis smiles wide.

A few years ago, this kind of attention might have made me uncomfortable, but I know these guys. I know they have my back even when they're making fun of me.

"It's nothing, Coach," I finally say. "Focused on the team. Focused on the game. I promise."

"I don't doubt that at all," Coach says. He lifts his hands to dismiss us. "That's all, men. See you tomorrow."

I skate past Coach with everyone else but pause when he calls my name. "Hey, Jamison."

I spin around and face him.

He smiles. "You know you *can* have a little fun when you aren't on the ice."

I duck my head in acknowledgment. "I'll do my best."

I appreciate Coach's encouragement, but that's easier said than done. Especially if the woman I'm interested in isn't interested back.

But the way she looked at me...I swear there's something there, something I'm not making up.

I hurry through showering and getting dressed, ignoring the guys as they rib me over my "mystery woman," several of them mentioning Ivy by name and asking if she's jealous.

Logan meets my eyes and smirks, and I make a mental note to make sure, if things ever go anywhere with Gracie, to explain to her what *Ivy* actually references before she meets anyone else on the team. Talk about creating unnecessary trouble for myself. Nothing like creating a cheating scandal when the only thing I'm "cheating" with is *books.*

Weirdly, my conversation with Gracie last night was so focused on music, we didn't even get into books, but I'm betting on Logan's assumption that she likes to read with my next move.

As soon as I'm in my car, I look over at the stack of books I swiped from Gracie's apartment this morning. It wasn't like I was sneaking around—I had to meet the disaster repair people over there anyway. They were able to remove all the standing water last night, but they came back first thing today to take care of the ruined drywall, door casings, flooring, furniture, and anything else damaged beyond repair. They didn't think it would take longer than today, so I'm hopeful I'll find the space cleaned out, fans in place to dry out the subfloor, by the time I get home.

But ruined books, pages swollen and warped from exposure to so much water—that's not something the disaster repair people will fix. That's why I grabbed them this morning.

Book repair—or book replacement, really—that can be my job. And if I happen to improve or expand her library while I'm at it, who's going to stop me?

I find a parking space right outside of Book Smart. Downtown Harvest Hollow is decked out in all its fall glory, and the front windows of Book Smart are no exception. Everything is pumpkin spice and fall leaves and splashes of red, yellow, and orange. I push through the front door, a bell jangling above my head as I do.

A woman behind the checkout counter smiles warmly and says, "Welcome to Book Smart. Let me know if you need help finding anything."

My first impulse is to ignore the woman's offer of help, to browse the store myself and talk to as few people as possible. That's how I functioned when I was a kid. But years of experience managing my anxiety has taught me that isn't necessarily the *best* thing for me, even if it does feel easier. Besides, I still want to stop by the grocery store to grab a few things for dinner, and letting this woman help me *would* be faster.

I walk right up to the counter, setting the wet books down in front of me. "Hi. I could definitely use your help. These books were damaged when a pipe exploded in my neighbor's apartment yesterday, and I'd like to replace them for her if I could. Could you help me find them all?"

"You're Felix Jamison," the woman blurts.

"Oh. Yeah. Hi?"

"Sorry. I didn't mean to make that awkward." The woman, Emmy, her name tag reads, smiles warmly. She has nice eyes and long brown hair and a face that looks vaguely familiar. "I mean, I'm a fan, but also, you volunteered at my house a while back. There was a fire, and the fire chief recruited volunteers, and I remember seeing you among them. *Thank you* for helping."

"Oh. Yeah, absolutely. I'm so sorry about your house."

She waves away my concern. "It could have been so much worse. Anyway, I'm making this all about me, and you need help finding these books?" She scans the titles, her brow furrowing. "Huh," she finally says. "Is your neighbor Gracie Mitchell?"

My eyebrows lift. "You know her?"

Emmy smiles. "She comes in here a lot. Normally, I wouldn't remember a random book stack, but this one is curated from a new list of recommendations that was just published in the New Yorker. She had the article with her when she came in, and a gift card she'd just gotten from one of her students. We picked out the books together, and I remember her being so thrilled when she had enough on the gift card to cover it."

"Perfect. Hopefully you still have copies in stock?"

She taps her chin. "Pretty sure. Let's see what we can find."

I follow behind her as she meanders through the bookstore, pulling books off the shelf and dropping them into my waiting hands. "The latest romance by Amelie De Pierre," she says, adding another book to the growing stack. "I've heard amazing things about that one."

She turns down another aisle into what looks like the historical fiction section. It's generously stocked, and I have a sudden itch to browse, but I'll have to come back later for that. Right now, I am a man on a mission.

"How long have you and Gracie been neighbors?" Emmy asks.

"Um, six months or so?" I say.

"She's great, right?"

"So great," I say, a little too eagerly, based on the knowing look Emmy tosses over her shoulder.

She drops one more on the top of the stack, bringing the total up to ten. "Okay. That's all of them."

"Perfect. Thank you. I'm going to grab a few more. Do you mind holding these for me for a minute?"

"Not at all." She lifts the book stack out of my hands. "I'll have them at the register for you. Just come on up when you're ready."

It takes about ten minutes to pick out three more books for Gracie, one I've read before and loved, one I've never read but it's about a cellist and the reviews are great so it feels like a safe bet, and a copy of *A River Runs Through It,* because it feels fitting considering what just happened to her apartment.

I quickly move to the counter, anxious to get home and see Gracie, and set the three additional titles in front of Emmy.

She picks up *A River Runs Through It* and smiles. "Because her books were ruined by an exploding pipe?"

"You think she'll get the joke?"

"She definitely will," Emmy says. "It's really nice of you to replace the rest of these."

"It's a long story," I say as she rings up the books, "but the pipe exploding in her apartment was sort of my fault. This feels like nothing."

"It's *not* nothing," Emmy says. "I'm sure Gracie will be touched."

I run a hand through my hair, my eyes drifting to the case of baked goods beside the checkout counter. There's no way to ask without showing my hand here, but Emmy seems like the kind of woman I can trust.

I motion toward the case. "Do you know if Gracie has a favorite?"

Emmy's expression softens, her lips shifting like she's fighting a smile. "If she drops by in the morning, she usually gets an apple cinnamon scone. If it's after work, she'll get the danish."

"Right." I nod. "Maybe one of each?"

"Excellent choice," she says.

Five minutes later, I'm back in my car, books and pastries stowed safely in my passenger seat. Emmy was nice enough to throw away the damaged copies. They really were beyond salvageable, the binding falling apart, the pages ripped and disintegrating.

Once I finish at the grocery store, I expect to find Gracie already at home. But her car isn't in its usual spot.

She went to bed so fast and left so early this morning, I didn't have the chance to check in about whether she'd need the apartment for her private lessons. She's welcome to it, but maybe she has somewhere else she'd rather teach?

I stop at the mailbox, shifting all the groceries to one hand so I can open her mailbox. The envelope I left her containing a key to my apartment is still there. So she hasn't been home since this morning at all.

Maybe this is better. Now I can cook and have food ready by the time she gets home.

Not that I'm turning this into something it's not. I'm cooking for *myself*, something I frequently do, especially during the season when getting enough protein and carbohydrates is so important. If there happen to be leftovers, of course I'll offer them to her. I'm chill. I'm totally casual about this.

I glance at the books sitting in my passenger seat. *It's too much.* Maybe *I'm* too much?

The last thing I want to do is scare her off, but also, *I like her.*

I lower the books and my groceries onto my kitchen counter, then drop the bag I take to and from practice onto the floor.

I sink onto a barstool and pull out my phone to text Logan.

Felix: This is hard. I feel dumb. I don't want to come on too strong.

Logan: Have you strewn your apartment with flower petals? If you have, ABANDON SHIP.

Felix: No flower petals. But I replaced some books that were damaged when the pipes in her apartment burst, and I was thinking about making enough dinner to share.

Logan: That seems chill. Parker agrees. You're fine, man.

Felix: I also asked the woman at Book Smart if Gracie has a favorite pastry, and I bought some of those. Her favorites. Is that weird? Am I being creepy?

Logan: Parker says you sound thoughtful, not weird. As long as you don't spread the books on her bed in the shape of a heart, or leave the pastries on her pillow, you're fine.

Felix: Definitely not doing that. Thanks, man.

Logan: Good luck.

Turns out, I don't need any luck because Gracie never shows.

I cook dinner—a mean chicken marsala with mashed potatoes and roasted green beans—I clean up after dinner, I read for an hour, and still, she doesn't come home. By 9:30, I'm starting to wonder if I should worry. It's totally unreasonable for me to feel like this.

If she were still next door instead of in my guest room, I'd have no idea she wasn't home, and I *wouldn't* worry. She's a grown woman, one who has zero obligation to let me know where she is or what time she's going to be home. She could be at a rehearsal or out with friends or on a date.

That last thought makes my stomach pitch, but why couldn't she be on a date? We barely held hands...for barely ten seconds. Not exactly a high-stakes commitment.

Still. I could text her and let her know there's leftover dinner in the fridge, the books on the counter are hers, and could she please lock the door once she's home?

That wouldn't be weird, right?

I reach for my phone, then groan.

I *can't* text Gracie. I don't have her number.

I lean back into my couch in frustration. Except, *wait*. I do have her lease agreement.

Somewhere, anyway. I'm not sure I ever printed it out, but I did save it in a digital folder on my laptop. I move to the desk in my bedroom and sit down, booting up my laptop. It takes a couple minutes of searching, but I finally pull up the lease agreement and find the number.

I scribble it out on a post-it note and carry it back into the living room, where I stick it to the trunk full of my grandmother's vinyl and sit down.

It is not lost on me that I'm in a standoff with a post-it note.

And it feels like I'm losing.

I open the trunk and pull out a record—Copland's *Appalachian Spring*—and load it onto the turntable. Music fills the room, immediately calming my nerves, but making me no less certain about what I should do here.

Probably nothing.

I'm overthinking.

"*To hell with it,*" I mutter, reaching for the post-it. I quickly type the number into my phone and send a text.

Felix: Hey. Sorry if this is weird. I grabbed your number off your lease agreement. Just wanted you to know there are leftovers in the fridge if you get hungry. And the key on the counter is yours.

Felix: Assuming I'm already in bed when you get home.

Felix: Not that you need to rush. Wherever you are is cool.

Felix: I mean, I hope it's cool?

Felix: I'm going to stop now.

I read back over my texts and groan. Could I sound any more ridiculous?

When the dancing dots show up at the bottom of my screen, I jump up, then sit down again. She's typing. The dots disappear. She's *not* typing?

They appear again.

I scrub a hand across my face and wait.

Gracie: Hey! I'm so glad you found my number. I've been wanting to text you all night.

Okay. That has to be a good sign.

Gracie: I'm actually at the hospital with my dad.

Felix: Is everything okay?

Gracie: We think so. He had some chest pains, and they've done a bunch of tests, but so far, everything has come back normal. They want to monitor him for another hour or so before they let him go.

Felix: I'm glad it's nothing serious. How are you holding up?

Gracie: I feel like maybe they need to monitor *ME* for an hour, but I'll be okay. I get a little stressed hanging out with my family, but it's nothing I'm not already used to.

Felix: I know that feeling.

Gracie: It'll probably be late when I get home. But I promise I'll lock up.

Felix: Will you let me know if there's anything I can do for you?

Gracie: If you're serious about the leftovers, that will be more than enough. I never did get dinner.

Felix: Chicken marsala, garlic mashed potatoes, roasted green beans

Gracie: Oh my gosh I might cry.

Gracie: You're spoiling me.

I want to spoil her. If she'll let me.

Felix: Eat as much as you want.

Gracie: Thanks, Felix.

After her last text, she sends one of those emojis that I think is supposed to be a hug, the one surrounded by hearts?

I don't know what it means. I'm not young enough or hip enough to know how to interpret emojis beyond knowing that I should never, under any circumstances, send anyone an eggplant or a peach.

I just know that this one makes me smile for the rest of the night.

Chapter Eleven
Gracie

"Are you texting a guy? Please tell me you're texting a guy."

Josh drops into the chair beside me in the back corner of the ER waiting room with the kind of flourish that typically marks all his movements. The man is never subtle. Wherever he goes, he goes loudly. Whatever he says, he projects for an entire room to hear. He's always been that way.

I hold my phone close to my chest. "Why do you care who I'm texting?"

Read: if I am texting a guy, I'm definitely not telling you about it.

"Because I'm *bored,* Gracie. And I hate hospitals and you texting a guy would be a nice distraction when I really need one." He reaches for my phone. "Come on. Spill it. You've been staring at that thing for the last ten minutes."

I shrug out of his reach. "Stop it. You can't have my phone. Who I'm texting is none of your business."

He smirks. "So it *is* a guy."

Josh would honestly lose his mind if he knew who I was texting. Which is all the more reason to keep my phone far out of his reach.

I drop it into my bag and zip up the outside pocket—even Josh isn't bold enough to go digging in a closed bag—and tighten the scarf I'm still wearing around my neck even though I've been inside the Mercy General emergency room with my family for going on—I glance at my watch—five hours now? Since I left the school. I don't know if the hospital really has been chilly or if it's only my uneasiness making me cold. I don't like hospitals, but then, does anyone really?

"Any new updates on Dad?"

Josh shakes his head no. "I was just talking to a guy outside—a Doctor Sharpe? He isn't Dad's doctor, but he said he'd check in and see if he could figure out why we're still waiting."

"I'd rather we wait and know for sure than have them send him home so he can have an actual heart attack in an hour."

Josh is quiet for a beat before he nudges my knee and says, "Do you think this will scare him into making some changes?"

"Like what?" My stomach grumbles, and I press a hand against it. The vending machine coffee and pack of crackers I split with Josh an hour ago haven't done much to quell my hunger. We should have just gone over to the hospital cafeteria to grab something to eat, but Mom has texted us at least a dozen times that they're "almost finished" so we kept putting it off, thinking we'd much prefer to get better food *outside* the hospital.

Now, though, I wouldn't go to the hospital cafeteria even if it *was* still open, which it isn't.

Because I have leftover chicken marsala waiting for me.

Warmth fills my belly, a tingling sense of anticipation skating down my limbs and out to my toes and fingertips, one that doesn't have anything to do with the food. It's all I can do not to pull out my phone and see if Felix has texted again.

I look at Josh and frown. *Stupid nosy brother.*

"I don't know," Josh finally answers. "His diet is terrible. All that fried bar food. And the most exercise he ever gets is jumping out of his chair every time his team scores." Josh runs a hand through his hair, real concern reflecting in his eyes. "I just want him to be around, you know?"

There could not be a more accurate description of my dad. I've never met a man whose life more fervently revolves around sports. That means weekends at the sports bar and evenings on the couch watching hockey, or football when there isn't a hockey game on, or baseball if he's really desperate.

"Maybe we could put a treadmill in the living room?" I ask. "Make him walk while he watches?"

Josh chuckles. "Sure. And then you'll start dating an Appie, Mom will start rooting for the Red Wings, and Jadah and I will have a set of triplets."

I don't even process the last half of Josh's sentence. Because—*what* did he just say? "Me date an *Appie*? Why would you—where did you get that idea?" My tone is defensive—too defensive—and Josh gives me a funny look.

"You *wouldn't* date one," he says. "That's the point. All those things are basically impossible, and they're still more likely than Dad using a treadmill in his living room."

My stomach drops. "Right. *Oh.* Right. You're so right. So totally unlikely."

A week ago, those words would have felt like truth. But now they feel hollow and, I don't know, almost like a betrayal somehow? Is it really fair that I'm sitting here dreaming about Felix's homemade chicken marsala while insisting to my brother I would *never* date him?

Last night, I mostly forgot Felix even *was* a hockey player. When we were laying on the floor and listening to music, talking about his grandmother, he was just...*Felix.* When I woke up this morning in the most comfortable bed I've ever slept in, wearing his clothes—clothes that still smelled like him—I was *not* thinking about the fact that he's an Appie.

Across the room, a doctor pushes through the double doors that lead into the ER, pauses, then moves again as soon as his eyes land on us. He looks youngish, probably Josh's age, and he's definitely the most handsome doctor I've ever seen in Harvest Hollow—handsome enough that if my head wasn't so full of Felix, I might feel a spark of interest.

But do I *want* my head to be so full of Felix? As a test, I focus all my attention on Doctor McDreamy and try to feel...I don't know. Something? Anything?

"Doctor Sharpe," Josh says as the doctor finally reaches us.

"Hey. I checked on your dad and did some digging," the doctor says. "Looks like we're waiting on an attending cardiologist to take one final look at the EKG to make sure everything checks out. The one at the hospital right now is currently in surgery, so they've paged the one on call and are waiting for him to call in. It could be any minute, but..." He weighs his hands in front of him. "It could just as easily be another hour. Sorry you're still waiting."

Josh nods. "Thanks for giving it to us straight."

Doctor Sharpe nods, his eyes drifting to me, and he lifts his lips in a polite smile.

I wait for that tingling that usually happens when I make eye contact with an attractive man, but I could be making eye contact with my grandma for all the tingling I'm feeling right now.

I watch the doctor walk away and sink into my chair, immediately thinking of the way my skin lit on fire when Felix wrapped my hand in his last night. Or even just the way my pulse skyrocketed when his first text message came through.

I like him.

He plays professional freaking hockey, and I still like him.

I always said I'd never do it, but honestly, that feels like such a dumb line to draw now that I'm really getting to know Felix. Summer *did* say I shouldn't prevent myself from getting to know someone amazing because of some arbitrary rule I made when I was basically still a child. I'm *not* a child anymore.

I'm a grown woman, and I really *want* to like Felix.

A flurry of excitement fills my chest. Even just acknowledging this is what I want has me flustered. What's going to happen when I see him again? When I'm face-to-face with his gorgeous hair and incredible brown eyes? And the tattoo! *Oh.* That tattoo is possibly the sexiest thing I have *ever* seen.

I manage to keep my phone out of my hands and my thoughts (mostly) PG—my brother *is* sitting directly beside me—until half an hour later, when an orderly pushes Dad through the big double doors in a wheelchair, Mom walking behind him carrying his coat and her purse and what I'm guessing is a stack of discharge paperwork.

Josh immediately fusses over Dad, so I move to Mom's side, pulling her into a quick hug. "How are you holding up?"

She gives me a startled look, like she's surprised by the gesture, but it only lasts a moment before her expression shifts into something warm and tender. "Oh, I'm okay. Got a list a mile long of changes we're supposed to make, and we've got an appointment with a cardiologist next week."

"Changes?" I tilt my head toward Dad. "How do you think he feels about that?"

"Oh, you know your father," she says knowingly. "But so do I. I'll get him moving one way or another. And Lord knows he only eats what I put in front of him as long as he isn't at the sports bar, so I've got more power than he thinks."

A surge of...something...moves through me. Warmth, I guess? I have always loved my parents—I know this. But that love has always been sort of abstract and intangible. Not quite obligatory, but also not something I'm actively practicing. I love them because they are my parents and that's what we do. We love family even when it's hard. Even when it's complicated and messy and uncomfortable.

But I've definitely kept them behind a wall the past few years. A thick one. One I needed if I had any hope of figuring out what I wanted my life to look like. I was so sure I didn't want it to look like theirs, and honestly, I still feel that way. But for the first time, I'm wondering if maybe, *possibly?* it doesn't have to be all or nothing. Maybe it's the thought of losing Dad that's done it. Do I wish he cared a little more about classical music? About the cello? Sure. Would I rather have him as he is than not at all?

Absolutely.

I reach out and squeeze Mom's hand. "Will you let me know if there's anything I can do? Come over and take walks with him, maybe?"

She holds my gaze, her eyes turning glassy as they fill with moisture. "I will, Gracie. Thank you."

I lean down and kiss Dad on the cheek, then punch my brother in the arm before heading toward my car.

It's after eleven p.m., late enough that it would be normal for Felix to already be asleep, or at least in bed, when I get home. I'm only just getting to know him, but I'd put money on him being the type of man who goes to bed early and wakes up with the sun so he can go on a long run, meditate for half an hour, then make a protein smoothie out of wheatgrass and other inedible green things, all before seven in the morning.

Sure enough, when I finally make it into his apartment, the lights are all off save one above the stove.

There's a note on the counter, and I immediately recognize his orderly handwriting from the poster he signed for Maddox.

Is it bad that I remember what his handwriting looks like? That I'm filing away all these little details about Felix like tiny keepsakes?

I pick up the note and read it slowly.

I made a plate for you and left it in the warming oven. The books are also for you. I saw that your original copies were ruined

*in the Great Pipe Explosion, so I took the liberty of replacing them
for you. I hope that isn't weird.*

I grin at this line. He said the same thing when he texted
me. That he hoped he wasn't being weird. Someone needs to
tell this man that if being kind and considerate and charming
makes him *weird,* he needs to lean in for all it's worth. Because
it's working.

Still smiling, I read the rest of the note.

*I also picked up a few additional titles I thought you might
like and grabbed a few pastries for you. Emmy said they were
your favorites. I hope your dad is okay. –Felix*

He bought me pastries.

He. bought. me. pastries.

I peek into the bag, seeing both an apple cinnamon scone
and an apple danish. I'm not at all surprised that Emmy re-
members my favorite pastries. But I am completely *smitten*
over Felix thinking to ask. And he replaced my books?

I run my hands over the glossy covers. There is nothing quite
like the feel of a brand-new book. I immediately recognize
the three books Felix added. The first two are contemporary
novels, neither of which I've read, but it's the third that makes
me laugh out loud.

A River Runs Through It.

I open the front cover and see Felix's familiar handwriting.
To commemorate the occasion. –Felix

Okay. It's official.

The man is actually perfect.

Slipping off my shoes, I make my way around the island
looking for my dinner. Which is...well, I don't know where it

is. I don't actually know what a *warming oven* is. I shake my head over the fact that Felix is the type of man who *does* know, then pull out my phone to google.

Eventually, the internet helps me discover a small sliding tray thing that extends out from under Felix's wall oven. The plate sitting on the tray is perfectly warm, and I practically groan as the smell of the food hits my nose.

For the next five minutes, I'm actually *glad* Felix is already in bed because my eating is more like *scarfing*. I'm so hungry, and the food is so good, and it's all I can do not to lick the plate clean.

I glance over my shoulder at Felix's bedroom door, which is firmly shut, no light shining underneath.

Oh, what the hell. I *do* lick my plate clean.

Fifteen minutes later, my belly full of dinner and danish, and my new stack of books on the nightstand beside me, I snuggle under my covers and send Felix a text.

Gracie: I know you won't get this until tomorrow, but thank you. Dinner was amazing. And the pastry was delicious and the books—that was sweet of you. I laughed out loud over *A River Runs Through It.*

Gracie: If you were awake, I'd give you a hug to say thank you.

Felix: Still awake. But I sleep in my underwear, so we should probably save the hugging for tomorrow.

I gasp when his response comes through. He's awake! And just on the other side of the apartment. *And in his underwear.*

I almost text him that I've already seen him in his underwear, so why wait? But that feels a little too suggestive for a man I still haven't actually dated, so I refrain. But that doesn't stop me from bringing the visual to mind. The smooth planes of his chest, the ridges of his abdominal muscles, the curves and dips of his shoulders and biceps. *The tattoo.*

Oh, I love that tattoo.

Felix: Wait. Maybe that was too much.

Felix: Sorry. Filter is broken.

Felix: I'm not in my underwear. I'm in my full hockey pads.

I laugh out loud for the second time tonight.

Gracie: That does not sound comfortable. I have no idea how you even walk around in those things. I can't imagine trying to sleep.

Felix: Goalie pads are particularly cumbersome, for sure.

Gracie: I'm already in bed, but tomorrow sounds like an excellent day for (fully clothed) hugging.

Felix: How's your dad? Is he home from the hospital?

Gracie: Yes. He's okay. Meeting with the cardiologist next week, and in desperate need of some changes to his diet and exercise routines. Hopefully Mom will whip him into shape.

Felix: Do YOU like to exercise?

Felix: No judgment. You look like you do.

Felix: Or like you don't need to?

Felix: Either one is fine. I'm only asking because I'm curious.

Felix: Even though now I realize it might sound like I think you NEED to exercise, which is not the case because I think you look amazing.

Felix: And also I wish I could unsend ALL those messages.

I send him a winking emoji because he's adorable and I love that he's so flustered.

Gracie: I do exercise, but only because I love pastries so much. I go to a spin class a couple of times a week and do tons of hot yoga. My sister-in-law is an instructor, and she's brutal.

Felix: Never done hot yoga. Should I try?

Gracie: Most definitely. I'll take you with me sometime.

The image of Felix doing hot yoga next to me, sweat dripping down his very beautiful body makes me close my eyes and sigh. Except...

I reread my text and feel a beat of trepidation. Did I just ask him on a date? Is that how he'll take it? Will he care? Before I can overthink things even further, he replies.

Felix: I would love that. Nothing like embarrassing myself in front of the woman I'm trying to impress.

I drop my phone and curl my hands into fists, practically squealing with excitement.

What is even happening to me? I have never been this woman. The woman who *squeals* over a man.

Gracie: Nah. I'm not buying it.

Felix: That I want to impress you?

Gracie: That you would embarrass yourself. You play hockey, which means you have great balance. And you probably have incredible core strength because goalies stand in the WEIRDEST positions during games. I don't think you have anything to worry about.

Felix: I appreciate the assessment. I'm already feeling more confident.

Gracie: I mean, Jadah will still BREAK YOU. But no more than she does everyone else.

Felix: Now I want to go just because I'm curious.

Felix: But honestly, you could invite me to try competitive duck herding and I'd still want to go if you were going to be there.

Gracie: Did you just make that up?

Instead of responding, Felix sends me a link to a video.

I watch it, one hand pressed against my mouth the entire time. It looks like it's some sort of team-building exercise where people have to work together to usher a group of ducks from one enclosed pen to another enclosed pen on the other side of a field. It's totally ridiculous and weird and I can't stop laughing.

Gracie: Well. That's three minutes of my life I can't get back.

Felix sends a winking emoji, which makes my belly swoop and my heart beat a tiny bit faster.

Felix: I'm glad your dad is okay and that you're home safe. Sleep well, Gracie.

Before I even think about what I'm doing, I respond with a single red heart.

CHAPTER TWELVE
Felix

AFTER PRACTICE ON TUESDAY, cello music floats out of my apartment as I climb the stairs. It only takes a moment to discern that Gracie isn't the one playing. The music is a little too stilted, the tone not quite deep enough to be Gracie, which means she must be teaching.

Before going inside, I let myself into her apartment and check on the progress of the repairs. It looks like the disaster response crew finished up today. Their fans are gone, and the place looks completely dry and mostly put back together, minus the damaged furniture, which they hauled away, and the exposed subfloor since the new floors haven't gone in yet.

"Okay," I say to myself as I look around the space. "It could have been worse."

I pull out my phone and find the email my dad sent earlier with recommendations regarding how and with what the plumbing should be replaced. He also included the name of a plumber based in Asheville, a cousin of one of his contractors in Chicago who he recommends I use. I might have balked at the idea of pulling someone in from Asheville when there are perfectly good plumbers in Harvest Hollow, but I'm a little gun-shy after having made such a bad call the first time around, so using Dad's recommendation is probably the safest route, no matter how much it pains me to admit it. Especially since Dad said he'd cut me a deal.

To his credit, after our initial conversation, our subsequent interactions have been a little easier. It's like he almost seems excited about having something for us to talk about. Like he's happy I actually *need* him.

It's not him coming to a hockey game. But it's something.

I pull out my phone and give the plumber a call. He answers on the first ring, and we quickly set something up for next Wednesday. I hate to wait so long, but I'd rather not have people in and out of the building while Gracie's here alone, and that's the first availability he has next week.

Hopefully Gracie doesn't truly mind staying at my place. It's encouraging that she's teaching lessons in my living room. It at least makes me feel like she's comfortable in my space.

With everything at Gracie's squared away, I head next door, letting myself in quietly so I don't disrupt her lesson.

Gracie looks up as I enter, and I nod my head in acknowledgment. She lifts her lips in a small smile without breaking the rhythm she's clapping out on her knees, her student playing along.

"Much better," Gracie says when the piece ends. "You nailed the rhythm through those final measures."

Her student—a boy who looks like he's maybe twelve or thirteen—breathes out a sigh as he lifts his bow off the strings. "Can we be done now, Miss Mitchell? My fingers are tired."

"Absolutely," Gracie says, her tone warm. "We're out of time anyway."

"Your fingers wouldn't feel so sore if you practiced more," a woman says from the couch in a tone that could only come from the kid's mom. I hadn't noticed her sitting there until now.

"More practicing will help," Gracie says, her tone extra gentle like she's trying to balance out the mother's scolding tone. "But you've worked hard today. You're totally fine to give your fingers a rest."

I'm impressed with the way she managed to both agree with the mom but also validate the kid's efforts. That takes a level of finesse I admire.

I pull the Italian sausage I plan to use for dinner out of the fridge, as well as an onion and a bell pepper, while Gracie's student packs up his cello. His mom moves to the door, her gaze fixed on me the entire time. If her expression is any clue, she doesn't trust me even a little bit.

I look at Gracie, lifting my shoulders as if to say, *What did I do to her?*

Gracie bites her lip. "Mrs. Henderson, you remember I mentioned I was staying with my neighbor while the plumbing in my apartment is being replaced. This is my neighbor, Felix."

The woman purses her lips. "Gracie, dear, do you think this is wise? When you told me, I assumed your neighbor was..." Her eyes dart to me for a quick second before she shifts them back to Gracie. "Well, another *woman*. This feels very...*untoward*," she finally finishes.

Before Gracie can answer, her student stands up, cello case in hand, and his eyes finally fall on me. "Holy Shi...itake mushrooms," he says, his eyes darting to his mom.

"Carson!" she scolds. "Watch your language."

"I said shiitake mushrooms," he says defensively. "Besides, that's..." He looks back at me. "You're Felix Jamison."

His mom looks at me with narrowed eyes. "Is that...someone I should know?"

"Felix plays hockey for the Appies," Gracie says. She looks at Carson. "Are you a fan?"

He nods and swallows, his eyes never leaving me.

Suddenly sensing I ought to do more than just stand here, I move around the counter and extend a hand. "Hi, Carson," I say. "It's nice to meet you."

"You look a lot bigger in person," he says.

"Yeah, I get that a lot."

He holds out his cello lesson book. "Will you sign my book?"

"I think I can do better than that." I move to my kitchen table where the jerseys Logan and Parker brought over are still sitting inside a giant, cardboard box. Next to the jerseys, there's a stack of team posters, and I pull one out, then grab a sharpie out of the junk drawer in the kitchen. I sign it to Carson and hand it over.

"Cool, thanks!" he says.

His mom finally smiles at me, though it's still tight. Is she *that* worried about what I might do to Gracie while she's staying here? "Should we expect to be here for lessons again next week?" she asks, directing her question to Gracie.

"I'll text you and let you know," Gracie says, ushering her out the door.

When they're finally gone, she slides the door closed and slumps against it. "Sorry about that. Carson's mom goes to church with *my* mom, and she's always been a little bit...buttoned up."

"I got that impression."

She drops onto a barstool. "Believe me, it could have been worse. You're lucky she didn't mention fornication or deflowering. I promise both those words were crossing through her mind."

I chuckle. "Deflowering, huh? That sounds...archaic."

"Tell me about it. What are you cooking? And please tell me you aren't *only* cooking for me. I can just warm up a pizza or something."

I glance at her over my shoulder. I like the idea of cooking for her, but I don't want to come on too strong. "I'm making spaghetti, and I'm happy to be cooking for you. But also, I'm going to be on the road for the next five days. I'd rather eat something home-cooked and good for me while I can."

"You're leaving already?" she asks, disappointment heavy in her tone. Her shoulders slump the slightest bit, which makes my heart pound harder in my chest.

Is she sad I'm leaving?

I'm *definitely* sad I'm leaving.

Gracie clears her throat, and when she speaks again, her words are bright and cheerful. "Where are you headed?"

I hide a grin. She *is* sad I'm leaving.

"Up to New York," I say. "And yeah. We leave first thing tomorrow morning. We're playing three in three, Thursday through Saturday, then driving home Sunday morning."

"Three games in three days," she says. "Sounds brutal."

"It will be."

She's quiet for a beat before she says, "Is it bad that I...?" Her words trail off, and I turn down the heat on the Italian sausage browning on the stove so I can face her.

"Is it bad that you what?"

She bites her lip and shakes her head. "Never mind."

I fold my arms over my chest. "Is it...bad that you hate spaghetti?"

She rolls her eyes. "I love spaghetti. I was just going to say that...I'm sad I won't see you all weekend."

I hold her gaze, sensation dancing over my skin like there's some kind of electrical current stretching across the space between us, lighting me up, waking up every nerve ending in my body. It's all I can do not to cross the room to her, touch her, *taste her.*

Instead, I keep my feet planted. The fact that we're even having this conversation feels big. I don't want to react too eagerly and scare her off.

"Me too," I finally say, realizing that for the first time, the words are true. I love hockey. I *really* love hockey. There aren't very many things I would choose to do instead.

But hanging out with Gracie? I don't even have to think about it.

"We can always text," I say.

"And we can make the most of the time we have before you leave," she says.

Don't freak out, Felix. Don't. Freak. Out.

She could be talking about friendship. That's what she said, after all. I was a good *friend*.

"We absolutely can," I say.

She stands and stretches her arms over her head. "Is there anything I can do to help?"

"Maybe make a salad? Just use whatever is in the fridge."

"Perfect. I'm going to change into something more comfortable first, but it will only take me a second. I'll be right back."

"No rush. I still have to cook the pasta."

While she's gone, I can't stop thinking about how much I love the idea of us cooking together, hanging out in the kitchen like it's no big deal. That's what it needs to be tonight: no big deal, which means I need to get my erratic emotions under control.

My pregame mantra pops into my head, and I repeat it a few times.

I'm steady. I'm focused. No one controls me but me.

Before a game, it helps me get in the zone, shut out all distractions. Tonight, I just hope it will help me keep my cool.

When Gracie returns to the kitchen barefoot, in black leggings that hug her curves, an oversized sweatshirt that's already fallen off of one of her shoulders, and glasses, her hair piled on top of her head, I give up. There is no way i'm keeping my cool tonight.

This deconstructed version of Gracie—I didn't even know she wore glasses—is incredibly sexy.

She opens the fridge and pulls out a bag of mixed greens. "I assume we're starting with this? What else?"

We fall into an easy rhythm as we cook, talking, laughing, moving around each other as we pull the meal together. As nervous as I am, Gracie is really easy to talk to. She's generous with her praise, she's quick to laugh, and though her bare pantry shelves made it seem like she doesn't do a lot of cooking, she's obviously comfortable in the kitchen.

More importantly, she seems comfortable around me. Like she's genuinely happy to be here.

Even though I've learned how to minimize my social anxiety, it still works to convince me that even when social situations seem to be going *right*, they are probably only seconds away from going *wrong*. If someone says to me, "I had a really great time tonight," my first impulse is to think, "Did you, though? Or are you just saying that to be nice?"

It's not healthy. And recognizing that makes it easier for me to dismiss the thoughts when they come and focus on being present in the moment instead.

I'm loving being present with Gracie, feeling every sensation, every pulse of my heartbeat, every thrill over the small touches we share as we move around the kitchen.

Once the meal is ready, I finally shift the box of youth hockey jerseys to the floor under the window so we can eat at the kitchen table like civilized humans. Gracie carries our plates over, setting them on either side of the same corner instead of on opposite ends of the table. She grabs the bowl of salad next, and I retrieve a bottle of wine from the fridge and two glasses from the cabinet.

She smiles warmly as we finally sit down to eat. "This is a really beautiful meal, Felix. Who taught you to cook?"

"Would you believe it was the same grandmother who taught me to love classical music?"

"Sounds like she was a really big part of your life."

"She was," I answer before taking a bite of spaghetti. "She didn't live with us, but she was close by, and she made a point to see me a few times a week. And she was always intentional about the time we spent together. Looking back, I think she had a pretty specific agenda. She recognized the privilege I was growing up with—more than she'd had growing up, even more than my dad had. I think she worried I would become spoiled or entitled, especially since my own parents didn't seem all that worried about it. They were all about living a life of luxury. I think my grandmother wanted me to understand it might not always be that way. And she wanted me to know how to function if it wasn't."

Gracie scoops some salad onto her plate. "So she taught you to cook."

"And to shovel snow," I say with a chuckle as Gracie passes me the salad. "To make myself a sandwich whenever I was hungry even if there was a chef in the kitchen willing to make it for me. To do my own laundry."

"Those are things you wouldn't have done without her influence?" Gracie asks. "You lived in a house where people would have done your laundry and made you sandwiches?"

I wince. "Trust me. I like the life I've built here a lot more."

She takes a bite of spaghetti, and her eyes close for the briefest moment. "Oh my word, that's really delicious."

Warmth spills from my midsection out to my limbs, which is silly. I made food, and she likes it. Why does that feel so good?

"When did you start playing hockey?" she asks after taking another bite.

I take a long sip of wine. "In middle school. My parents pushed me into it because they thought it would make me more social, help me get better at interacting with kids my age instead of hanging out with my grandma all the time."

"Did you like it?" Gracie asks.

"Not at first. But then I figured out if I was the goalie, I didn't have to talk to anybody."

She chuckles. "How convenient. I bet your parents loved that."

I grin. "That's when the sport really clicked for me. I think my parents actually regretted signing me up at that point because suddenly, it was all I wanted to do."

She huffs. "Yeah. I know a little something about how obsessive hockey players can be."

I lift my eyebrows. "Tell me more."

As Gracie starts to talk, I begin to understand a little more of where she's coming from. She told me before that she grew up watching her brother play hockey, and that had something to do with her aversion to the sport. But at her house, hockey was a lot more than just the sport her brother happened to *play*.

"So like, the entire room is dedicated to hockey?" I ask through a bite of spaghetti.

She nods. "One half is Carolina Hurricanes every-thing—red, black, and gray everywhere. The other half is dedicated to the Appies."

"That sounds like a lot of bold colors in one room."

"Oh, you have no idea," she says. "There are also puck-shaped coasters, hockey sticks mounted in a giant X above the fireplace, framed team posters that they update every year, and a signed Cam Ward jersey mounted inside a special shadow box that Dad keeps locked."

"And this is your parents' *living room*?"

"Not the garage or the man cave or the den. The actual living room where they welcome guests into their house. If you can believe it, my mom was the one who did all the decorating. Dad is the more loyal Appies fan, but I think Mom would literally crawl naked across a highway to see the Hurricanes play in person."

"That's some serious fandom."

She's quiet for a beat before she says, "It's not that I *hate* the sport, you know? I used to really like watching it, especially when Josh was playing. But now, it just...I don't know. It defined my existence for so long, I just wanted to get away from it all. To occupy a space where dinner conversation wasn't always about shooting percentages or the draft lottery or even the quality of the hotdogs they serve at the Summit. I'm not kidding you, Felix. It is literally all they talk about."

The hotdogs they serve at the Summit are particularly good, but that feels like a horrible thing to point out *now*. I understand Gracie's frustration. It might be different for me because hockey is my job, but even as much as I love it, I also love having a space where I don't have to think about it. Where I can leave it behind and read books and listen to music and cook and relax and just be Felix, without being Felix Jamison, Appies goalie.

I can't imagine living so completely immersed in the hockey world, especially if it kept Gracie from exploring her own interests.

"What did your parents think about your music?" I ask.

She winces the slightest bit, but then she shrugs and breathes out a long sigh, the hurt in her expression melting into something more like resignation. "I mean, they tried. They always encouraged me to do whatever made me happy. But they didn't really understand. If they *did* come to hear me play, it was only because it was me. Not because it was anything they actually enjoyed. They never come to any of my performances now. It's just not their thing."

"But *you* are their thing. You're their daughter," I say. "That should count for something."

She quickly shakes her head. "I've made peace with it. And we get along fine now. The fewer expectations I have, the easier it is to not get my feelings hurt."

I don't like the idea of *anything* hurting Gracie's feelings, but she clearly doesn't want to talk about it anymore. "If it matters," I say slowly, my eyes lifting to hers, "I love to hear you play."

"A point in your favor," she says with an easy smile. But then she bites her lip, her eyes flashing as her expression shifts into something flirty. "And something that made me finally decide I was being a little shortsighted by dismissing *all* hockey players."

It's not quite a declaration of interest, but it's close. "It's that so?" I say. "Want me to send you Eli's number?"

She purses her lips. "You're not funny."

I smirk. "I'm a little funny."

"And I'm sure Eli is a nice guy. But he's definitely not the hockey player I'm interested in."

"Felix!" A voice calls from the other side of my front door. *Eli's voice.* "Are you home?"

Gracie's eyes go wide, and I shake my head.

"No way," I say.

She starts to laugh. "Is that actually Eli? How did he even do that? He literally showed up seconds after I said his name!"

"Leave it to Eli." I sigh and put down my fork. I never should have given my teammates the code to the outside door. I stand and step away from the table, then pause and turn to face Gracie. "Just in case, I apologize for anything that's about to happen."

I slide my door open to find not just Eli, but Nathan, too.

"Hey," I say. "What are you—" My words cut off as Eli pushes into my apartment, clapping me on the back on his way. "Sure, come on in," I say dryly. "I don't have anything else going on."

Nathan shrugs and gruffly says, "You know Eli."

I've actually been known to *admire* Eli in the past. The man enters every room with absolute certainty that he is one, always welcome, and two, everyone's favorite person. Not in a cocky way. He's just...happy and comfortable in his own skin in pretty much every environment.

Right now, I wish he'd be happy and comfortable somewhere else.

I step out of the way and motion Nathan into the apartment. He's the exact opposite of Eli. Honestly, he'd probably prefer waiting in the hallway, or even outside in the car.

"Oh, hey...you have company," Eli says as Nathan follows me into the kitchen. "Hi, Gracie. Nice to see you again."

Eli moves to the stove, sniffing around the remaining spaghetti. What he doesn't do is *flirt* with Gracie, which, based on her raised eyebrows, seems to surprise her.

I'm not surprised, though. Eli won't overstep now that he knows I'm interested in Gracie. He's too good a guy for that.

"Yeah, I do have company," I say as I run a hand through my hair. "I could have told you that had you texted."

Eli pulls a spoon out of the drawer and takes a bite of spaghetti sauce. "I did text. You didn't answer."

I pat my pockets looking for my phone, but it's not even on me. It must be in the kitchen somewhere, but I've been so focused on Gracie, I haven't even noticed or missed it.

"Dude, this is amazing," Eli says, motioning to the sauce. "Did you make this?"

"I did," I say. "Why are you here again? We were kind of in the middle of..." I don't finish my sentence because it's not like I'm on an actual date with Gracie. We ate dinner, and now we're done. We aren't in the middle of anything except a conversation, and it feels a little too pointed to shove my friends out of the apartment just because of that.

"We're here for the jerseys," Eli says. "Seriously, can I have a plate of this? I'm starving."

"We *just* ate," Nathan says, tugging at his ponytail.

"Two hours ago," Eli counters. "And it looks like there's plenty. You want some too?"

I was hoping Gracie might enjoy the leftovers while I'm out of town, but I motion for Eli to go ahead anyway.

Nathan looks at me, a question in his eyes, and I nod. "Go for it." I move back to the table and gather the empty plates. Gracie and I make eye contact, and I mouth a quick, *"Sorry."*

She smiles and waves a dismissive hand like this is no big deal.

"So, what jerseys are we talking about?" I ask as I put our dishes into the sink.

"Parker said you had them," Eli says. "For the youth clinic? I guess we're helping now too, so we're supposed to sign them."

"The youth clinic isn't for another month," I say.

"But we had time tonight. And you know how hard it is to remember crap like that once we're on the road."

Eli and Nathan both move to the table, plates heaping with the last of the spaghetti, and fill the chairs directly opposite Gracie. She looks more amused than annoyed, so I sit down too, hesitation melting into acceptance, and listen as Eli introduces Gracie to Nathan, then starts peppering her with questions.

It doesn't take long to realize that Eli has a very specific purpose. Every question he asks Gracie somehow leads back to me.

When she mentions her nephew, he talks about how great I am with kids whenever we're signing team merch or helping out with youth clinics.

When she mentions her favorite food—barbecue chicken pizza, and yes, I'm taking notes—he claims my homemade pizza is the best he's ever had. I've never made homemade pizza at all, much less made it for Eli, but I appreciate his efforts anyway.

Even if he's being about as subtle as a semi plowing down the highway.

"I agree," Gracie says after his next comment, the amusement in her tone saying she's picked up on Eli's endgame as well. "Felix does have excellent taste in music."

"Is there something you need to confess, Eli?" Nathan asks, his deep baritone rumbling across the table. "Cause it sounds like you got a thing for Felix."

Eli winks at Gracie. "I wouldn't stand a chance. Pretty sure his attention is engaged elsewhere."

"Okay! How about we sign some jerseys now?" I say, clapping my hands together as I stand and reach for the box. "Are you guys done eating? It looks like you're done eating."

"I'll just get out of your hair," Gracie says as she stands. "I've got some work to catch up on anyway." She looks at Eli and Nathan. "It was nice to meet you, Nathan. Eli, you're an excellent wingman, and I like you much better now." She passes me on her way to her room, a coy smile on her lips, and brushes her hand along my shoulder.

It's barely a touch. The smallest gesture.

But I can't stop smiling anyway.

CHAPTER THIRTEEN
Gracie

I'M STRETCHED OUT ON my bed, reading one of the novels Felix added to my book stack yesterday, and let me tell you, this book is *not* for the faint of heart. It is *so good*—about what I think is a murderous ghost haunting a symphony hall—but it is also *so scary*. I'm only five chapters in, and my heart is pounding so quickly, I might as well be running a marathon.

A knock sounds at my door. I squeal, tossing the book into the air, and clutch my chest.

"Gracie?" Felix calls. "Are you okay?"

I stand up from the bed and retrieve the book from the floor, then open the door. "You cannot knock on my door when I'm reading this thing," I say, pressing the book into his chest. "And probably I shouldn't do any more reading at night, or else I might have to sleep in your room with you."

He grins. "The bed is big enough, so I wouldn't say no."

I blink, my brain tripping over Felix's *very flirty* tone. But then he holds up the book, moving on like he didn't just make a casual reference to us sharing his bed.

"It's good, right?" he says, and I force my focus back to the book.

"So good. Totally gripping. But I feel like I need a nap."

He puts the book on the edge of the dresser and crosses his arms over his chest. "How about a distraction?"

I lift my eyebrows. His tone is still incredibly flirty, which...does he mean what I think he means? I swallow against the sudden dryness in my throat. "Did your teammates leave?"

He nods. "It's just you and me now."

"So we're alone," I say slowly. "And that means we could..." I hesitate, hoping he'll fill in the blank so I don't have to. Not that I have any idea what I would say in response.

"We could go downstairs and see the first floor of the warehouse?" he says, clearly confused by my behavior.

Relief flows through me, and I let out an audible breath. "Oh. Oh! That's a great idea. Let's definitely do that."

He studies me, his brow furrowed. "What did you think I was—wait, did you think I was suggesting sex?"

I hide my face behind my hands, my cheeks hot under my palms. "No! I mean, yes? Maybe? I didn't know what you were suggesting. But now I'm really embarrassed so probably you should go so I can hide under the bed."

"What kind of a man do you think I am?" he says. Only the lightness of his tone keeps me from worrying.

I peek one eye out from between my fingers.

Felix has his hands propped on his hips, his expression playful, if not a tiny bit disbelieving. "Who knew your mind spent so much time in the gutter?" he jokes.

I scoff and drop my hands. "You started it when you talked about sharing your bed."

"*You* mentioned sleeping in my room first," he fires back.

Well. He's got me there. I think I might actually die of mortification. Right here in the middle of Felix's perfectly perfect guest room. I lift my hands again, this time using my entire arms to hide my face. "Okay. Just kill me now. If you call my brother, he'll come collect my belongings. And the body."

Felix chuckles and I feel him moving toward me. Sure enough, his hands wrap around my wrists, and he gently tugs them from in front of my face. "*Or,*" he says gently, "we can go downstairs."

I blow a wisp of hair out of my face. "And forget this conversation ever happened?"

"Oh, I'll never forget," he says. "But I promise I won't make fun of you anymore." He grins. "At least for tonight."

I groan and pull my arms back, using them to hide again.

"No wait, I'm sorry," Felix says, laughing harder this time. "I'm sorry, I'm sorry. I promise. No more teasing."

I still don't move, but then Felix's hands fall onto my shoulders. "Please?" he says, and I drop my arms, lifting my gaze to his.

"Hi," he says.

I breathe out a grumpy sigh. "Hi."

"Do you want to go downstairs with me?"

"Yes, thank you."

He nods. "Good. But Gracie, I want you to know..." He squeezes my shoulders, his brown eyes holding mine. "I'm *not* that kind of guy."

It's not like I've ever seen women coming or going from Felix's apartment, and I feel like I probably would have if he were any kind of player. But his admission still sends a swirl of heat through my belly.

"Downstairs isn't heated, so you might want to grab a coat," he says, his hands finally falling from my shoulders. He slips them into his pockets. "And you'll definitely want to have some shoes on."

I do as he suggests and grab my coat off the chair in the corner and a pair of Uggs from the closet, slipping them both on before following Felix out the door. "I've seriously wondered so many times what's down here," I say as we head down the stairs.

He looks over his shoulder and smiles. "It isn't that exciting. At least, not yet."

We pause at the base of the stairs, and Felix uses his keys to unlock the enormous metal door I've been walking past for months. Once we're inside, he hits a series of switches on the wall, and faint yellow light floods the cavernous space.

There isn't much to look at. There are several stacks of pallets pushed against a back wall, a single table sitting in the center of the room, and concrete columns every twenty feet or so, making the space feel a little like a parking garage.

A very empty, very boring parking garage.

I don't know what I was expecting—this is just a warehouse, after all—but Felix did say he wanted to show me something. Why would he want to show me this?

He reaches for my hand, lacing our fingers together. "I know it doesn't look like much. But come see."

He tugs me toward the table while I try not to freak out that we're actually holding hands. When we reach the table in the center of the room, he drops my hand, then reaches for several large rolls of paper. He unrolls them, using his phone to hold down one side, and his hand to hold down the other.

I pull my own phone out of the pocket on my leggings and offer it to him as an additional paperweight.

"Thanks," he says. Once the paper is stretched out and secure, he steps to the side so I can lean in and take a look.

It looks like some kind of design rendering of a clean, open office space. It must be what he intends for *this* space because I immediately recognize the pattern of the columns. There are couches and chairs, long conference tables surrounded by chairs, as well as smaller workspaces, little alcoves where someone might work privately. On the other end, there are a series of smaller rooms—offices, maybe?—but the walls are fully glass, keeping with the open concept vibe of the rest of the space. A wide hallway cuts between the offices, ending at what looks like some sort of large kitchen space.

"It's beautiful," I finally say. "What's it going to be?"

Felix pushes his hands into his pockets, a hint of vulnerability passing over his features. "The Elizabeth R. Jamison Creative Center."

"Your grandmother?"

He nods. "It was her money. Seemed like a good idea to name it after her." He points at the drawing on the table in front of us. "The idea is to provide a space for start-ups and other entrepreneurs and freelancers to work." His fingers slide over the drawing. "So, larger tables over here for collaborations, a conference room for when people need privacy, and plenty of spaces where people can sit and work or write or whatever it is they need to do. Then over here, these little private rooms I thought could be used for musicians, maybe. For practicing, or even teaching lessons. I just emailed the architect to see if we could also add a recording studio—nothing fancy, just a basic booth with minimal equipment, but it would be enough if someone wanted to make a demo. I should have those drawings back next week."

Finally, he points at the kitchen space at the far end. "And this would be a commercial kitchen. When people are just getting started, selling baked goods or making cakes or whatever, you have to have a kitchen that's commercially certified, which is a barrier for a lot of entrepreneurs in the food business. A lot of bigger cities have kitchens people can rent out for a certain amount of time, but they're often cost prohibitive, and there's nothing like that here in Harvest Hollow." He breathes out a shaky breath. "And I guess I just...thought there should be."

My eyes drift back to the soundproof rooms he mentioned, and I point. "So, if I wanted to teach cello lessons in one of these, I could?"

"That's the idea."

"There's a music store on the other side of town that has teaching rooms you can rent," I say. "But you have to contract through the store and agree to teach at their advertised prices, which, when I only have a few students, it doesn't really feel worth it."

"So something like this would be perfect for you," he says.

"What will you charge?" I ask. He probably hasn't thought that far in advance, but it's the first place my mind goes because my budget is already so tight.

"Hopefully nothing," he says. "Or, I don't know. I might have to charge something, maybe something tiered based on income, if there are too many people wanting to use the space." He runs a hand through his hair. "I'm still working through the logistics, but I plan to apply for grants from the Jamison Foundation and use those funds to keep it running. I just don't want anyone who wants to start a business to be stifled because they don't have adequate workspace."

My eyes move over the drawing one more time, and I imagine what it might feel like to have a place like this to meet my students, or even to record a few things with my quartet. A little over a year ago, we spent close to a thousand dollars to rent a studio to record a few sample pieces for our website. We only had the space for two hours, and it was so stressful trying to get everything done in such a limited amount of time.

"This is amazing." I lift my eyes to Felix's. "It's an incredible idea."

He smiles, his eyes dropping for the briefest second, like he's genuinely happy to have my approval. "You really think so? You're actually the first person I've told. Aside from my architect."

A flush of heat rushes through me. I'm the first person he's told? "I really think so. I love it. I love all of it."

More than the space and idea, what I really love is the care and thoughtfulness behind it. The more time I spend with Felix, the more I'm starting to see the layers to him, each one revealing more of a good, good man. The kind of man who, if I'm not careful, I could fall way too hard for, way too fast.

He breathes out what sounds like a sigh of relief, and I wonder how long he's been sitting on this idea, planning, hoping he might be able to make it happen.

"Will you still love it if you know it's the reason I agreed to keep the old plumbing when I was renovating upstairs?" His mouth lifts into a sheepish smile. "I wanted to save as much money as possible to make sure I had enough to make this happen."

I prop my hands on my hips. "Finally, something to blame for my ruined furniture."

He smirks. "You couldn't just blame me?"

"Nope. You might have made me stay somewhere else, and the bed I'm sleeping in at your place is a million times more comfortable than mine was."

This is possibly the understatement of the century. The bed I was sleeping on before was something I bought from a fellow teacher when they downgraded to a smaller house and got rid of the guest bed they'd had for years. The mattress was old and springy and creaky in all the worst ways, but it was free, and free trumps just about everything else.

"I'll make sure your replacement is the same kind of mattress," Felix says, his tone shifting from playful to a little more serious. "Everyone deserves to be comfortable when they sleep."

"Felix, you don't have to buy me a new mattress," I protest. "I read over my policy yesterday, and my rental insurance will cover it."

He's shaking his head before I even finish my sentence. "We already talked about this, Gracie. If you *caused* the flood, I might be okay with that. But this wasn't your fault. You aren't filing any insurance claims. This is on me."

Felix's tone is still warm, but there's also a bossiness to it that sends a thrill skittering down my spine. Clearly, he's not going to compromise on this. Is it weird I find that so sexy? That the tiny bit of commanding firmness in his tone is making me feel weak-kneed and flushed? But then, that seems to be the trend lately. *Everything* about Felix makes me feel weak-kneed and flushed.

"So you're leaving tomorrow," I say, needing something, *anything,* to ground me. Otherwise, I might climb this man like a literal tree and settle myself into his arms.

There's a palpable tension crackling between us. I don't think I'm the only one buzzing with attraction, but I also get the sense that Felix is holding back.

If he tried to kiss me, I'd let him. And I don't *think* he'd stop me if I made the first move.

But I also think we'd be rushing things. And if this is happening between us, I want to make sure we get it right.

Felix nods as he rolls the architectural drawings back up. He pockets his phone, then hands mine over to me. "The bus leaves at six a.m. sharp."

"Oof. That's early," I say. "Do you always travel by bus?"

"Not always. We'll fly if we're going all the way across the country. But if we're staying on the east coast, it's always a bus."

We walk side by side across the room and to the stairs. Our arms brush, and Felix looks over, catching my eye and smiling.

Does that mean he feels it too? The energy that sets my skin on fire whenever we touch?

I wait while Felix turns off the lights and locks the door, then we head up the stairs together. "What do you do to make it through the long bus rides?" I ask. "I don't mind a road trip, but it has to get old as much as you guys travel."

"It's not too bad. I sleep a lot. Watch movies," Felix says. "Mostly I listen to music." He slides open his apartment door, but he doesn't move out of the way, so when I cross into the apartment, I brush up against his chest, close enough that I catch his scent. It's all I can do not to lean in and draw in a deep breath of spicy Felix-scented air. I *do* want to get things right between us, and I'm pretty sure that means going slow. But going slow might make me spontaneously combust.

"Last season, for every bus trip, I picked a different composer and listened to all their works chronologically," Felix says as he follows me into the kitchen.

I grab my water bottle from where I left it on the counter and move to the fridge so I can refill it and cool off. "You did not."

"I did, too." He leans against the counter beside me, so close we're all but touching. "I have to do *something* to drown out the sound of Eli and Van bickering."

I swallow and take a steadying breath. "What composers have you covered?" This is what it's come to—me talking about composers to try to cut the tension and keep me from doing something I might regret tomorrow.

He wrinkles his brow and purses his lips to the side, giving me a fleeting glimpse of the dimple in his cheek. *Ohh that dimple.*

"Aaron Copland was first," he says. "Then Gershwin, then I started on Brahms, but I ran out of hours before I finished."

"Will you start where you left off this year?" I ask.

I lean against the fridge door, loving how close we are, how focused he is on our conversation even if the tension is killing me. In the shadowy kitchen, his light brown eyes look darker than normal, but they still draw me right in. I feel like I could stand here and talk to him all night long.

Or...stand here and *not* talk to him, but I'm determined to keep those thoughts at bay. At least for now.

"I might," he says, his lips lifting into a sly grin. "Though I'm hoping I'll have someone texting me, giving me something else to look forward to."

"Texting, huh? You think that could actually be more exciting than Brahms's complete catalog?"

He holds my gaze, his expression turning flirty in a way that makes my stomach swoop. "Only if the texts are from you."

CHAPTER FOURTEEN
Felix and Gracie

Felix: Unpopular opinion: Brahms's second piano concerto is trash.

Gracie: Shut. Up. I feel the same way, and no one ever agrees with me!

Felix: You don't like it either? That surprises me. I thought you might, just for the cello solo.

Gracie: Trust me. I know. I've argued with so many cellists about this. But despite the solo, overall, the piece is just boring.

Felix: And a little repetitive, right? It feels like it takes forever to get through it.

Gracie: Fun fact about Brahms. He wrote his second piano concerto twenty-five years after he wrote the first one. I love the first one. It's big and bold and gorgeous and interesting. Especially the third movement. But by the time he wrote the second one, I don't know. Maybe he was taking himself too seriously by then? It's like he forgot how to be brave.

Gracie: Or maybe he was just heartbroken over his unrequited love.

Gracie: By the time he wrote it, he'd probably been in love with Clara Schumann for decades.

Felix: Clara Schumann? As in the composer Schumann's wife?

Gracie: YES. She was a composer and performer of note in her own right. And she was brilliant. Also fourteen years older than Brahms. Clearly, he didn't care. I'm probably not being very nice to poor Brahms. I stand by the brilliance of his first concerto. The second one just makes me tired.

Felix: Give me more reasons to like you, Gracie. I'm not sure I have enough.

Gracie: Question. Is there anything in your fridge I can't eat?

Felix: Have at it. My food is your food.

Gracie: Your food looks like it was shopped by a professional and arranged by one of those organizers on TikTok.

Felix: Organization keeps me calm.

Gracie: I can see that. Your food matches the rest of your apartment. In a good way. Your apartment is really beautiful.

Felix: That's thanks to my sister. She loves interior design. I gave her free rein.

Gracie: I don't buy it. This apartment looks just like you.

Felix: Vivie has a good eye. And whenever I had opinions, she listened.

Gracie: I didn't know you had a sister. She's older? Younger?

Felix: Older. Vivian. She's married. Her husband is my father's CFO. She's very much the perfect daughter.

Gracie: A contrast to the rebel son?

Felix: You have no idea.

Gracie: I want all the stories!

Felix: It's mostly just the hockey. I went to Loyola to play on scholarship instead of going Ivy League. I don't work with my dad. I don't have a high-paying job.

Gracie: You're also a business owner. An entrepreneur.

Felix: But I didn't do it Dad's way. So.

Gracie: I know a little something about that.

Felix: Here's to finding our own way?

Gracie: And to building bridges wherever we can?

Felix: I'm trying, actually. We've been talking more since the Great Pipe Explosion. And it hasn't been terrible.

Gracie: I love that you refer to it with capital letters, like it ought to be commemorated in history books or something.

Felix: It should be. At least in our history book.

Gracie: Ours?

Felix: Yours? Sorry. Ours was probably presumptive.

Gracie: A little. But I didn't mind.

Gracie: Congrats on the win! And another shut-out.

Felix: Thanks. It took all my willpower to focus on the game.

Gracie: Yeah? Why is that?

Felix: There's just been this person I've been thinking about a lot lately...

Gracie: It's Brahms, right? He can be *so distracting...*

Gracie: FELIX. You have a surprising number of romance novels on your shelf.

Felix: And?

Gracie: And I'm very impressed. But it IS unusual. I'd be lying if I didn't say I expected more historical war novels.

Felix: My mom loves romance. She's gotten me hooked. But I think I also have a very impressive collection of historical war novels.

Gracie: Very. But I'm just saying. Their spines don't look nearly as worn.

Felix: Have you ever read Amy Harmon's *From Sand and Ash*?

Gracie: I haven't.

Felix: It's a historical war novel that's *also* a romance. Read it. It's one of my favorites.

Gracie: I will read and report back.

Felix: I can't wait.

———

Felix: Hey, can I ask a favor?

Gracie: Of course!

Felix: Across the street, there's a blue house on the corner. The one with white shutters?

Gracie: Yes. I see it.

Felix: That's where Mrs. Dobson lives. She goes to the grocery store every Saturday morning, and I always keep an eye out for her when she gets home. She's not very steady on her feet, and I like to help her get everything inside.

Gracie: You watch for her every Saturday morning?

Felix: Only if I'm home. It's not a big deal, and I don't think she really expects it. But if you're around, will you run over and make sure she's okay?

Gracie: Of course I will.

Gracie: Also, I finished the book—read it in one day—and I LOVED it. So far, you're two for two with your recommendations. Excellent work.

Felix: Keep stroking my ego, and you'll get book recommendations for life.

Gracie: I like this plan.

—ele—

Gracie: Mrs. Dobson says hello! Her groceries are inside and she's the sweetest ever. She made me lemonade, and we talked all about her grandchildren and how much she loves it when they come to visit.

Felix: Thanks for doing that for me.

Gracie: And congrats on another win! You guys are killing it.

Felix: You're watching the games?

Gracie: No? But I AM checking the scores, which, considering I used to have hockey entirely blocked on all my internet browsers, I'd say that's making progress.

Felix: I appreciate the effort.

Gracie: I really am happy you guys are doing so well.

Felix: The last win was sloppy. It wouldn't have happened without Logan. And I let too many goals through.

Gracie: You can't lose a game on your own, Felix.

Felix: I can. It's happened before.

Felix: Distract me. What are you doing right now?

Gracie: Practicing, actually.

Felix: Right this second?

Gracie: Right this second.

Felix: Can I listen?

Gracie: Seriously?

Felix: Seriously.

Gracie: Give me a second, and I'll call you.

Felix: I got the recordings! Thank you for sending them. It's not quite as magical as it was to listen to you playing on the phone last night, but it's a very close second.

Felix: Now I've got a problem, though.

Gracie: What kind of problem?

Felix: You've spoiled me, and now the only classical music I want to listen to is you.

Gracie: Stop it.

Felix: I'm serious. Somehow, knowing you're on the other end of the music I'm listening to makes me like it more.

Gracie: Now you're spoiling ME.

Gracie: I'm sorry about the loss. How are you feeling?

Felix: Mostly just ready to be home.

Gracie: How's Brahms? Have you made it through yet?

Felix: Not yet. But we've still got...nine more hours on the road? There's still time.

Gracie: Want to play a game?

Felix: Sure.

Gracie: So trusting...

Felix: Should I not be? What kind of game are we talking?

Gracie: I'm teasing. It's nothing scary. I ask you a question, and you can either answer or pass. But if you answer, then I have to answer the same question too. And you can only pass three times, then you have to answer everything.

Felix: Ahh. So we shouldn't ask anything we aren't willing to answer ourselves.

Gracie: Right. And use your passes wisely.

Felix: Okay. Let's do it.

Gracie: YAY. First question: are you a cat person or a dog person?

Felix: Hmm. I've never actually been either. We never had pets growing up. But if I had to pick, I'd say probably a dog person? You?

Gracie: Definitely a dog person. I don't trust that a cat won't turn on me and eat me in my sleep.

Felix: Even with my limited cat experience, this...feels like it tracks. Okay, next question. How old were you when you had your first kiss?

Gracie: Wow. You're really going for it with that one.

Felix: I've never been the kind of man who messes around.

Gracie: Noted. I was seventeen. It was horrible and I wish I could take it back.

Gracie: Actually, that's not true. The kiss itself was fine. I still liked the guy at the time, and I felt all the fun, tingly things you feel with a first kiss. But the memory is tainted by how badly he behaved later.

Felix: Now I'm curious. And angry on your behalf.

Gracie: He was just a stupid kid. A hockey player on my brother's team who stood me up on prom night to sleep with a college girl who had come to see him play and waited outside the locker room like some kind of weird, junior league puck bunny. I mean, he was eighteen. But she was in college and it just...felt awful. I got all dressed up and waited for him to pick me up, but he never showed. I saw pictures of him on Instagram the next morning, lounging shirtless in her dorm room.

Felix: That's...really not cool. No wonder you don't want to date hockey players.

Gracie: He definitely didn't help.

Felix: I'm sorry he did that to you. Did you end up going to prom at all?

Gracie: Not my junior year. But I went my senior year with a group of orchestra friends, and we had a great time.

Gracie: Okay, your turn! Thinking about Gavin is making me feel gross.

Felix: How about thinking about a fourteen-year-old Felix kissing a girl and making her cry?

Gracie: You did not.

Felix: I did. Caroline Williams. She cut her lip on my braces. She dripped blood onto her sweater, then freaked out because it was her favorite sweater and started ranting about how she hadn't wanted to kiss me anyway. I was so mortified, I ran away and threw up in the bushes outside the school.

Gracie: That's a really terrible first kiss story.

Felix: Here. Photo evidence. You might as well get the whole picture.

Felix: *<jpg.1842>*

Gracie: FELIX YOU WERE SO CUTE. Look at all your fluffy hair!

Felix: Trust me, no one thought I was cute then. I was so awkward. The only reason it even happened was because a bunch of guys on my hockey team put her up to it. I was the only one on the team who hadn't been kissed.

Gracie: Man. Growing up is really hard work.

Felix: Sometimes I wonder how I made it.

Gracie: Next question?

Felix: Sure.

Gracie: Last girlfriend?

Felix: Her name was Sarah. We were together for six months while I was playing for the Wolves up in Chicago.

Gracie: You played for the Wolves?

Felix: Started there right out of college. Then I had the chance to go up to the NHL and play for the Hurricanes, but I came to the Appies instead.

Gracie: You *didn't* go play in the NHL? Isn't that the whole point of the minor leagues? To send people up to the majors?

Felix: Usually. But. That kind of life. It wasn't for me.

Gracie: Too stressful?

Felix: Too public.

Gracie: Gotcha.

Gracie: What ended your relationship with Sarah?

Felix: That, actually.

Gracie: Not signing with the Hurricanes?

Felix: She wanted the life, I guess.

Gracie: Boo. Sarah's loss for not recognizing your value.

Gracie: Also, how could anyone not want the life you offer?

Gracie: Though, as the woman who is currently snuggled up on your very comfortable couch in your very beautiful apartment with a bag of apple cider donuts and a very delicious latte...I could be biased.

Felix: Okay. Your turn again. Last boyfriend?

Gracie: Anton. A very broody violinist in college, then off and on for a few years *after* college. He was very dramatic. And loved himself more than he ever loved me.

Felix: We've covered some serious ground.

Gracie: And we didn't even use any of our passes!

Felix: I'll tell you anything you want to know, Gracie.

Gracie: Really?

Felix: I kind of want you to know everything.

...

...

...

Felix: Did I scare you away? It's been a minute.

Gracie: I'm here! You didn't scare me. My brother called to give me a dad update.

Felix: He's okay?

Gracie: Still being stubborn about exercise, but it sounds like he's eating a little better.

Gracie: Also.

Gracie: I want you to know everything too.

CHAPTER FIFTEEN
Felix

IT'S AFTER MIDNIGHT WHEN the Appies bus finally pulls into the Summit parking lot. By the time I make it home and let myself into my apartment, I assume Gracie has already gone to bed. It's Sunday night, which means she has to teach early in the morning, but the lamp is on in the living room, illuminating the outline of her sleeping form stretched out on the couch.

I walk quietly across the living room and crouch down in front of her. She looks beautiful sleeping like this, but it feels creepy to just sit here and stare at her. I pull the blanket a little higher on her shoulders, and she shifts slightly, a lock of her hair falling over her cheek.

Slowly, I brush it off her face, my fingers grazing lightly over her skin.

Her eyes blink open, and her lips lift into a sleepy smile. "You're home," she says softly.

"I thought you'd be in bed," I say.

She yawns. "I thought I would be too. I didn't mean to fall asleep here." She pauses. "But now I'm glad I did. What time is it?"

"Almost one."

She groans. "Oh man. I'm going to hate life in the morning."

"Come on," I say, standing up and holding out my hand. "Let's get you to bed."

She slips her hand into mine and squeezes it gently, and I immediately wince.

"What is it? What did I do?" she says.

"Nothing," I say. "It's not you." I switch hands and tug her to her feet. "It's my fault. I forgot this hand is bruised."

She lifts my palm, cradling it while she inspects the puck-sized bruise covering the side of my thumb and wrist. Her fingers graze over it gently, and she bites her lip. "That looks like it hurt."

"Little bit," I say.

"Did you make the save, at least?"

"I did. Though we lost the game anyway."

Her fingers are still on my skin, her touch feather soft. Honestly, I'll take a slapshot to the palm any day if it means her touching me like this.

"I'm sorry I made it worse," she says.

I shake my head and gently say, "You couldn't make anything worse, Gracie."

She smiles as she yawns again, letting out a little laugh as she tries and fails to stifle it.

"Okay, you *really* need to go to bed." I drop my hands onto her shoulders and steer her toward her bedroom.

Funny how after just a few days, it already feels like *her room*. Not the guest room. When Logan stayed here for a while last month, it definitely never felt like his room. But Gracie just seems to fit here, like she belongs in my space.

As soon as we're there, she spins around and leans into the doorframe, her gaze locked on mine.

It feels so good to see her, to be with her after such a long weekend.

The final leg of our bus trip home was long, made even longer by the subdued mood of everyone on board. Our last loss was brutal, and we all took it pretty hard. But now, with Gracie in front of me, all that frustration melts away.

"Hey," I say, "before you go to sleep, can I ask you a question?"

She nods. "Of course."

I lean a little closer. "Can I take you to dinner, Gracie?"

She licks her lips, her eyes sparkling in the faint light emanating from the lamp in her bedroom. "Like, on a date?"

I nod. "There's a place downtown Logan recommended. It's called Harvested, I think? Word is it's hard to get a table, but if I can swing it...will you go with me?"

She reaches up and tugs at the strings of the Appies hoodie I'm wearing. "I have a feeling the Appies star goalie could get a table anywhere he wanted."

"The only thing that matters to me is that you're at the table with me."

She smiles. "I would love to have dinner with you."

"Maybe we can talk tomorrow and figure out when?" I reach forward and hook a finger around her pinky.

Only her pinky. One tiny finger, and my heart is galloping out of my chest like a freaking horse at Churchill Downs.

She nods, her lips parting as she leans into me the slightest bit.

I hold her gaze for another long minute, then take a step backward. I hate to leave her, but I'm determined to do this right. We wouldn't be having this moment if she weren't staying here, and I don't want that proximity to push us into things too fast. Especially when I know Gracie had reservations about me in the first place.

"Goodnight, Gracie," I say, then I turn my back and head across the apartment.

I only make it a few paces before she calls out to stop me. "Felix, wait."

I turn around to face her, and she darts forward. When she reaches me, she lifts one hand to my chest and the other to my shoulder. Then she pushes up on her toes and presses a long, lingering kiss to my cheek. "I'm glad you're home safe," she whispers, her breath fanning over my cheek.

Then she turns and disappears into her bedroom.

I lift a hand to my cheek, still warm from her kiss. I smile as I grab my bag and make my way to my room.

I've got a date with Gracie Mitchell.

And it can't get here fast enough.

Monday morning, Gracie and I compare schedules to see when we can go out to dinner. She's got a rehearsal with her quartet Monday night, then I've got the goalie clinic on Tuesday, then a game on Wednesday. Thursday, she has an open house at the middle school, so Friday is the first evening we're both free.

Of course, we still see each other throughout the week. But it's really only when we're coming or going. One morning I sneak out early and surprise her with a latte from Cataloochee Mountain Coffee, and the night of the game, she makes a chicken stir fry big enough to feed half my team, then texts me to let me know, saying I can bring home anyone who's hungry.

When I show up with half a dozen hungry hockey players, she meets me at the door wearing baggy jeans and the Chicago Art Institute hoodie I gave her the night the pipes burst in her apartment. Her hair is long and loose over her shoulders, and she's swapped her contacts for her glasses. She looks like a dream—and the fantasy only intensifies as I watch her interaction with my teammates, talking to them like they're her friends too.

Every time Gracie and I make eye contact, Eli elbows me or makes fake kissing noises or cracks a joke under his breath, but I don't even care. The ribbing is worth her being here, though I'm still having a hard time shaking the feeling that she's too good to be true. That whatever this is will slip right through my fingers.

The nagging worry is particularly potent while I'm getting ready for our date on Friday night, a remnant of the anxiety I fought so hard to conquer rearing up and ruining my good mood. But it doesn't have to be that way. I take a few steadying breaths.

I'm steady. I'm focused. No one controls me but me.

I grab a dress shirt off a hanger in my closet and shrug it on, but before I can button it, a knock sounds behind me on my open bedroom door.

I spin around to see Gracie standing in the doorway, one hand pressed against the door jamb. She's wearing a dark red dress that's wrapping around her curves in all the right ways.

My eyes rove over her body, drinking her in, but when I finally force my eyes to her face, she's doing the same thing to me, so I don't feel quite so bad.

"Hi," I say, and she startles the slightest bit, like she just remembered why she's even here.

"Hi. Is this too fancy?" She looks down at her dress. "I've been freaking out for the past ten minutes because I want to wear something perfect because I want our date to be perfect, and I couldn't decide between this one and a black dress that I really love, but honestly, I wear black all the freaking time, so do I really want to wear black when I'm not on stage? But the lace on this one feels fancier than the black and I don't want to be too fancy." She finally takes a breath. "So I'm asking you."

It takes me a minute to respond. Because she's adorable. And her dress is stunning. And the way she barreled in here demanding an opinion feels so domestic, so comfortable, I can't focus on answering because I'm too busy imagining a life where talking to Gracie like this is the norm. Just a regular day.

Gracie's eyes drop to the floor and a hand presses to her stomach. "It *is* too fancy. I knew it was." She turns to leave.

"Gracie, stop." It takes three long strides to reach her, then I catch her wrist, tugging her toward me before she can escape. Her hands press against my chest—my *bare* chest—and for a moment, I let myself hold her, my hands falling to the curve of her waist.

I close my eyes as the warmth from her palms seeps through my skin and settles in my heart. "It's not too fancy," I say softly. "You look beautiful."

"Are you sure?" She lifts her brown eyes to mine.

I slowly drop my hands and step backward, pushing them safely into my pockets. "I mean, I'm biased," I say, "so you could come in here in sweats and I'd still think you look beautiful. But yes. I'm sure."

She slides her hands down the front of her dress. "Okay. Thank you. I'll be ready in ten minutes."

She spins around and darts out the door, but then she pauses and sticks her head back in. "Hey Felix?" She grins and looks me up and down. "You aren't looking so bad yourself."

Everything about our date is perfect. Dinner at Harvested is delicious, our conversation is easy and natural, and we're touching every chance we get. Just little things. A brush of her arm against mine, my hand on the small of her back, her foot nudging mine under the table. But even these small gestures are ratcheting up the tension between us. If I don't kiss this woman soon, I might lose my mind.

We talk about everything. Our families, our likes and dislikes, even what we hope our own futures look like. (Just for the record, our plans for the future totally align.)

The only thing we don't talk about is hockey. I'm not sure it's intentional, but the conversation doesn't lead us there, and I'm hesitant to bring it up. I'd like to think it's not an issue for Gracie anymore. My profession hasn't changed in the last few weeks, and she's giving me plenty of signs that she's interested in pursuing whatever is happening between us.

But in the back of my mind, I can't help but wonder. If we *do* wind up in a relationship, will she come to my games? Support me in that way?

It's this thought that finally makes me recognize the connection between hockey and my earlier anxiety. Back when Eli crashed our dinner, Gracie hinted that she was changing her mind about hockey players, but does that mean she's changed her mind about the sport in general?

By the time we finish our dessert, I manage to push the disquieting thought to the back of my mind. I don't want to get ahead of myself, and Gracie hasn't given me any reason to worry.

Outside, the temperature has dropped several degrees, the wind picking up the fall leaves and tossing them around us in tiny cyclones.

Gracie leans into my side, slipping her arm through mine. "Ugh, does this feel like winter to you? I'm not ready for winter."

I tug her a little closer. "As long as it isn't a Chicago winter, I'm okay."

"Hey, Felix!" Logan calls, his voice cutting through the cool night air.

I look up to see him and Parker approaching us on the street, hand in hand.

We walk toward them, pausing in front of Cataloochee Coffee's front window. The shop is closed already, but the window casings are wrapped in twinkle lights, highlighting the fall leaves and pumpkins decorating the entire storefront. All of Maple Street is decorated for fall with an enthusiasm that surprised me when I first moved to Harvest Hollow. But now, it just feels like home. White lights crisscross back and forth all the way down Maple Street, and hay bales and pumpkins adorn every street corner.

"Hey, man," Logan says as he reaches out to shake my hand. He pulls me in for a quick hug, slapping me on the back. "Looking good."

"Hey," I say. "You remember Gracie."

They quickly say hello, then Logan introduces Parker.

"We've never officially met," Parker says to Gracie, "but our brothers played hockey together years ago. Do you remember a Brandon Douglas?"

"That definitely sounds familiar," Gracie says. "It's nice to meet you."

The two of them start up a conversation about high school and all the people they know in common while Logan pulls me to the side, eyebrows raised.

"So this is happening?" he says, his voice low. "How's it going?"

I run a hand through my hair. "It's happening. And it's good. Great, even."

Logan's gaze narrows. "But?"

I shrug, my eyes cutting toward Gracie and Parker. "No buts. It's good. Everything's good. Just hoping the hockey thing isn't actually a big deal."

"The hockey thing?" Logan deadpans. "You mean that thing you do as your profession?"

"Shut up."

"Don't make it complicated. Just invite her to a game and see how she responds. Invite her to tomorrow's game, even. She might have fun."

"Tomorrow's game has been sold out for days," I say.

Logan grins. "Yeah, Parker's last viral video went bigger than the norm. Who knew Alec in a bikini would get such a response? But dude, that's not a problem. Parker could get her in."

We turn our attention to Parker and Gracie, who, it sounds like, are already talking about tomorrow's game. "You could sit with me," Parker is saying. "I absolutely have an extra ticket."

"That's really sweet of you," Gracie says. "But I've got a gig tomorrow afternoon. I don't think I'll be finished until after the game starts."

I rack my brain, trying to remember if she's mentioned a gig this weekend. She has an audition with the Knoxville Symphony in a few weeks, something I remember specifically because she was so excited when the email came in, confirming her audition time, and there's another symphony concert here in Harvest Hollow next weekend. But I don't remember anything about a gig.

I quickly check my thoughts. I'm not Gracie's keeper—or even her boyfriend. It's totally reasonable to think she has something on her schedule that she hasn't discussed with me. I'm just acting weird because I really would love for her to come to a game.

"Next time, then," Parker says. "Have Felix give you my number. Text me anytime."

Gracie and Parker hug—it always amazes me how quickly women can connect—we say our goodbyes, then we're alone again.

"She seems great," Gracie says as we approach my car.

"Yeah. And she and Logan are great together." I open the door for her and offer a hand while she lowers herself into the passenger seat.

I crank up the heat once I'm in the car, and Gracie reaches up to turn on her seat warmer. I love that she doesn't ask—she just does it. Like she's comfortable—familiar enough that she knows she doesn't need to. She settles back in and wiggles her butt around a little. "Hmmm, I love your fancy car, Felix."

My heart stretches and pulls. I love having her in my fancy car.

As I ease the car onto the main road, Gracie sits up a little taller, shifting her body so she's facing me. "Okay, so I have a surprise for you. And I've been wanting to tell you all week, but I thought it would be fun to save it for tonight."

"A surprise?"

She nods. "Yes. And if you have something else planned, that's totally fine, too. But if you don't...I was hoping we might head back to the apartment so I can play something for you."

My eyebrows lift. "On your cello?"

"Nope. On the tuba," she deadpans.

I grin. "I walked right into that one, didn't I?"

"I've been working on it at school because I didn't want you to hear it. But it's finally ready, which means *I'm* finally ready to share."

"I didn't make plans beyond dinner, so heading back to the apartment sounds perfect."

Honestly, I can't think of anything I'd enjoy more.

But if she thinks she's going to play for me, looking as beautiful as she looks right now, without me kissing her senseless, she's got another thing coming.

Chapter Sixteen
Felix

As soon as we're in the apartment, Gracie's warm hand wraps around mine, and I let her lead me into the living room. She sits me down on the couch, her hands falling onto my shoulders like she's guiding me down.

"Okay," she says. "I have to go change first because I can't play my cello wearing this dress. So you just wait here, and I'll be right back."

I watch her walk away, my eyes lingering on the sway of her hips and the curve of her slender waist. The woman has mad curves, and I am here for it.

She's back in less than five minutes in a loose black tank top and a pair of jeans that are just as flattering as the dress she wore to dinner. I wipe a hand across my face and focus on Gracie's intentional movements as she pulls her cello from the case and gets ready to play.

I'm not sure she's ever looked so beautiful.

"Okay, so I'm just going to qualify this by saying I had to transpose this piece into bass clef, so there are a few places it might sound slightly different than what you're used to. Still. I'm pretty happy with how it turned out."

She tilts her head to either side, stretching her neck, then lifts her bow to the strings. "Ready?"

I swallow against the knot in my throat. I thought I loved watching Gracie all dressed up, playing on stage with the rest of the Harvest Hollow Symphony. But here, in my living room, playing for me—*only* me—I just hope she doesn't need me to talk. Because my words are gone. Disappeared.

Or maybe there just *aren't* any words.

Not for this. Not for how she's making me feel right now.

I nod. "Whenever you are."

The first notes ring out into the quiet living room and immediately fill my soul—then I realize what she's playing. It's a few octaves lower to fit the cello's register, but I recognize the melody. It's the only piece I know completely by heart. Every note. Every dip and swell of the music is as familiar to me as my own name.

She's playing Bach's first violin sonata—my grandmother's favorite piece.

My favorite piece.

I'm not prepared for the onslaught of emotions this brings. It feels big that Gracie would do this for me. It's incredibly thoughtful and touching, but it's also incredible to hear my favorite piece played on my favorite instrument. I've always loved the deeper, rich tones of the cello, so this is something I never would have thought to ask for, but now, I'm not sure I'll ever want to hear it the original way again.

Even more than that, I can't stop thinking about how much my grandmother would love this. How much she would love *Gracie.* She's only been gone a few years, long enough that missing her tends to come in waves. I'll go days, even weeks without thinking of her. But then I'll hear a certain piece of music and she'll pop right into my mind.

I don't have particularly strong feelings about what life after death might be like. But I do know that in those moments, I feel like she's close by, like I'm thinking of her because she swung by to say hello.

Right now is definitely one of those moments. Maybe it's silly, but I'd like to think she's here, listening right along with me.

Gracie finishes the piece, the final notes echoing into the silence, and then takes a deep breath. "That's only the first movement, but..." Her words trail off, and I can hear a question in her tone.

I'm still sitting on the couch, my elbows resting on my knees, my head down. I want to look up, tell her how beautiful it was, but if I do, she's going to see the tears in my eyes, and that just feels...are we ready for that? We've only been on one date. Do I really want to cry in front of this woman?

"Hey," Gracie says, and suddenly she's in front of me on the floor, her hands sliding over my knees as she tilts her head, trying to meet my eye. "Felix, I'm sorry. I didn't think about the possibility of the song being emotional for you, but of course it would be. I should have asked before I just played it like that—"

I shake my head, cutting off her apology. "That's not it. I'm glad you played it," I say shakily. "It was perfect." I sniff and clear my throat with a gruff *arrgh,* turning my face away from Gracie. I don't want her to see me like this—to feel responsible for making me feel this way when what she did was so thoughtful, so incredibly amazing.

I clear my throat again, a little more forcefully this time, and try to rein in my emotions. "Would you—do you think you could record it for me?" I ask.

Before she responds, she reaches up and takes my face in her hands, her fingers brushing over my beard, her thumbs sliding across the moisture under my eyes. "Of course I'll record it for you," she says. "But Felix, please don't hide how you're feeling right now. Not from me. You feeling this way about someone who meant a lot to you doesn't make you look weak." She licks her lips, then lifts them into a coy smile. "It does make you sexy as hell."

This makes me chuckle, and I close my eyes, relaxing into her touch. "Men really don't know how badly we get it wrong sometimes, do we?"

"I won't speak for all women, but as a romantic at heart who is driven by passion and love stories, I'm totally into this," she says. She pushes off the floor and settles onto the couch, sitting sideways so she's facing me, and immediately pulls me into a hug.

I didn't really know I needed a hug, but as her smaller body melts against mine, her arms threading around me, tension eases out of my shoulders. My nose presses against the exposed skin of her neck and shoulder, and I breathe her in. She smells incredible—a little citrusy, but more like the Carolina jessamine that grew on the trellises outside my grandmother's Hilton Head beach house. Her body is warm, yielding, arching into me as I pull her closer.

There is a moment—a *specific* moment—when the hug shifts from an offering of comfort to something else entirely. I feel it in the way Gracie's movements slow, her hands sliding over my shoulders to the base of my neck. I feel it in the air, the tension crackling between us. And I see it in her eyes when she pulls back and looks at me, her eyelids heavy, her lips parted.

"Gracie?" I say on an exhale—because I need to make sure we're on the same page.

Is this okay? Is *she* okay? Is this what she wants?

Desire flashes in her eyes, and then she leans forward, pressing her mouth against mine. There isn't an ounce of hesitation in her movements. Her lips are warm and soft, and she tastes like the wine we drank with dinner, and I cannot get enough of her.

Her fingers tangle in my hair, and she tilts her head to deepen the kiss, but sitting like this, it's hard to get close enough, to—

Gracie's movements silence my thoughts as she shifts and settles herself on my lap, straddling me, making it possible to lean even further into the kiss. The warmth and weight of her sends heat racing through my body as my hands slide up her thighs, over the swell of her hips to her waist, then up to her back. I relax into the couch cushions, tugging her with me, nipping at her bottom lip while I capture her face with my hands.

"Gracie," I say again. This time, her name feels like a plea for whatever this is, whatever is happening between us, to last forever. Her lips move from my mouth down to the side of my neck, tracing a line of tender kisses up to my ear while her hands slide over my beard. Her thumb brushes across my bottom lip, then we're kissing again and again and *again,* her tongue brushing against mine as we taste each other, move together, our bodies in sync in a way that I've never experienced before.

When she finally leans back, her chest rising and falling as she catches her breath, there's a question in her eyes. "That was…Did that feel…?" She exhales slowly. "I'm not crazy, right? You feel it, too?"

Her hands are resting on her thighs, and I pick them up, threading our fingers together. "Like that was a lot more than just a first kiss?" I ask.

She nods. "I've never had a first kiss feel like that before."

"I've never had *any* kiss feel like that before."

She chuckles and leans forward, dropping my hands so she can wrap her arms around me. Her head rests on my shoulder as her body relaxes against mine. "No, me neither," she says, her breath brushing against my neck.

I lift my hands and rub slow circles over her back. "Does that scare you at all?"

She tenses the slightest bit, then she sits up and looks at me, her bottom lip caught between her teeth.

I brace myself for her response, but there's an easy confidence in her expression. "It terrifies me. But I think it's supposed to, Felix." She leans down and presses a lingering kiss to my lips. "That's how we know it's good. When we're already scared of losing it."

I *am* already scared of losing whatever this is. It feels too big for a first kiss. The fact that Gracie senses it too makes me slightly less scared—at least I'm not reading more into things than she is—but it also makes me *more* scared. Because the stakes are suddenly higher, and I don't want to do anything to screw this up.

Gracie tilts her head and lifts a finger to my forehead, tracing it between my brows. "You look like you're thinking really hard right now."

I lift my lips in a small smile. "Just...hoping I don't screw this up."

She gives her head a little shake. "You won't."

I tug her toward me and kiss her one more time.

I can only hope she's right.

CHAPTER SEVENTEEN
Gracie

I AM ABSOLUTELY READY to admit that my reasons for not dating hockey players have completely dissolved, at least when it comes to Felix Jamison.

Hockey? I love hockey. Best sport ever.

But there is one thing I don't love.

And that's the number of times we're having to say goodbye.

It's been just shy of two weeks since our first date, and Felix has been gone as many days as he's been home. Once we get through this weekend, he'll have several home games in a row, so we'll have two solid weeks of uninterrupted time together, and we're both counting down the days.

Not that the last two weeks have been anything but amazing. You can get to know a person really well through texts, something we do almost nonstop whenever he's on the road. At least as nonstop as it can be when I have students to teach and faculty meetings to attend.

We've also managed to squeeze in a few more dates, including a fundraising event for the symphony, during which Felix made my stand partner Joyce's hockey-loving husband cry real actual tears when he called Logan Barnes on his phone and had him say hello.

It's been so good. But that just makes the goodbyes so much harder.

Felix leaves first thing tomorrow morning for back-to-back away games in Ohio, then Texas, which means we have to make the most of tonight.

Well, what's left of it. I'm on my way home from symphony rehearsal and it's already after nine. The plan is to see a late movie, but I'm not sure I have enough steam left. Rehearsal took it out of me tonight. I'd just as soon stay in, lounge around the apartment, and read or watch something at home.

Especially since tonight is my last night in Felix's guestroom. The repairs in my place are officially finished, which means there's no reason for me to keep living with him, no matter how much I'm enjoying myself.

And I really *do* need to move out. While it has been incredibly sexy making out in every square inch of Felix's apartment, our relationship is only a couple of weeks old. But sharing the same space—it's making me feel like it's been much longer. It's making me forget I'm the kind of woman who likes to take things slow.

Especially when it comes to sex.

Summer would argue my pace isn't just slow, it's ancient-sloth-with-a-bad-hip slow. But I'd say I'm more like a very healthy turtle, one with enough self-awareness to recognize that physical commitment only magnifies my level of emotional commitment. I've been burned before—when I *didn't* move slow and my heart got too invested, too fast—and

I've learned to better protect myself. I *do* take things slow. But the right man isn't going to have a problem with that.

Besides, we're only just getting to know each other. Just because I can imagine what it might feel like to fall asleep with my head pressed against Felix's chest, my leg hooked over his, his fingers trailing up and down my back, doesn't mean I'm ready to actually experience it.

But one more night trying to sleep, knowing he's just on the other side of the apartment with his soft lips and his strong hands and his very warm body...it might break me.

Moving out is my only remaining defense.

I finally pull my car into my parking space at the apartment and gather up my things. When I grab my phone, I notice a text message from Summer, so I pause long enough to read it and respond.

Summer: How are things? Are you madly in love yet? Please tell me you're madly in love.

Gracie: I'm madly in like? But I can definitely see love as a possibility in our future.

Summer: OH MY GOSH. THIS MAKES ME SO HAPPY.

Summer: Have you gone to see him play yet?

Gracie: Not yet, but only because he hasn't had any home games, and I'm not sure we've reached "fly across the country to watch his games" status just yet.

Summer: But you're willing to go? To watch him play?

Gracie: Summer. If we're together, I'm watching him play. No childish hangup is going to keep me from supporting him.

Summer: It makes me really happy to hear you say so. I think he's good for you, Gracie.

Gracie: Me too. But cross your fingers for me anyway because I think I'm going to take him to Maddox's birthday party next week. As long as he wants to go.

Summer: Meeting the family feels big.

Gracie: Especially meeting my family. They're going to worship-level love him. But Maddox will lose his mind, and that feels worth any awkwardness with my parents.

Summer: It will be! It totally will be. How's your dad?

Gracie: He seems okay. Mom's still worried about him. But I also feel like this whole thing has mellowed him somehow. We're all getting along a little better now.

Summer: I'm glad! I'm sitting down to watch a movie with Lucy, but tell Felix I said hi! And keep me posted on all the things!

Summer: Oh! I meant to ask—how's your old lady sloth? Has she gotten her hip replaced yet?

Gracie: SUMMER.

Summer: It's a valid question! Just making sure she isn't dead.

Gracie: I'm a turtle, not a sloth. Nothing is dead, and we are not having this conversation.

Summer sends back a series of emojis that have me rolling my eyes and laughing as I haul my cello up the stairs. She's completely ridiculous, but I'm grateful for her anyway. Everyone deserves a friend like Summer in their lives.

Felix meets me at the door, taking my cello from me and carrying it into the living room.

I drop my purse to the floor and shrug out of my coat, then he's back in front of me, pulling me into an embrace.

"Hi," he says, a smile stretching across his face. "How was rehearsal?"

I let out a tired groan. "Exhausting. We're playing *Don Juan*, and the cello part is so hard and super exposed."

"I hate that I'm going to miss this concert," he says. "But at least it's not *Death and Transfiguration*. That's the best thing Richard Strauss ever wrote."

"Just put on the album then. I'm going to spend all day tomorrow practicing, and I'm still worried I might have to fake my way through a few tough sections."

He chuckles, his hands sliding over my shoulders and down my arms. "I'm sure you'll get it."

He bends down for a kiss, and I push up on my tiptoes to meet him.

I am a big fan of passionate, fiery kisses that make my blood heat and turn my limbs to liquid jello. But this kind of slow, tender kiss—I like these too. Because there are words in kisses like this one—words that go beyond basic desire.

This kiss doesn't just say *I want you*. It says *I like you*.

And right now, that kind of kiss matters too.

When I finally ease away, my lips still tingling with sensation, I lean forward and press my head against Felix's chest. He wraps his arms around me, practically engulfing me in his embrace. It's not like I can forget how incredibly enormous he is, but I'm definitely more aware of it in moments like this one. Not that I mind. I could stay here forever. Breathing him in, savoring the sweet and spicy scent of his very expensive cologne.

There must be some sort of magic pheromone thing happening though because Felix doesn't just smell like cologne. He smells like soft leather sofas and pine trees dotted with snow and warm fires and old books and coffee with cream and safety and happiness and contentment all at the same time.

Because my brain and body are equally tired, we forgo the late movie we were planning to see and wind up on opposite ends of the couch, Copeland's *Appalachian Spring* playing softly in the background, each of us with our own book in our laps. Felix is flipping pages at a pretty normal pace, but I'm mostly just pretending to read.

Maybe because I'm so tired. Or maybe because he's so incredibly distracting.

I really don't want him to leave tomorrow.

He must sense me staring because he puts down his book and levels me with a questioning look. "What are you thinking over there? Whatever it is, it's very loud."

I nudge my toe into his ribs. "You're prickly when you're reading."

He catches my foot and pulls it into his lap, abandoning his book in favor of giving me a foot rub. "Only when I'm interrupted."

I moan and close my eyes. "Oh my gosh. Please don't stop. If this is my punishment for interrupting you, you're never going to read in peace again."

"That's quite the sacrifice," he says as he reaches for my other foot. "What do I get for all the interruptions and foot rubs?"

I sit up a little straighter so I can look into his eyes. "Ummm, how about I take you home to meet my family?"

He looks up, surprise overtaking his expression. "Are you serious?"

I shrug. "I know that's kind of a big deal, so I don't want you to freak out. And you can absolutely say no. Actually, you maybe *should* say no, because it's very possible that if you say yes, you will be exposing yourself to a variety of discomforts and awkward moments."

He chuckles. "Are you trying to tell me you want me to say no?"

"No, no," I quickly say. "I really want you to say yes. I just want you to be informed. I don't want to gaslight you into thinking it will all be sunshine and rainbows."

"You already told me your family are Appies fans," he says. "Is that all we're talking about here?"

Ha. He thinks they're like normal fans.

"Felix, my dad is going to grill you on all your stats. Dissect every save, every goal you let through in any game you've played this season. Mom will probably cry when she meets you. Then she will want to feed you. And hug you. And she will probably ask you to sign every single piece of memorabilia she owns, which is a lot."

"That's better than people asking me to sign their boobs," Felix says dryly. "I get asked that all the time."

I am momentarily horrified by his confession. I don't like to think about how many women have hockey player fantasies, so reminders like this one always feel like a punch to the gut. But this is not the time to get hung up on that, so I squash down my jealousy-fueled rage and force my mind back to our conversation.

JENNY PROCTOR

"The most important thing is that you're Maddox's favorite player," I say. "That's the real reason I want you to come. Josh told me to get him an Appies hoodie for his birthday, and I will. But if I also bring you? I think he'll be really excited."

Felix shifts so he can lean over and press a kiss to my lips. "I would love to meet your family, even if your parents are the most obnoxious fans out there. They're your family. That means they're important to me."

Oh, be still my fluttering heart.

I nod. "The party is next Sunday."

"So I'll be home," he says, grinning wide enough to make his dimple pop. "I'll make sure my schedule stays clear."

We pretend to read for another hour, something that looks a lot more like laughing at TikTok videos and goofing around than actual reading. We don't do much kissing, and though we haven't talked about it, my guess is we both sense that every time we start, it's getting harder and harder to stop.

We haven't had a conversation about sex, though, so now it's like we're being more careful with each other. Not tiptoeing around the subject necessarily, just giving ourselves the room to figure out our pacing without pressure.

Still, I can't ignore how keenly my body is tuned into his. Every move, every touch. Even just his looks are making my skin crackle with heat. By the time he walks me to my bedroom door to say goodnight, a habit we've developed over the last few nights, the air between us is thick with tension.

He leans down and kisses me long and slow. "Will you text me while I'm gone?" he asks as his lips trail kisses along my neck.

I let out a little laugh. "Do you even need to ask?"

"I'm going to miss you," he says, shifting to the other side of my neck, his hand lifting my hair and moving it out of the way.

I lean back, giving him better access, and close my eyes. "I'll miss you too."

His lips move up to my earlobe, then start a slow journey across my jawline, finally landing on my lips. "Every second I'm not on the ice," he murmurs, "I'll be thinking of you."

Goosebumps break out across my skin, and a shiver of desire moves through my body. My hands slip under the hem of his T-shirt, pressing against the skin at the small of his back. He's so incredibly warm, so solid under my palms.

Then his lips are on my neck again, and *oh,* this man.

Everything about this feels so right, so easy, so...essential, I'm not sure how I survived before this moment right now. How did I breathe without him next to me? How did I sleep when I didn't have this to look forward to?

I let out a little whimper, and Felix shifts, his grip on me tightening as his mouth more fully captures mine. My hands grasp his shirt as I tug him closer, *closer,* deepening the kiss. When his tongue brushes against mine, the heat in my belly turns molten, and finally, my brain catches up with the rest of me.

My hands slide from his body, and I press them against the door at my back, letting the cool wood anchor me. "We have to stop," I say, my voice airy and soft. "Because if we don't, I'll want you to come in." I slowly lift my eyes to meet his. "And I'm not ready for you to come in yet."

He nods as he runs a hand through his hair, his demeanor immediately shifting, but not in a bad way. I've had men react poorly when I've set boundaries, but Felix doesn't seem bothered at all.

He's still close, still touching me, and his eyes are still full of warmth. The only difference is that now there's a measure of careful control in his movements.

I have never felt anything but safe in Felix's presence. But seeing him now, recognizing the respect in his eyes, I realize how deeply I trust him. And how much that matters to me.

Felix lifts a hand and slides it over my cheek, tucking a loose strand of hair behind my ear. "Thank you for being honest with me."

I nod and take a deep breath, an attempt to slow my still-racing heart. "Thank you for listening."

His brow furrows, and his expression darkens for the briefest moment. "Gracie, any man who doesn't listen isn't worth a look, much less a single minute of your time."

I lift my hands to his face, cradling either side while I press one final kiss to his lips. "You're a good man, Felix Jamison. The best, even."

You're a good man. And I'm already halfway to falling in love.

CHAPTER EIGHTEEN
Gracie

FELIX IS WAITING FOR me in the hallway when I step out of my apartment on the Sunday of Maddox's birthday party. He's leaning against the wall, his ankles crossed in front of him, and his hands are pressed into his coat pockets.

I *love* the coat he's wearing. How well it fits him. How soft it feels under my hands. How much it complements his complexion and his dark hair and eyes. He's also wearing a forest green scarf—Felix is definitely the kind of man who can pull off wearing a scarf—and his beard has been freshly trimmed.

He is legitimate perfection from head to toe, and a flutter of nerves pushes through my belly. I'm still not used to the fact that he's mine.

Or, I don't know. Sort of mine?

I guess we're technically still just dating—we haven't made anything official—but that feels like a minor technicality because we're together every free moment we have.

"Hi," he says as he leans down to kiss me hello. He tries to pull away after a tiny peck, but I hook a hand around his scarf and hold him close for something longer. *Deeper.*

He chuckles against my lips. "This is not the way to make me want to go hang out with your family."

"It's your fault. You're the one who was standing here looking all delicious and perfect."

He smirks and holds up a gift bag. "For Maddox."

I pull the Appies hoodie out of the bag and hold it up, then let out a little gasp. "Felix, did the whole team sign this?"

"They did," he says.

"Maddox is going to lose his mind." I look up and meet his eyes. "Josh is going to lose his mind. *My parents* are going to lose their minds, enough that they might steal Maddox's sweatshirt and put it inside another shadowbox."

"That's quite a track record. Your entire family with their minds blown?" He presses me up against the wall, and I let out a little gasp. "What's it going to take for you to lose your mind, Gracie?"

He kisses *me* this time, long enough that I'm the one pushing back. "No! Stop it," I tease. "You just said it yourself. We have to go to this party."

He smirks and reaches toward his feet, picking up a second bag, this one just a regular one from the Appies merch store. "There's a signed jersey in here for Josh, too. And one for each of your parents. I didn't want them to feel left out, but I thought we might give them to them after the party so it doesn't overshadow Maddox's big day."

My heart squeezes the tiniest bit. "Felix, you didn't have to go to all this trouble."

He shrugs. "It wasn't any trouble. I see my teammates every day. I just threw a few things on the table in the locker room, put my goalie pads on, then blocked the door until they gave me what I wanted."

"Right," I say, though I can't help but grin. "That doesn't sound like any trouble at all."

I stare at Felix for a long moment. Sometimes, I'm not even sure he's real.

This morning for breakfast, I had homemade apple butter on my toast because yesterday, when Felix ran across the street to help Mrs. Dobson with her groceries, she gave him a jar to say thank you. When he replaced everything in my apartment, he used top-of-the-line materials and bought the very same mattress he has in his guest bedroom to replace my ruined one. He even replaced my stove, since one of the burners was acting up, and he wanted to make sure everything in my apartment worked perfectly. Then there's the youth clinics with the hockey team and the way he's constantly feeding his teammates and making everyone feel seen and welcome. All of it is amazing. *Of course* it's amazing. But it's also a lot. And I don't want Felix to think this level of going above and beyond is what I expect or need.

I love that he's always taking care of people, but is he taking care of himself? Does he ever say no?

I take the bag of extra Appies jerseys and lean up to kiss him one more time. "This was really sweet of you, Felix."

Together, we head down the stairs and to Felix's car.

I'm glad he's driving for two reasons. One, my car started making a very weird sound on my way home from school on Friday, and the less I drive it, the better I feel. And two, I'm a nervous wreck.

My parents know I'm coming to Maddox's party, but they have no idea I'm bringing Felix. That alone will be shocking enough. But when they learn that we're dating...I can't even imagine what might happen.

Actually, that's not true. I can perfectly imagine it. I just don't want to. Because in their eyes, it will mean I've finally come back to the fold. They will treat me differently because now, I will have given them evidence that I'm one of them. That I don't actually hate hockey after all.

I don't love how much I want that feeling.

I also don't love that I've never had it before just by being me.

"Turn left right up here," I say to Felix as we approach Josh's neighborhood. I point to a house with navy blue shutters and an Appies team flag hanging off the front porch. "That house right there is actually my parents' house," I say. "And this one here is Josh's. The one with the balloons on the mailbox."

"Have they always lived so close to each other?" Felix asks.

"Not always. Josh and Jadah moved in probably two, maybe three years ago?" I say. "They lived with Jadah's parents before that, saving up money until they could afford their own place. When they moved in here, it made my mother ridiculously happy."

Felix cuts the ignition, then reaches over and takes my hand, lifting it to his lips and pressing a quick kiss just above my knuckles. "I'm excited to meet everyone."

Before I can respond, his gaze shifts, and he looks out the window behind me. "Looks like we've already been spotted."

I turn and see Josh crossing the yard, his eyes narrowed like he's trying to see who I've brought with me to the party. "Oh boy," I say slowly. I give Felix one more look. "Better brace yourself."

I climb out of the car and smile at Josh.

"Hey!" he says as he pulls me into a hug. "I didn't know you were bringing a..." His words trail off, and I can only assume it's because Felix has gotten out of the car.

He steps up behind me, and Josh's eyes dart from me to Felix, then back again.

"Josh," I say slowly, "this is my—"

"Felix Jamison," Josh says, his eyes wide. "You're Felix Jamison."

For once, I don't mind that Josh cut me off because I'm not sure how I would have finished that sentence. This is my...date? That probably would have been easiest. But the word that popped into my head? Pretty sure it was *boyfriend.*

Would Felix have been okay with that?

"How are you, man?" Felix says, extending his hand to Josh.

Josh shakes it and starts to laugh. "I can't believe this is happening." He looks at me. "I told you to get Maddox an Appies hoodie, and you bring him the freaking goalie instead?"

I smile with feigned nonchalance. "He *did* tell me Felix was his favorite player."

"He is!" Josh says. He looks at Felix. "You are. Seriously. It's such an honor. We're big fans."

"I appreciate it," Felix says. He holds up the gift bag holding Maddox's new hoodie. "We brought the sweatshirt, too. Signed by the whole team."

"You're lying. The whole team?" Josh shakes his head, his smile wide as he leads us toward the house. "Seriously, best present ever. Gracie, you win the award. I'm not sure how much you had to pay him to come for Maddox, but *man*, nothing will ever compete with this."

I catch Felix's eye, and we share a quick smile.

Josh chuckles. "Man, I hope she paid you a lot because you're about to be swarmed by a dozen hockey-obsessed ten-year-olds."

"I've done enough youth clinics to be comfortable with that crowd," Felix says. "But she's not paying me anything. Gracie and I are neighbors." His eyes dart to me, a question in his expression, and I realize for the second time that we really should have talked about how I was going to introduce him to my family. Probably shouldn't spring boyfriend on him before we have an actual define-the-relationship talk, but surely he'll be okay if I tell them we're dating.

I lift my shoulders in a tiny shrug, and Felix nods as if to say whatever I want is fine with him.

"Neighbors who are also...dating," I add slowly, and Felix reaches over and takes my hand, giving it a quick squeeze.

Josh pauses, spinning around to face me.

"You're dating?" He props his hands on his hips, his gaze narrowing. "*You* are dating Felix Jamison?"

"That *is* what I just said," I answer.

Josh frowns, the furrow between his brows deepening. "But...he plays hockey."

Oh geez. I knew my family might be surprised, but Josh is going to bring this up here? Right in front of Felix?

"Yep," I quickly say, grabbing Josh's shoulder and steering him toward the front door. "Can we go inside now? How's Dad? Has he been doing the exercises his doctor gave him?"

Josh shoots me a look, but there isn't time to say anything else because the front door opens and Maddox appears.

My nephew's eyes land on me, and he smiles, then they lift to Felix.

"What?!" he says, with an exaggerated emphasis that makes me fight to stifle my laughter. "Felix Jamison is at my birthday party?!"

Felix drops to one knee in front of Maddox. "Hey, Maddox," he says. "I hope you don't mind me dropping by."

Maddox nods, his wide eyes and stunned expression identical to what I saw on my brother's face not five minutes ago.

"You came here for me?" Maddox asks.

"I sure did. I'm a friend of your Aunt Gracie's. She told me you're an Appies fan."

"Are you serious?!" Maddox yells, his hands lifting to either side of his head like he can't believe what's happening. "*Of course* it's okay. My friends are going to freak!" He grabs Felix's hand and tugs him back to his feet and toward the door. "Come on! Everyone is in the backyard!"

Felix looks over his shoulder and grins, even as Maddox is dragging him through the house. Josh and I follow behind, quickly enough that we hear Maddox yelling to my parents, "Grandma! Grandpa! Gracie brought Felix Jamison to my birthday party!" Then he's pushing through the back door and yelling to his friends.

"I'll go make sure Felix doesn't get mauled," Josh says, but then he turns back and lifts a finger, pointing it right at me. "But we're going to *talk,* sister."

He disappears into the backyard, leaving me with Jadah and my parents who are staring at me, their eyes wide.

Mom presses a hand to her chest. "Was that *actually* Felix Jamison who just walked through the living room?"

"It was," I say.

Dad immediately moves to the window and raises the blinds, practically pressing his face against the glass.

"Don't stare, Sam!" Mom says. "He'll see you!"

"What do I care if he sees me?" Dad says. "He came to the party, didn't he?"

Mom is at the window now, too, and she nudges Dad out of the way. "Let me see. Jadah, where's my phone? I want to take a picture. Ohhh, just look at him! He's bigger in person, isn't he? The size of those hands!"

"Those are goalie hands," Dad says. "What is he, six-three? Six-four?"

"Six-four," I say. I look at Jadah and roll my eyes, but her expression says she's a lot more interested in why I know the exact height of the Appies star goalie than she is in my parents and their ridiculous antics.

"Look at that, Sam," Mom says. "An actual Appie in our neighborhood! Do you think he likes pie? Maybe I could run home and bake him something."

"He can't eat pie," Dad mutters. "He's right in the middle of his season. Plus, he's not getting pie if I'm not getting pie. Why aren't you offering to make *me* pie?"

"Because your arteries are clogged and you need to drop forty pounds," Mom says. "But I bet Felix Jamison's are just fine."

"Oh geez," Jadah says under her breath. She walks over and stands next to me. "If we don't do something, they'll keep this up for an hour."

I chuckle. "They aren't hurting anything. Let them have their fun."

She shoots me an odd look. "Are you feeling okay, Gracie?"

I meet her curious gaze. "Will you believe me if I tell you I really am?"

"Okay, you're coming with me so we can talk."

I quickly shrug out of my coat, then follow Jadah into the kitchen.

She nudges a bowl of frosting toward me and holds out a spatula, pointing to a tray of cupcakes sitting in the middle of the counter. "Want to help?"

I take the spatula. "As long as you don't need them to be pretty."

"Are you kidding? For a bunch of ten-year-olds? I could drop the bowl of frosting in the middle of the backyard, pour in the candy corn, and throw a bunch of spoons at them and they wouldn't care. I definitely don't need them to be pretty."

I smear a glob of orange frosting over a cupcake, then decorate it with candy corn from a bowl next to the frosting. "How's that?"

"Perfect," Jadah says. "Better than I can do." She hands me another cupcake. "So," she says, "You wanna tell me about the pro hockey goalie you happened to bring to my house unannounced?"

I look up, suddenly worried she's offended I didn't mention my plans. "I'm sorry I didn't tell you," I quickly say. "I was just thinking about how much Maddox would love the surprise. But I should have—"

"Girl. Breathe," she says, cutting me off. "It's fine. You know I don't care like that. I'm asking about *you*. How did you meet him? Are you dating? He's a *hockey player*, Gracie. We both know that's worth a conversation." Her voice drops low. "And spill the tea quick before your mama comes in here and takes over the conversation."

I let out an easy chuckle, a surge of gratitude and affection for my sister-in-law filling my heart. She loves hockey a lot more than I do, but she's never made me feel like a weirdo for how *I* feel. In this family, that's a pretty big deal.

"He's my neighbor," I say. "And yeah. I know he's a hockey player. But he also listens to classical music, and he has the most insane collection of books, and he's..."

"Insanely beautiful and sexy as hell?" she finishes.

"Yes, and *yes*," I say.

She grins and sets another finished cupcake down on the platter between us. "And a really excellent kisser?"

I open and close my mouth, and a blush climbs up my cheeks.

Jadah grins. "Girl. You've got to tell me everything."

I smile and shake my head. "It's only been a few weeks, but I had to stay in his guest room while my apartment was being repaired, and...I don't know, Jadah. I really like him. We've basically been together every night that he hasn't been on the road for games."

"How are you feeling about it? About the hockey and everything."

"Most of the time, I forget he even plays hockey. There's so much more to him than that," I say. "I mean, yeah. It's a little weird. Like I'm having to deprogram myself because I was so anti-hockey for so long. But that was just a childish hangup, and this is real life. *He's* real life."

She smiles wide. "Have you gone to see him play?"

"Not yet. But..."

"But you might soon?" she finishes when I don't.

"Let's not get ahead of ourselves," I say. "I don't have plans to turn into a puck bunny or anything. But if I end up falling in love with him, I'll definitely start going to his games."

Jadah's eyes widen, and she presses her lips together as her gaze darts over my shoulder, then back to me.

I turn around slowly, knowing exactly who I'm going to see. Sure enough, Felix is standing in the kitchen doorway, and I can tell by his expression he's been there long enough to have heard me.

Before I can say another word, he crosses the kitchen to where I'm standing and leans a hand on the counter on either side of me, trapping me in between his arms. He leans close and presses a long and lingering kiss on my lips. Somewhere in the back of my mind, I hear Jadah chuckling, but I don't even care. Felix *owns* me right now. The familiar scent of his cologne, the confident way he just walked over to kiss me, the warmth of his lips as they brush against mine.

The kiss only lasts a couple of seconds, but I feel it all the way into my toes, on every inch of me.

When Felix pulls away, he holds my gaze, his eyes bright. "Challenge accepted," he says, then Josh calls his name, and he turns and heads back into the living room.

I slowly turn around and look at Jadah, who is staring at me, her mouth wide in a disbelieving *O*.

"What just happened?" I say, and she starts to laugh.

"I think he just told you he plans to make you fall in love with him," Jadah said.

I reach for another cupcake, willing my heart to slow.

I guess the joke is on him, because it suddenly occurs to me: I think I already have.

Minutes later, the pizza arrives, and a dozen ten-year-olds push in from the backyard, cheeks and noses pink from the chilly fall air. They're all talking over each other and grabbing for plates while Jadah sets up the food, and it takes all the adults present to keep everything running smoothly.

Felix is definitely the star of the party, as I knew he would be. My parents are surprisingly tame in their adoration, though I think that's mostly because they know the day is supposed to be about Maddox. It could also be that they're still in shock that I'm dating Felix in the first place. It's not like I built a giant wall and painted a "No Hockey Allowed" sign, but it only took a few months for my parents to realize that once I moved out of their house, I was never going to accept their invitations to hockey games or tailgate parties.

For me to just bring Felix to the party like it's no big deal?

It's not something they ever would have predicted.

Still, as the party progresses, it becomes clear just how *happy* they are to have Felix here.

At one point while Maddox is opening his presents, Dad corners Felix in the living room and starts a conversation about the Appies' defensive pairings this season. Felix listens like the gentleman he is, contributing to the conversation and complimenting Dad on his insight.

I've never seen Dad so animated.

When Felix excuses himself and heads to the bathroom, Dad looks over at me and smiles wide, warm affection radiating from his gaze.

It should make me happy. It *does* make me happy.

But it makes a part of me sad, too. Because I've never made my parents this happy on my own. I don't want to dwell on that sadness though. It's been good today, being together like this. It feels like it's time to move on, and maybe, for the first time, I realize how much I want to.

Soon, it's time for the kids to all go home, a process I quickly realize is going to take much longer since Felix is here. I doubt Felix is *always* recognized whenever he goes out. When we've gone out over the past couple of weeks, no one has really stopped us or acted like they knew who he was. But the majority of the kids Maddox invited to his party are friends from his youth hockey league. It stands to reason that parents with kids who play hockey know a little more than average about Harvest Hollow's hockey team.

Felix must stand in the front yard talking and taking selfies for close to an hour. At first, it's fun to see so many people excited to meet him and take a picture. But the longer it goes on, the more uncomfortable I feel.

Felix doesn't have to be doing this. He could go hide in the backyard and say goodbye to exactly zero guests, and no one would fault him for it. But he just keeps standing there. Shaking hands. Talking to everyone like they deserve his undivided attention. He doesn't even waver when several dads want autographs and come into the house looking for something they can have Felix sign. Or when one single mom gets handsy enough that I contemplate heading out into the yard so I can punch her right in her pert little nose. Eventually, Felix manages to untangle himself, but one more second, and I definitely would have been running to his rescue.

"It's awfully nice of him to talk to everyone like that," Mom says from her rocking chair beside me. "And in this weather, too."

It's almost too chilly to be sitting outside, but I love the crispness in the air. Plus, it's beautiful out here. The sun slanting toward the mountains in the distance is turning the maple trees in Josh's front yard a blazing, golden yellow.

"He's always like this," I say. "He's very generous with his time."

She shakes her head like she's in awe. "I don't know how you did it." She lets out a little giggle, her eyes still on Felix who is standing a few yards away talking to Josh, waving as the last kid finally pulls away from the curb. "Snagging a man like that. Especially with how different you are."

I immediately bristle. I was feeling pretty good about my efforts to be mature and move past the differences I've had with my family, but all that effort flies straight out the window when Mom hits right at the heart of what it is I'm struggling to get over.

How *different* I am? What is that even supposed to mean?

Felix shoots me a worried look, his brow furrowed.

Did he hear her comment?

The thought floods my cheeks with embarrassment. I don't want Felix to know how much this gets to me, how much I wish I had my parents' approval *without* a hockey player on my arm. I close my eyes and force a slow breath in through my nose, then out through my mouth.

"It was her music."

My eyes fly open to see Felix stepping onto the porch.

"It was her music that made me fall for her," he repeats. He holds out his hand, and I slip my fingers into his, letting him tug me to my feet. He sits down in my chair and pulls me onto his lap, wrapping his arms securely around me. "Before we started dating," he says, "I would move my most comfortable chair right up to the wall that separates my apartment from Gracie's just so I could sit and listen to her playing her cello. I've been listening to classical music since I was a kid but hearing someone as gifted as Gracie playing—there's nothing like it. There's no one like her."

Felix is looking directly at my mom, so I can't meet his eye. But...he really did that? He listened to me practicing? The thought almost makes me cry. If that doesn't, the way he just defended me to my mother definitely will.

Something shifts in Mom's expression. "Oh, well. That's—we've always been proud of how talented Gracie is."

Felix's arms tighten around me. "Being such a gifted musician—a *professional* musician—it's not all that different from being a professional athlete. It requires the same level of dedication, the same hours of practice, the same commitment to excellence. Your daughter inspires me, Mrs. Mitchell. You really should be so proud."

Okay. Tears are definitely falling now.

"You know," he continues, "Gracie has a symphony concert in a couple of weeks. Right here in Harvest Hollow. Maybe we could all go together and listen to her play. I can only imagine what that level of support would mean to her."

"Felix," I whisper, my voice trembling. "Please don't."

Mom's face blanches the slightest bit, but then tears spring to her eyes and she nods, a hand lifting to her chest. "I...uh...actually, that sounds nice." She looks at me, her blue eyes brimming with tears. "We always loved hearing you play, Gracie."

Felix gives my waist a gentle squeeze. It isn't much, but it's the encouragement I need. "Honestly, Mom. It never really felt like it."

She nods, her gaze dropping to the floor for a long moment. Finally, she looks back at me and nods. "No, I suppose it didn't. But...I know it probably doesn't matter now. But if I could go back...Gracie, I'd do things differently." She motions toward the house. "It was Josh who made me realize. When he walked away from hockey to be there for Jadah, for Maddox, without even a second thought, well...they do always say your children are your greatest teachers." Mom sniffs one more time, then stands up, wiping her cheeks with the backs of her hands. "If you'll excuse me, I think I'll make some coffee for everyone."

Josh has already gone back inside, so when Mom leaves, Felix and I are alone on the porch.

I immediately drop my head onto his shoulder. "You didn't have to do that."

"Yes, I did," he says.

I sit up so I can look into his eyes. They are intensely serious, focused only on me.

"I appreciate that your mom apologized. But they owe you more than that. They need to understand how truly incredible you are."

I shake my head and look away. "Am I, though? I hear what you're saying, but Felix, I didn't make it easy on them. I was snobbish and rude and acted like I was so much better than they were. It's not a wonder they didn't want to watch me play."

"No," he says. "You were a kid who was protecting herself. If you pushed them away, it would hurt less when they let you down. That's not your fault. That's not on you."

"I don't know. I think we pushed each other away. But I don't want to do that anymore."

He shrugs. "Then don't. But it's still okay for you to have boundaries. For you to rebuild the relationship on terms that you're comfortable with."

I sniff and wipe the tears from under my eyes. "How do you know so much?"

He lifts his lips into a small grin. "Ten thousand dollars in therapy can make you pretty smart."

I lift my hands to his cheeks, my fingers brushing against his beard, and lean forward, pressing my lips against his. "Thank you," I whisper when I pull away. "For coming and for dealing with all the chaos and attention."

"I'm happy to be here," he says. "I've had a good time."

The front door pushes open again, and Maddox steps out wearing the hoodie Felix and I brought him. He holds out his arms and spins around. "Looking good, right?" he says, and we both laugh.

"Amazing," I say. "But you'd look cool in anything."

Maddox runs his hand over the side of his head in an exaggerated gesture of coolness, then pulls out a pair of finger guns, shooting at us with dramatic flair and looking way too much like his dad. Serves Josh right, I guess, to have a kid with even more personality than he has.

"Hey, Felix?" Maddox asks. "We're thinking about going over to the rink so I can try out my new skates. Want to come?"

Felix looks at me, his eyebrows raised.

I shrug. I never mind hanging out with Josh and Jadah. Especially if Maddox is along. "It's okay with me," I say.

Felix nods, his look turning mischievous. "I'd love to go skating, but I've got an idea about where we might go instead."

CHAPTER NINETEEN
Felix

I'VE NEVER BEEN SO grateful I didn't make a big deal about Gracie not going to my hockey games. Not that she's really even had a chance yet. But after spending the afternoon with her family, I get it.

The last thing I want to do is pressure her.

She's quiet in the car beside me, and I get the sense she needs to be for a while longer. Even though it looked like the hug she shared with her mom was pretty cathartic, I'm sure she still has a lot to process.

We're on our way over to the Summit, Josh, Jadah, and Maddox following behind us. It only took one phone call to Malik, the Appies manager, to get the okay, then a second to Javi, head of maintenance at the Summit, to get the arena opened for us. This way, Maddox can try out his skates, and I can give him and Josh a behind-the-scenes tour of the Appies' official stomping ground.

Maddox is a cool kid, and I like Josh and Jadah. But a bigger part of me is excited to bring Gracie to the Summit—to show her where I work every day. I may understand why she feels the way she feels. That doesn't mean I don't still want her to be a part of my life. And the Summit is a huge part of my life.

"This is really sweet of you, Felix," Gracie says from the passenger seat. "You've already done so much for my family today. More than you needed to."

"I don't mind," I say as I turn into the back parking lot reserved for players and staff. "Maddox seems like a great kid."

"I think you've made his entire life," she says. "Or at least given him a birthday he'll never forget."

As soon as we get out of the car, Maddox comes charging over. "Am I really gonna get to skate at the Summit?!" he yells.

"Yeah, you are. But you have to listen to everything I say, all right? No messing around."

He immediately sobers and straightens up, his face taking on a very serious expression. "Got it. I'll be good."

I reach over and tussle his hair. "I'm sure you will."

Javi meets us at the door, and I shake his hand. "Thanks for doing this," I say. "Can we hit the ice while we're here?"

He nods. "I thought you'd want to. Everything's open and ready for you." He looks at Maddox. "If the kid wants to ride the Zamboni, let me know. Otherwise, just call when you're ready to head out, and I'll lock up behind you."

We start at the locker rooms first, and Maddox makes solid work of exploring, reading the names off of each locker and reverently running his hands over the sticks, helmets, and other gear that occupies the space. After Maddox has explored the weight room, the PT room, and the coaches' offices, his dad trying, and failing, to seem much less enthusiastic than his ten-year-old kid, we finally make our way to the rink.

We pause in the tunnel, and Josh helps Maddox into his skates. He seems like a good dad, and for a quick minute, I wonder if I would have done the same thing. Would I have walked away from a potential career had I been in the same situation?

I'd like to think I would have. Mostly because watching Josh with Maddox, it's clear I want the same thing. I want a family. Maybe not right this second, but...maybe sooner than later.

My eyes drift to Gracie who is wearing a pair of Jadah's old skates—she says it's been years since she's had her own—and is laughing about how wobbly she feels. She may *feel* wobbly, but she doesn't look it. In fact, the sight of her in skates is doing strange things to my heart.

I'd be lying if I said she wasn't the main reason it's so easy for me to think about fatherhood. It's always been a sort of vague, nebulous thing in the back of my mind. But Gracie makes it seem more tangible. More possible.

I make my way over and hold out my hand. "Ready?"

She nods as she slips her fingers into mine. "Promise you won't laugh at me if I fall?"

"I'll definitely laugh," Josh says as he leads Maddox out onto the ice, passing us both.

"Don't worry," Jadah says. "If he laughs, I'll body-check him and take him out."

Gracie is a little unsteady at first, but skating is a lot like riding a bicycle. Once you learn how, it's hard to forget. Soon, we're circling the rink, hand in hand. I look down at her and catch her gaze, and she smiles.

I had no idea this was a dream of mine, but clearly, it's triggering some kind of dormant desire because I can't stop smiling, can't stop thinking about how good it feels to have her on the ice beside me.

"I like having you here," I admit.

"What, at the Summit?" she says. "Or just...skating?"

"Both, I guess?" I answer. "I'm here every day. It's just...nice to have you be a part of it."

She looks away, her cheeks flooding with pink, and I wonder if she's thinking about that moment in the kitchen when I all but told her I wanted her to fall in love with me. She may not know it, and I don't want to get too far ahead of myself, but those words to her sister-in-law, that once she was in love with me, *then* she'll start watching me play, snuffed out the last vestiges of doubt still lingering in my mind.

"I like being here with you, too," Gracie says, squeezing my hand. "You know, after talking to my mom today, I think what really hurt me all those years growing up was that I just felt like an afterthought."

She slows her skates, and I adjust my pace to match hers, sensing that what she's saying right now is really important.

"I think I just wanted to be seen. It wasn't really about hockey," she says. She stops altogether, and I turn so I'm standing right in front of her. "Or hockey players. Except for Gavin, who was absolutely a jerk."

I reach forward and squeeze her hands. "Agreed. I wish I could meet him in a game and let him know exactly how I feel about what he did to you."

She rolls her eyes. "Would you bodycheck him as the goalie?"

I scoff. "You doubt me? I could play offense for one game."

"Hey, Felix, watch me!" Maddox calls.

I look over my shoulder, watching as Maddox skates a puck toward the net and slams it in.

Gracie leans up and presses a quick kiss to my lips, then nudges me away. "Go on," she says. "Go play with him. I'll skate with Jadah."

I cross the rink to Maddox, who has recovered the puck and slides it toward me. Josh hands me a hockey stick, and I take control of the puck.

Maddox has pretty solid moves for a nine-year-old. He said something about wanting to be a goalie at the party, and I suddenly wish he had his pads with him so we could shoot around for real. He's a little young for the goalie clinic I did a few weeks back, but watching him skate, he's better than a lot of the kids four, even five years older than he is. With a little bit of one-on-one coaching, he could probably grow into a solid goalie.

I make a mental note to talk to Josh about it, see if they might be interested, then spend a few minutes helping Maddox with his grip. After that, we shoot around a little bit, Josh and I laughing as Maddox basically puts on a one-man show, scoring goal after goal and commentating his own moves.

"If personality were all it takes," Josh says, "I think he'd be well on his way."

"Agreed," I say through a chuckle. "But I think he's got some pretty solid skills, too. If he sticks with it, and if he's lucky enough to be big enough, I think he's got a pretty good shot."

Josh stands a little taller. "Really?"

"Yeah. I do. And I'm happy to help him anytime. Maybe do a little one-on-one coaching? But only if he wants it."

Josh quickly nods. "That would be amazing. If you're willing, then, yes. Absolutely yes. I'm sure he wants it."

His sudden enthusiasm gives me pause, and I reach over and clap a hand on his back. "Do me a favor, all right?" I say. "Ask Maddox first. Make sure it's what *he* wants, too."

Josh's expression sobers, but he nods.

"You know your kid better than anyone," I say, "but he's young, and he might change his mind. If he does, let him."

Josh finally smiles. "You sound like Gracie. Please tell her if Maddox decides he wants to try the cello, I *promise* I'll let him try, even if it means quitting hockey."

"Gracie knows what she's talking about," I say.

Across the rink, her laugh rings out, echoing through the cavernous room and making my heart squeeze.

I look at Josh and tilt my head toward his sister. "I'm going to..."

"Yeah, yeah," Josh says, smiling. "I see where your priorities lie. But listen. I know you're Felix Jamison, but I still need to tell you if you do anything to hurt my sister, I *will* mess you up."

"I would expect nothing less," I say.

I skate toward Gracie, gaining speed as I pass her on the inside, then spin around, skidding to a stop and sending a flurry of ice toward her and Jadah.

"Is this you showing off, Felix?" she asks playfully.

I skate backward so I'm facing her as she moves around the rink. "Is it working?"

"Okay, I'm finding Josh," Jadah says. "You guys are just cute enough to make me barf."

I grab Gracie's hand and tug her toward me, then spin us both around so her back is to the wall and I'm hovering in front of her.

Gracie lets out a surprised yelp, her arms gripping my biceps until we're finally still, her breathing coming in shallow gasps.

"Hi," I say.

She smiles and gives her head a little shake. "You scared me."

"If you can trust me anywhere, it's on the ice."

"I can see that." Her nose is slightly pink with cold, her eyes are bright and happy, and I'm...falling in love with her.

The realization hits me with peaceful certainty, spreading through me with comforting warmth. My grandmother used to tell me the story of how she met my grandfather, how quickly they got engaged. It was a ridiculous story—less than two weeks from when they met to when he proposed—but she always told me, sometimes you just *know*. I couldn't imagine how that was possibly true, but now, I believe it. I finally understand what she meant.

I lean down and kiss Gracie, and her hands slide inside my jacket, pressing against my chest. "How are you always so warm?" she asks, her face pressed against my chest. "You're like a big sexy furnace."

I chuckle. "I'm going to take that as a compliment."

Her hands slide up my chest, and concern flashes in her eyes, one palm pressing against my heart. "Felix, your heart is racing."

I chuckle. *Yeah, I bet it is.* "Gracie, I want us to be official," I blurt out.

Her eyes widen, and she catches her bottom lip between her teeth, a question in her gaze.

"I don't want us to just be dating. I want us to be exclusive. I want..." My words trail off, and I close my eyes, suddenly feeling stupid.

Gracie's palms slide up and around my neck. "Felix, I've been with you every spare second for weeks. I don't want to date anyone else. I want exclusive, too." She smiles. "I want official."

We kiss one more time, this one lasting long enough that her brother finally yells at us from across the rink. "Hey, there's a child present," he says. "Might want to dial things back a little."

Gracie laughs against my lips, then pulls away and smiles up at me.

I lift my hands to either side of her face. "Today has made me very happy," I say.

She holds my gaze for a long moment. "Me too."

I almost tell her I love her. Right here on the ice with her family watching. But then she shifts and moves away from the wall, skating away from me.

"Come on, *boyfriend*," she says over her shoulder. "I'm tired. I think I'm ready for you to take me home."

Fire flashes in her eyes, and I get the distinct impression she isn't as tired as she claims. Which could mean very good things for me.

I follow quickly behind, powerless to do anything else.

I'll follow her anywhere. Whatever it takes. Whatever she wants.

I'm hers.

CHAPTER TWENTY
Gracie

"I DON'T WANT TO jinx it by saying things with Felix are perfect," I say into my phone, "But Summer, I really think things are perfect."

It's only been a week since we made things official at the rink after Maddox's party, so I'm willing to own that I'm very much in the honeymoon stages of a brand-new relationship. But it's just so easy with him. Like our relationship was always meant to exist. Like we were always meant to be together.

"Girl, you ride that perfect wave as long as it lasts," Summer says. "And please start telling me all the dirty details whenever you're ready."

I roll my eyes. "*Or,*" I say pointedly, "you can tell me your favorite Christmas song and help me plan my winter orchestra program."

"Boooring," she sing-songs. "But fine. How about *Angels We Have Heard on High*?"

"Okay, let's make this easier. Your choices are *Jingle Bells* or *Up on the House Top.*"

"Wow. So many great choices," she says.

I sigh and push away the bin of middle school orchestral scores. "You're right. These are terrible choices. I think I have to buy new music this year."

"Well, you've got a sugar daddy now," Summer says. "Just mention you're in the market, and he'll probably buy you every middle school Christmas arrangement ever arranged."

"You know, I get the sense that you're making fun of me right now, and I don't think I like it," I say.

"You love *me* though, and you always will," Summer says. "Gotta go. Call me after your audition! I wanna know how it goes."

"Will do," I say. I hang up my phone, happy to have talked to Summer through at least most of my seventh-period planning. Twenty more minutes before the bell rings, then a faculty meeting that hopefully won't last longer than an hour, and I'll be on my way to my audition with the Knoxville Symphony.

It's not that I don't love playing in Harvest Hollow. I do. And I'll keep playing with them whether I get the spot in Knoxville or not. But Knoxville is a bigger city. That means better pay and more frequent gigs. More gigs? More money.

Summer was right when she implied Felix would spoil me if I let him, and believe me, *I do.* But it's still important to me that I make my own way.

Abandoning my sheet music, I scroll back up to my last text message exchange with Felix, in which we argued about the top five greatest authors of the twentieth century. We agreed on John Steinbeck and Toni Morrison, but there's no way I'm keeping Ernest Hemingway over F. Scott Fitzgerald and James Joyce, no matter what Felix says.

I thought Felix was sexy when he talked to me about classical music. And he definitely is. But we usually agree about what we like. We tend to debate about books a little more, something that's becoming one of my favorite things to do. He gets so impassioned, so animated, and more words come out of his mouth at one time than they *ever* do on any other subject.

It's adorable.

He's adorable.

Wrong about Ernest Hemingway, but that doesn't mean I don't enjoy watching him deliver his arguments. It's hard to believe when he looks like he does, all hard muscle and chiseled jawline, but I actually like his brain even more than I do his body.

As soon as the bell rings, I pocket my phone and gather the rest of my belongings, taking everything with me to the faculty meeting so I can go straight to my car as soon as the meeting is over.

I love my job. I do. And I don't even mind the occasional faculty meeting. I'm just on edge and anxious about my audition. It's a big deal that I even got the spot, and I don't want to blow it by showing up late.

When the meeting finally ends, the principal pulls me aside to chat for an extra minute about my budget request for a new bass. The school only has one, but I have two students who both want to play, and having them share is getting a little ridiculous.

Once I remind the principal—*again*—that the football team gets four times the money I do even though my program serves just as many kids, I finally make it to my car. Pretty much everyone else is gone by now, which is only a problem because...my car won't start.

My. car. won't. start.

I grip the steering wheel a little tighter.

"Come on, come on, come on," I say as I try again.

Nothing. Not even a tiny sputter. My lights will turn on, so I don't think it's the battery. Either way, I don't know how to fix it, there's no one left in the school parking lot who can help me, and I'm supposed to be in Knoxville in less than three hours.

Sweat breaks out along my brow, despite the cold temperature inside my car, and my heart pounds in my chest. I just have to think. There has to be something I can do right now. Some way to fix this.

I force a deep breath, willing my mind to slow.

Think through your options, Gracie. Just think!

I drum my phone against my palm, mentally sorting through everyone I know who both has a car and has absolutely nothing to do right now.

Felix is obviously who I think of first, but he's at a hockey thing—the youth skills clinic he committed to weeks ago—and he won't finish until six.

I could try my teacher friend, Abby. I've given her rides before, and she probably *just* left the school. She has tiny kids at home, so I wouldn't ask her to take me all the way to Knoxville, but she could at least get me home and to my cello. And maybe I can find a ride on the way.

I quickly call her, and she immediately agrees to swing back and pick me up.

While I'm waiting, I call Josh, but he and Jadah are already on their way to Asheville for Maddox's hockey game.

I knew that Maddox has a game because if not for my audition, I'd be going to watch him play, too. There's no way my parents will miss Maddox's first game as goalie, which means my entire family is unavailable to help me.

My shoulders sag. What on earth am I going to do?

Abby pulls into the parking lot, and I quickly jump from my car into hers, locking mine behind me. "Stupid thing has been making weird noises for weeks," I say as I settle into her passenger seat. "But why did it have to pick *today* to finally die?"

"You need the name of a good mechanic?" Abby says. "My friend Hazel is great."

"Definitely," I say. "But I've got bigger problems to solve right now." I pull out my phone, staring at the screen like an answer might pop up on its own.

"You've got somewhere important to be?" Abby asks, concern filling her voice.

I nod. "An audition in Knoxville. Sorry. I'm so distracted right now, and I'm being so rude. Thank you for coming back for me."

She waves away my concern. "Of course. I hadn't even made it to the corner, so it's not a big deal at all."

I breathe out a sigh. "You don't happen to have an extra car lying around, do you?"

Her eyebrows lift. "For real?"

"Yes? I mean, *no.* I don't expect you to give me your car. It's just that this audition is a really big deal, and I have no idea how I'm supposed to get there."

Abby frowns, her hands tightening on the steering wheel. "Gracie, I would totally let you use my car, except we're having dinner with Steve's parents tonight, and my car has the car seats in it, and—"

"No no, Abby," I say, reaching out to touch her arm. "I really didn't expect you to say yes. I was just grumbling. I'm sure I'll figure something out."

"Have you asked Felix if he can help?"

I haven't called Felix because I know he won't be finished in time. And he would bend over backward trying to solve the problem for me, even to his own detriment, because that's just how Felix is. But I'm running out of options. I won't ask him to leave his hockey thing early, but maybe I could at least borrow his car.

"Let me try him now," I say.

He doesn't answer the first time I call, but once I text him and let him know what's going on, he immediately calls me back.

"Hey! Where are you now?" he asks.

"Abby's taking me home," I say. "But if you're okay with me taking your car, I could see if she could drive me by the community center to pick it up." Beside me, Abby nods, and I add, "She just said she can."

"Don't do that. I'll just come meet you at home, and I'll drive you to Knoxville," Felix says.

Warmth fills my chest. I would *love* to have Felix's calming presence with me all the way to Knoxville. Especially now that my nerves are even more frayed thanks to my dumb car issues.

"Are you sure? I thought you weren't finished until six."

"Eli and Nathan can finish up. If I'm home by 5:15, will that give us enough time?"

It'll be cutting it close, but if he's driving, I won't have to worry about navigating or parking will be so much easier. "That's perfect. Are you sure?"

"Of course I'm sure. Don't sweat it. I'll be there."

I breathe out a sigh as I hang up my phone. "Okay. Crisis averted. Felix can take me."

Abby smiles. "I still can't get used to the fact that you're dating an Appie."

"Trust me. Me neither."

"He seems really great though," she says as she pulls into the parking lot outside my apartment.

"He *is* really great," I say, not even trying to hide the grin that emerges whenever I think about him. I reach for the door handle. "But so are you for driving me home. Thanks again, Abby."

I only have half an hour before Felix will be home, so I change clothes, make sure my cello is packed and ready to go, then fix myself something to eat. I'm too nervous to want anything huge, and hopefully we'll stop for dinner on the way home, but I should probably have *something* in my stomach, even if it's something small.

After I scarf down a banana and a peanut butter and jelly sandwich, I carry my cello downstairs to wait for Felix.

It's 5:16, and he still isn't here, but it's already huge that he's cutting out early to take me in the first place. I'm not going to grumble about him being a few minutes late.

But then a minute turns into five, then ten.

When I try to call him, he doesn't pick up.

I send him another text, but that goes unanswered as well.

By five-thirty, I've called six times and texted ten. If I don't leave for my audition in the next ten minutes, I won't make it at all.

I don't know how to make sense of the messy cocktail of emotions swirling in my gut right now. I'm nervous, which is making me nauseous, anxious about being late, which is making my pulse pound in my head, and I'm worried about Felix.

Because he would never stand me up like this unless something were truly wrong.

We *just* talked forty-five minutes ago. Does that mean something happened to him?

The longer I stand here, the sicker I feel. Who cares about my audition? I just want to know that Felix is okay.

I'm on the internet looking for a number at the Summit, hoping there might be someone there who can get me in touch with Eli or Nathan when an email notification pops up for my school account.

I don't usually check school email when I'm not at school, but the subject line for this one catches my eye.

Subject: From Felix

I scramble to open the message and read through it once, then twice just to make sure I understand.

Gracie, I'm so sorry. I don't have my phone, and I'm not going to make it. I'll explain everything later. –Felix

I don't recognize the sending email address, and I can't for the life of me figure out why he would be emailing from some random address. But if he doesn't have his phone, how else would he reach me? I doubt he has my number memorized—I couldn't even tell you the area code of his—and we've never exchanged personal emails.

My school email is public, so it's reasonable to think he might have borrowed someone's phone to send me an email.

But why? What happened? And what am I supposed to do now?

Tears brim in my eyes as I pull up the Uber app on my phone and price a ride to the symphony hall in Knoxville. It's almost two hundred dollars one-way.

At this rate, I'm going to be eating ramen for the rest of the month.

I sigh and confirm the ride. A driver will be here to pick me up in less than three minutes.

It takes all three to force away my tears and breathe my way to a semi-normal heart rate. But no matter my breathing, I still can't shake the utter disappointment over how my afternoon has gone.

When I climb into the back of the Uber, my cello taking up two-thirds of the backseat, my mind drifts back to that lonely bus ride after All-State Orchestra my junior year.

I was alone while everyone I cared about was at a hockey game.

Now, I'm alone. And everyone I care about is at a hockey game.

Or at least, in Felix's case, doing something hockey-related.

The thought brings another round of tears, but that just makes me feel silly. The logical side of my brain knows better than to let old emotions from a long time ago impact how I react right now.

That was a different situation. My parents aren't choosing hockey over *me* right now. They're supporting my nephew. They had no idea my car was going to die, and if they had known, they happily would have loaned me a car. I know they would have.

And Felix—he's never done anything but show me that he only wants to put me first. Over and over again, he's prioritized my needs, made me feel seen, made me feel so deeply important to him.

But if that's true...then where is he?

He has to have a reason.

I'm *sure* he has a reason.

But that still doesn't stop me from feeling utterly, desperately *alone*.

Chapter Twenty-One
Felix

WHAT A COMPLETE AND total nightmare.

I pace back and forth through my kitchen, eyes on my open apartment door. I don't dare risk closing it, because I don't want to miss Gracie when she finally gets home. Every time I pass my counter, I look down at my phone, just to make sure she hasn't responded to any of my messages.

So far, she's been radio silent.

Not that I blame her for ignoring me.

There was no reason why I shouldn't have been able to leave the skills clinic early and drive Gracie to Knoxville. If I thought there was any reason why I couldn't, I would never have volunteered to take her. I would have just let her borrow my car.

Nathan, Eli, and the youth hockey coaches were fine with me ducking out an hour early, then a kid hit the ice and made contact with the blade of another kid's skate.

Then everything fell apart.

The kid's parents weren't on site, and the coaches were busy trying to track them down. Which is why, ten minutes later, I was in the back of the ambulance, riding to Mercy General, reassuring a thirteen-year-old wingman named Riley. He clutched my hand the entire time while I reassured him over and over that he wasn't going to lose his arm, he *would* play hockey again, and everything was going to be okay.

Meanwhile, my phone was back at the community center. I must have dropped it when I saw Riley cut his arm and raced over to help because it didn't make the trip to the hospital, leaving me with no way to reach Gracie.

No way to let her know I was about to let her down in the worst way possible.

It was after eight p.m. by the time I left the hospital and made it back to the community center to retrieve my phone.

Since then, I've texted Gracie at least a dozen times, giving her a very thorough explanation of exactly what happened, and called her three different times.

I can't imagine how she must have felt. What it must have taken to find a last-minute ride.

Maybe her friend Abby was able to take her? Or someone from her orchestra?

I have to at least hope she got the email I sent her. Without my phone, it was the only way I could think of to reach her. I don't have the actual digits of her phone number memorized, and we've never had reason to exchange emails.

But her school email is public.

It felt like a stroke of genius when I convinced one of the nurses at the hospital to let me borrow her phone long enough to find it. I was able to pull it right up, then the nurse suggested I send Gracie a message directly from her account. Logging onto my own email on a stranger's phone felt too complicated, so I did as the nurse suggested, then crossed my fingers Gracie would see the message.

Genius idea or not, it won't matter if Gracie didn't get it.

Growing tired of my kitchen, I move into the hallway and drop onto the top step. It's late enough now that she must have found a way to get to Knoxville, but it's also late enough that if she did, she should be getting back any second.

I groan and drop my head into my hands. The stairs are cold and hard and incredibly uncomfortable, but I'm not getting up. Not when I have to be on a flight first thing tomorrow morning for a game in LA.

If I don't see Gracie tonight, I won't see her until Sunday.

Maybe ten minutes later, the main warehouse door finally opens, and I quickly stand, my heart picking up speed as Gracie emerges. I race down the stairs, stopping in front of her and pulling her into my arms.

Her cello is on her back, which makes the hug awkward, but I don't even care. I just want to know that she's okay. Her body is stiff at first, but then she melts into me, her head pressing against my chest, and her arms lifting and wrapping around my waist.

"I'm so sorry," I say into her hair. "I'm so sorry, Gracie."

She slowly leans back and takes a deep breath. "I know. I saw your messages."

She moves past me, trudging her way up the stairs like her cello weighs ten thousand pounds. I follow behind her, but I don't touch her, suddenly sensing this is a moment Gracie needs to control herself.

When she finally reaches her apartment, she shrugs her cello off her back and leans it against the wall, then unlocks her door.

She looks exhausted—mentally, physically, emotionally.

My heart squeezes, and I swallow against the sudden dryness in my throat. "Did you find a ride?" I ask.

She lets out a little chuckle. "I paid for an Uber."

I close my eyes. An Uber to Knoxville couldn't have been cheap. "I'll cover the cost of the Uber, Gracie. This is my fault."

"It isn't," she says. "No more than it's my fault for ignoring the noise my car has been making for weeks. How could you have known some kid was gonna get his arm sliced open? I know you wouldn't have left me on purpose."

I hear the words she's saying, but I'm not sure I believe them. Because it doesn't really seem like *she* believes them.

She drops her eyes, her fingers running over the hem of her yellow scarf over and over again.

"But I still have to wonder..." Her words trail off, and she shakes her head, like she isn't sure how to finish.

"Just say it, Gracie," I prompt. "Whatever it is."

She looks up and holds my gaze. "Did you really have to get in the ambulance with him?" She wipes at the tears on her cheeks. "I know his parents weren't there yet, and I know how you are, how much you want to help people. But couldn't Eli have gone? Or one of the coaches? Why did it have to be you?"

The question hits me like a rib-crushing punch.

All I was thinking about when I climbed into the ambulance with Riley was Gracie. How I needed to get to her. How I didn't want to let her down. So why did I say yes? Why, when Riley begged me not to leave him alone, did I say okay? Even when I understood the dilemma it would create for Gracie?

I think back to that moment, to the expression on Riley's face, to the way the EMTs looked at me so expectantly. I didn't want to disappoint them. I didn't want to disappoint the coaches, who were driving behind the ambulance. The accident happened on my watch. I didn't want anyone to think I wasn't doing my part, that I wasn't doing a good job.

"I love that you're so generous," Gracie says. "I love that you're always volunteering and helping people and taking care of people. But I didn't love it tonight. Because I needed you. And you weren't here because you were helping someone else."

It was Parker who last talked to me about this, though I've heard the same thing from my therapist numerous times. *You don't have anything to prove, Felix. You're doing enough.*

Now, that need to prove myself, to measure up to some invisible yardstick, has hurt the person I care about most.

Gracie leaves her door and steps toward me. "I don't want to be mad about this, okay?" She slips her arms around my waist and tucks herself into my chest. "Rationally, I know you wouldn't have abandoned me unless you felt like the circumstances were truly out of your control. But I'm not feeling particularly rational right now. I'm so tired, and I'm pretty sure I blew my audition, and I just...I think I need to be alone for a little bit."

I nod, my hands rubbing up and down her back. I wish there was something I could say. Something I could do to fix things, but I'm not going to push her when she's telling me explicitly what she needs. Even if it means going to California before this is resolved.

Slowly, she steps away from me and moves back to her door, where she picks up her cello.

"Gracie, I fly to LA first thing tomorrow morning."

She briefly closes her eyes as she breathes out a sigh that's so weary, so heavy, I can feel its weight all the way across the hallway. "I forgot."

"I wish I didn't have to go," I say.

"It's your job, Felix. You have to go."

I *do* have to go, but that doesn't mean I have to like it. Maybe it'll be good for me, though. Clearly, I have some things of my own to sort out.

I've always justified my need to please because what bad can truly happen when I'm the only person who is impacted?

So I'm generous. Who cares?

But tonight, it impacted Gracie. And that can never happen again.

She has to be my number one. And I have to trust that setting boundaries to respect that priority won't make me a bad person. It *will* make me a better partner.

"Can we talk as soon as I get back?" I ask.

She nods. "Yeah. I'd like that," she says.

Then she carries her cello into her apartment, closes the door, and leaves me in the empty hallway.

I don't fault her. I brought this fully upon myself.

Now I just have to figure out how to make it up to her.

Chapter Twenty-Two
Gracie

W HEN I WAKE UP the morning after the worst audition of my life, I find a text message from Felix that arrived at 5:14 a.m.

Felix: My apartment is unlocked, and my car keys are on the counter. Thought you could use my car while I'm gone until we figure out what's wrong with yours. Miss you already.

I lean back onto my pillows and drop my phone onto my chest. It's sweet of him to leave me his car. I hadn't even thought about how I'm getting to school this morning, so he solved my problem before I even remembered I had one.

It's a very Felix thing to do. The man is *always* going above and beyond. I can't truly be mad about that.

But it still stung when he let me down last night. And I'm still not sure he should have prioritized a thirteen-year-old hockey player over me. Ask me in five minutes, and I might feel like he was completely justified. His text messages didn't give me all the details, but he did say there was a lot of blood, and one of the coaches was freaking out, and *all* the kids were freaking out, particularly the kid whose skate had done the damage, and everyone was just trying to calm the chaos any way they could.

It isn't hard to imagine.

But Felix isn't even one of the coaches. Surely there was someone else who could have jumped in the ambulance.

I blow out an exasperated breath, then pick up my phone and read Felix's text one more time. This time, my eyes catch on one tiny little word. He says I can use his car until *we* figure out what's wrong with mine.

Not until *I* figure it out. *We.*

My heart stretches and pulls.

I really want there to still be a *we.*

I stumble through getting ready for school, seriously considering the possibility of calling in and taking a sick day. But then I think about last year when I ran out of sick days and had to go to school feeling like actual death. There's no way I want to wind up in that situation again, so I toughen up, make myself drink a green smoothie because they always make me feel awake and healthy even if I hate them going down, then go next door to Felix's to grab his keys.

His apartment smells like him, and it makes my heart flip and tumble inside my chest.

As promised, his car keys are sitting on the kitchen counter. But they aren't sitting alone.

Next to the keys, there's a book wrapped in brown paper and an envelope with my name scrawled across the front.

I glance at my watch. As long as I leave in the next fifteen minutes, I'll make it to school on time.

I carry the book and notecard into the living room and drop into Felix's favorite chair. Once I'm sitting down, I unwrap the book first, finding a very old copy of Jane Austen's *Pride and Prejudice*.

I open the book, looking for some indication of the book's age. It isn't a first edition—that would have been three volumes anyway, but it was printed in 1894, which has to make it a collectible. And he's giving it to me?

I open the card next, leaning back into the chair as I read Felix's steady, careful handwriting.

Gracie—I know I can't compete with Mr. Darcy when it comes to written apologies. So I might be doing myself a disservice by giving you a gift that makes it possible for you to compare his words to mine. I also told myself I ought to leave you alone, give you some space to process how you're feeling. But I've been trying to sleep for hours, and it's clear I won't succeed if I don't tell you how I feel.

When you asked me why it had to be me who climbed into the back of the ambulance with Riley, I realized a few things. The first is hard to admit. Because it makes it seem like my priorities are out of order, but I want to be fully transparent with you, so I hope you'll stay with me while I work my way through.

The truth is...it didn't have to be me. At the time, I believed it did. I believed I could not look someone in the eye and tell them I couldn't be who or what they needed. I believed I had to say yes, to be present, to give all my time and energy to being enough.

For a very long time, I have been chasing that acceptance, that sense of purpose and accomplishment. I never found it when I was a kid. I was never good enough for my father, and that has made me overcompensate. I don't like to say no. I don't like to disappoint people.

But as the ambulance pulled away yesterday and I accepted I could not be in two places at one time, I realized the person I didn't want to disappoint most was you. I let you down. I hurt you. And that's the last thing I want to do.

My priorities have to be different now because I'm different now.

They have to be different, because I'm in love with you, Gracie.

I'm so sorry I left you on your own. I'm sorry I chose so poorly. I'm sorry I let my own insecurities interfere with how I take care of you.

I can't promise I won't ever screw up again. But I can promise I will live every day trying my hardest to put you first—to love you like you deserve.

Please forgive me.

Yours, Felix

Well.

How am I supposed to go to school now?

I sniff and wipe the tears from my eyes, then read Felix's letter one more time.

In the space of five minutes, whatever hesitations I had about forgiving him completely evaporate. Turns out, self-awareness and humility, and a really good apology, are incredibly sexy.

Also. I really, *really* love him, too.

A sudden desire to tell him overwhelms me, but it's not exactly the kind of thing I want to say in a text. I want him to look in my eyes when I tell him I understand. When I tell him that no audition in Knoxville or anywhere else is more important than he is, than what the two of us share.

But how?

A sudden thought pops into my brain, and a jolt of excitement pushes out to my limbs, making my hands tremble.

Felix *did* hear me say that once I was in love with him, I would go to his games.

I bite my lip as I stand and cross back to the kitchen so I can retrieve my phone.

I glance at my watch, then send Abby a quick text, asking her to cover the first few minutes of my first period. She has her planning period first, so it shouldn't be a big deal, and I'm definitely going to be a little late.

Then I text Summer.

Because I think I need to go to California to watch a hockey game, and if anyone will give me the courage to make it happen, it's her.

"This is seriously the most exciting thing we have ever done," Summer says as we wheel our suitcases through the Asheville airport.

"It's the craziest thing we've ever done," I say. "And I still can't believe you're coming with me."

"Are you kidding me? Taking a red-eye across the country so you can declare your love for a super sexy hockey goalie? This is the kind of thing people write books about. I wouldn't miss it for the world."

"And you're sure it doesn't have anything to do with avoiding your boss?"

"Oh, it has everything to do with avoiding my boss," she says back. "But this excuse is much more believable than the one I was coming up with on my own."

"Yeah? What excuse were you planning on using?"

"A brain-eating amoeba from my sister's lab escaped and slipped into my food, and now my frontal lobe is only partially functional?"

I roll my eyes. "Pretty sure amoebas can't escape or slip anywhere on their own. Also, I think the brain-eating kind are deadly."

Summer frowns. "See? This *is* a better excuse."

"Summer, you're going to have to talk to someone about him."

She presses her lips together. "I know. I will. I'm working on a plan." We reach our gate, already crowded with travelers, and drop into a couple of empty chairs. "In the meantime," she says, "I'm going to escape my own worries by dreaming about your soon-to-be magical happily-ever-after."

"Don't get ahead of yourself," I say. "I don't even know if we'll get into the game."

"Of course you will. Parker will come through."

Parker did say I could reach out if I ever wanted to go to a game. I got her number from Felix the night we ran into them on Maple Street, but I haven't texted her until today, and so far, she still hasn't responded.

It's possibly insane that I'm flying across the country when the entire plan is hinging on Parker getting us into an already sold-out game.

Worst-case scenario, I'll just hang out outside the team bus and wait for Felix to show up. But I really want him to see me *at* the game. Cheering for him. Wearing his jersey. Watching him play.

"Okay," Summer says from beside me, her phone in her hand. "Flint says everything is set for our hotel stay. And there will be a driver to pick us up at the airport as soon as we land."

I shake my head in disbelief. It's hard enough to accept the fact that Summer's brother-in-law is *the* Flint Hawthorne. But to imagine him caring enough about my stupid problems to get us a car and a suite in a hotel I could never afford on my own? It's too much.

Then again, I wouldn't be making this trip without Flint's generosity. After my stupid four-hundred-dollar Uber bill and my plane ticket, I'm double digits away from maxing out my credit card.

"I hate that he's paying for this stuff, Summer."

She waves away my concern. "Oh, I doubt very seriously he's paying for anything. I'm sure they're comping the room."

"Why would they do that? We're not important at all."

"But Flint *is* important, and if they give him a free room, the next time he's in town, he'll stay with them and bring them all kinds of positive press and more business. Crazy, right? That it's the celebrities who get all the free stuff when they're the ones who can actually afford to pay for it."

Our boarding group is called, and we both stand up, Summer dropping her phone into her bag before slinging it onto her back. "Still, even if Flint is paying for it, I promise he's not sweating it. He's generous like that. *And* he's an Appies fan."

"What? Is he really?"

She nods. "I mean, he grew up in Silver Creek. That's not so far from Harvest Hollow that he couldn't be an OG fan. But it could also just be the Appies social media. He's definitely not the only celebrity who's taking notice."

"I can't wait to tell Parker that Flint Hawthorne is a fan of her work."

"Oh, right. So the one who we're hoping can get us into the game is the social media manager?"

I nod, even as my phone buzzes in my pocket. I pull it out, smiling wide when I see Parker's text. "She is. And she finally just responded."

Summer lets out a little squeal. "This is going to be so great, Gracie."

I send Parker a quick text, then scan my boarding pass and make my way onto the plane.

It's going to be a long night.

But there's a certainty deep in my bones that it's going to be worth it.

CHAPTER TWENTY-THREE
Felix

"Seriously, what's wrong with you, man?" Alec says from across the locker room. "You're missing saves that my grandma could make."

"Hey, give it a rest," Eli says. "You're not looking so hot yourself."

"Eli's right," Logan says as he tosses down his stick. "But Alec's right, too." He looks right at me. "You're definitely off your game tonight."

I drop my head into my hands. I am *completely* off my game. My focus is gone, my reflexes are trash, and I'm distracted by things both in the game and inside my own head.

Mostly, I just can't stop thinking about Gracie. *Worrying* about her. Wondering what she's thinking. If she liked the book. If she read my letter.

But I can't be thinking about all that now.

It's been years since I've played this badly. One period in, we're down zero to three, and all three goals were easy shots I should have blocked.

Coach shows up in front of me, arms folded across his chest. "Felix, you know how much I preach about this being a team effort. No one player is ever going to lose a game on his own. But we're playing against a tough team, and we need you at your best. If that's not possible, tell me and we'll sub in Hendrix."

Hendrix is the newest guy on the team—the back-up goalie to our back-up goalie—and he's nowhere near ready to face the team we're playing tonight. If Peterson were here, he might could handle them, but his wife decided to have a baby this week, so we're playing without him.

It has to be me.

I have to get my head in the game.

"I can do it," I say. "I just need a few minutes to regroup."

Coach reaches forward and drops a hand on my shoulder, a gesture I appreciate even if I can't feel it through my heavy pads. "You sure you're okay? You know you can talk to me."

"I'm okay," I say. "I've got this."

He nods. "All right. I trust you. Take a minute and find your center. You've got the skills to block every single one of the shots they're going to fire at you out there." He taps the side of his head. "It's a mind game now." He claps me on the shoulder one more time, then turns his attention back to the rest of the team.

I pull my phone and headphones out of my locker and crank up the heavy metal of all classical compositions, Stravinsky's *The Rite of Spring*. It's not my regular go-to, but if anything will drown out the sound of my own thoughts while also firing me up, it's the dissonance and chaos of this piece.

Five minutes later, I'm still not as focused as I'd like to be, but I at least feel more like myself, more in control of my thoughts.

By the time I stand up, the team is already making its way out of the locker room and back to the ice for the second period. Parker is in the hallway outside the locker room, nodding at the guys as they pass by. When Logan reaches her, she leans up and whispers something to him. His eyes dart to me, then he nods, and Parker disappears down the hallway.

Logan hangs back, waiting for everyone else to leave before he falls into step beside me.

"What's going on?" I ask.

He pulls on his helmet and secures it under his chin. "Hang with me when we get on the ice," he says. "Just for a second. There's something I want to show you."

I don't have time to protest, because we're nearing the ice, and I'm still carrying my gloves. I slide them onto my hands, then I'm on the ice beside Logan, stick in hand. We circle the rink once, which is typical, but Logan stops short right beside the penalty box and points into the stands.

At first, I don't know what I'm supposed to be looking at, but then I see her.

Gracie.

Sitting just behind the glass, a huge smile on her face, wearing an Appies jersey.

Gracie is here—*in freaking California*—at my game.

I don't know how to process, how to make sense of her being here. She was in her apartment when I left yesterday morning, and now, she's *here*, not just at a hockey game, but at a hockey game on the other side of the country.

Because of me.

I can't help but think back to what she told her sister-in-law at Maddox's party, that she'd start going to my games once she fell in love with me. She might have been joking. But when she lifts her shoulders in a shrug, eyes glistening, I understand exactly what she's saying.

Those words were real.

And that's why she's here.

As I watch, Summer, who is in the stands right beside Gracie, hands Gracie a poster, motioning for her to hold it up.

Gracie laughs as she lifts it over her head, holding it up for me to see. The poster reads *MR. DARCY? NAH. GIVE ME FELIX JAMISON.*

Behind me, my teammates bang their sticks against the wall, and I turn to see them clustered around the bench, grinning and cheering. Even Coach Davis has a smile on his face.

Alec tilts his head toward the net, and I nod, understanding exactly what he's telling me.

Game on.

And this time, I'd better bring it.

I've never played with a girlfriend in the stands before.

Turns out, wanting to show off is a great motivator.

The opposing team brings the puck down fast, and I catch a shot in my glove in the first twenty seconds of the period. It feels good to make a solid save, but when two more shots come hard and quick, I'm ready for our defense to pick up and give me some breathing room. I block them both, then Logan takes the puck down, gaining speed as he enters the zone, before sliding the puck over to Eli who sends it flying past the goalie.

Getting a goal on the scoreboard is the morale boost we need, and we dominate in the second period. Eli ends with a hat trick, Logan scores once, and I block all but one shot, so we go into the third tied at four.

But momentum is on our side, so even though the LA team had a perfect record going into the game, we shut them out in the last period and end the game with a win, seven to four.

We're all flying high, but I'm soaring for a different reason than everyone else.

I can't wait to see Gracie, to have her in my arms.

I make fast work of stripping off my gear and getting showered. I even manage to smile through the ribbing my teammates give me.

"What are you hurrying for, Jamison?" Alec asks. "It's almost like you think there's someone here to see you."

"Pretty sure she's here to see me," Eli says. "I always knew she'd come around."

I grin and throw a towel at Eli's head. "Yeah, you wish." I pull my shirt over my head, then look up and make eye contact with Logan. "Did you know Gracie was coming?"

He shakes his head. "Not until Parker told me. I hope she keeps coming, though. If she makes you play like you did in the third." Logan looks down at his phone. "Speaking of Parker *and* Gracie, they're together and waiting for us in the family room. You ready?"

There have been more than a few moments when I've watched other players greet their wives and girlfriends after games and wondered what it might feel like. I've tried not to linger on the thought because it always feels a little caveman-ish to expect a woman to be here just so she can watch me perform and compliment my manliness.

But having Gracie here doesn't feel like that. I *do* want her to be proud of me, and I definitely played harder because I knew she was watching. But it isn't about *me*. It's about us. About sharing a life. It's about wanting something that's important to me to matter to her, too.

Still, I recognize it's no small matter that she's here. Especially after the hard day she had right before I left, after the way we left things.

As soon as we reach the family room where team members' wives and family members wait for the players, Logan immediately moves into the room and heads toward Parker, but I stop and watch Gracie from the doorway.

She looks beautiful, her face animated as she laughs at something Summer is saying.

Nathan, of all people, is standing between the two women, eyes locked on Summer, looking somewhere between stunned and totally captivated. Or maybe he's both?

With Nathan, it's always hard to tell.

Gracie is wearing the black, white, and teal jersey we wear for away games, and I feel a sudden urge to see her turn so I can read the number that's on the back, see the name blazoned across the top.

Maybe I am like a caveman because I really want that jersey she's wearing to be mine.

As soon as Logan reaches Parker, Gracie looks up, her eyes scanning the room until they land on me.

Then she's running across the room and throwing herself into my arms.

I pick her up, holding her against me as her hands fly around my neck. Her lips crash into mine. We've kissed countless times over the past few weeks, and all of them have been amazing. Kisses that say *I want you, I need you,* even just *I like you.*

But this is the first kiss to say *I love you.* And that makes it the kiss to rival all kisses.

Slowly, I lower her back to the ground, but I keep my arms around her.

She's here—*she's here*—and I don't ever want to let her go.

When she finally pulls away, she looks up at me, brown eyes shining. "Felix, you were amazing," she says, words tumbling out quickly. "When you were hugging the post, and the other team circled the net like they were gonna shoot through the back door, and you whipped around and caught the shot even though you weren't even looking at them. It was brilliant. It was—"

I cut off her words with another kiss. Because honestly, if she's going to talk hockey like she's some kind of professional sports analyst, what choice does she give me?

She smiles as she pulls away. "What was that for?"

"You're sexy when you talk hockey."

She smirks. "I'll have to do it more often."

I nuzzle my nose into her hair. "I can't believe you came to California."

"*You* are in California." She shrugs and bites her bottom lip. "And I wanted to see you play. *And* I wanted to see you in person so I could tell you...I love you."

I pull her closer and lower my forehead to hers, pausing long enough to breathe her in.

She's here, in my arms, and she loves me.

I take a steadying breath. "I love you, too. I've been so worried about you, Gracie. And I'm still so sorry about what happened. I never should have—"

"Stop it," she whispers. "Your letter was perfect. There's no reason to say more than that."

"Even better than Darcy?"

She smiles. "You saw the poster. I'll take Felix Jamison over Fitzwilliam Darcy any day of the week."

I kiss her again, losing myself in the taste of her, the feel of her mouth, the way her body yields to my touch and so easily molds against mine, until a few of my teammates start catcalling from across the room.

Gracie pulls away, her cheeks flushing pink as she tucks herself into my side and turns to face them.

"I'm hurt, Gracie," Eli calls, his smile wide and his tone teasing. "You told me hockey players were off-limits."

She shrugs. "They were. But...well, watch this." She looks up at me. "Hey, Felix, can you name three classical compositions for cello? And make them each from a different century."

My amusement over whatever Gracie is trying to prove is quickly eclipsed by my need to actually answer the question. Fortunately, it isn't a *hard* question, so it doesn't take long. "Bach's Cello Suites, which...that feels like too easy of an answer, but it's solidly eighteenth-century, so let's start there. Then any of Brahms's cello sonatas—those were all nineteenth-century. And...twentieth-century could be Prokofiev's *Cello Sonata in C Major*?"

Gracie smiles and pats my chest. "Excellent work." She looks back at Eli and smiles sweetly. "Do you want to try the same question?"

Eli laughs and shakes his head. "Man, you let your nerd flag fly that high and it actually made her like you *more*?" Despite his joking, he walks over and pulls us both into a crushing group hug. "I'm really happy for you both," he says, his tone genuine. "Your music sucks, but I'm still happy for you."

Soon, he and everyone else slowly trickle out of the room until Gracie and I are the only ones left. Even Summer disappears, and I get the sense from the exaggerated wink she tosses my way, that she isn't coming back any time soon.

Gracie and I move over to a sofa that's pushed up against the back wall, and I sit down, pulling her down beside me.

I lean over and press a kiss to her temple, and she looks up at me, the overhead light catching in her deep brown eyes. "Did I tell you how much I loved watching you play hockey?" she says, her voice low and soft.

I grin. "That's good to know because you look incredibly sexy in that Appies jersey."

"In *your* Appies jersey," she says, her expression turning coy. "Number thirty-one."

A sharp bolt of longing pushes through me, and I lean down, catching her lips with mine. "You don't know what you're doing to me," I whisper against her lips.

"Probably exactly what you did to me when I found Bach tattooed on your arm."

I chuckle in between kisses. "Should I make it a whole symphony?" I tease. "Cover my entire back?"

"Definitely not. Your back is perfect exactly the way it is. But I do have some ideas about how you could use music notes to decorate the creative center."

"You'd help me with that?" I say, meeting her gaze.

"Of course I would. I would love to. I mean, I'm no designer. You're better off asking your sister to do the heavy lifting when it comes to that. But I saw these hammered metal music notes on Etsy the other day and immediately thought they would look great in a bigger space like the creative center."

"That sounds amazing. You'll have to show me," I say.

I love that she's thinking about it, that we're talking about my life like it's her life, too.

The reality is a relationship isn't going to be easy—not so long as I'm still playing for the Appies. Or any other team, for that matter.

I'll be on the road a lot, and with Gracie's teaching and symphony schedules, I doubt she'll be traveling with me very often.

ABSOLUTELY NOT IN LOVE

But I've never been so certain I want to do whatever it takes to make it work. It still feels like something miraculous that she's in love with me in the first place.

Whatever it takes, whatever she needs, I'm all in.

I don't have a single doubt in my mind.

She's worth it.

Epilogue
Gracie

I HAVE ALWAYS LOVED being on stage as a part of a symphony. But being on an outdoor stage when the weather is perfect, the mountains are newly green, and my entire family is out on the lawn listening?

It's taking my love to an all-new level.

I'm balancing multiple symphonies now, Harvest Hollow *and* Knoxville—turns out my audition wasn't quite so dismal after all—but today, I'm happy to be playing in my hometown.

Well, mostly happy. I'm also a nervous wreck. My stand partner and former teacher retired last month, and when I auditioned for her principal seat, *I got it*. That means I'm playing a solo in our next piece, and if I think too hard about it, I might throw up, which, pretty sure that would ruin my solo.

As we finish our first piece and the audience breaks into applause, I look out into the audience, shielding my eyes against the late afternoon sun, and spot Felix standing off to the left. He's away from the rest of the audience, but he's perfectly situated in my line of sight. I'm positive he put himself there on purpose.

We make eye contact, and his lips lift in a small smile. His head dips in an almost imperceptible nod. *You've got this,* he's saying.

I take a deep breath, the nerves swirling in my belly finally settling from an all-out frenzy to a manageable flutter. Felix would know better than anyone because he's the one who has heard me practicing the last couple of weeks. He's the one who has been my north star, telling me over and over again that I'm perfectly capable of playing the solo, that I'm not going to screw it up.

My conductor looks at me, baton raised, and I nod.

Then I look at Felix, shut out the rest of the crowd, and pretend I'm only playing for him.

My entire family is waiting for me after the concert, as well as Felix, who pulls me into a hug and kisses me soundly. "You were amazing," he says. "Every note of your solo was perfect."

He lets me go, only for Josh to swing an arm around my shoulders. "Not bad, little sister," he says. "You sounded good."

After a few more minutes of small talk and hugs of support from both my parents, Felix and I say goodbye and make our way to his car.

His hockey season officially ended last weekend, and I'm soaking up all this uninterrupted time with him. We're both counting down the weeks to summer when I'll have a few months off from school and we can be totally lazy and lay around all day reading books and listening to music.

Annnnnd teaching private lessons and playing all kinds of wedding gigs and working on the remodel of the creative center. But still. We'll have more free time than we do *now,* and that's saying something.

I honestly don't even care if we are busy. As long as we're together more than we aren't, I'll be happy.

I drop my cello off at my place and change into sweats, then let myself into Felix's apartment. We've started leaving our front doors unlocked—no big deal since the one downstairs is always locked—because we're both in and out of each other's apartments so much.

Felix is already on the couch in the living room, feet propped up on the ottoman.

"Hey, have you seen my glasses?" I say as I kick off my Birkenstocks. "I can't find them."

He looks over his shoulder. "Maybe look in the bedroom? I feel like I saw them next to the bed."

I can't imagine anything getting lost in Felix's bedroom because it is as neat and orderly as the rest of his apartment. Literally the only messes that ever exist in this place are messes that I make, but I look anyway. Maybe they got swept into a drawer or something?

There's nothing out of place on either nightstand or the dresser, but the drawer on Felix's side of the bed is slightly ajar, just open enough that my glasses could have easily fallen inside. I sit down on the bed and open the drawer all the way. Sure enough, my glasses are sitting inside.

I pull them out, then freeze. Because in the back corner of the drawer, there's a midnight blue velvet ring box.

I glance over my shoulder at the door.

I shouldn't look.

It could be anything. His high school class ring. A set of fancy cufflinks.

I mean, it *looks* like a ring box, but that doesn't mean it's an *engagement ring*. It doesn't mean it's meant for me.

I bite my lip. I can't resist.

I'm going to look anyway.

With another surreptitious look over my shoulder, I slowly pick up the box and lift the lid.

Ohhh. This was a bad idea. Because this ring is literal perfection. If it is anything but what I get to wear on my left hand for the rest of my life, I might actually cry. It's not a traditional wedding ring, though it definitely looks like a diamond. But there are blue stones surrounding it, and the setting looks vintage and amazing and exactly like something I would choose for myself.

"Did you find them?" Felix says from behind me.

I gasp in fright and toss the ring box in the air, scrambling to catch it before I slam the box shut and toss it back in the drawer like it's literally on fire. I close the drawer next, slamming it so hard, the lamp sitting on top of the nightstand wobbles, and I have to reach out to save it, barely catching it before it falls to the floor.

I look up to meet Felix's wide, shocked gaze.

"Felix, I'm sorry. I didn't mean...my glasses *did* fall in your drawer, and I found them, and then I saw the box, but I shouldn't have looked."

He slowly moves into the room and sits down on the edge of the bed. He reaches past me and opens the drawer, takes out the box, then carefully opens the lid.

I steal a glance at his face, almost afraid to look, but he doesn't look annoyed or mad. Just...curious, maybe? Or even a little nervous.

"My mom sent it to me last week," he says. "It was my grandmother's ring."

He has to mean *the* grandmother. The one who taught him how to be nice and helpful and to make his own sandwiches. The one who taught him to love classical music. Who inspired his tattoo. Whose name will be on this building as soon as the renovations are done.

That makes the ring even more special. The fact that he's giving it to me—might be giving it to me?—means the world.

I bite my lip. "It's really beautiful."

He leans forward, propping his elbows on his knees. "This isn't how I was going to ask you, Gracie." He lifts his warm, brown eyes to mine, and my heart climbs into my throat. "But obviously, I want it to be yours."

"I would very much like for it to be mine, too," I say softly.

He chuckles and runs a hand through his hair, the slight tremble in his hands giving way to how nervous he is. "I wanted to come up with a plan," he says. "A grand gesture or something. Or even just to wait for the right moment. But..."

"I don't need a grand gesture," I say quickly. "I promise I don't. And right now feels like a really good moment." I don't even try to hide the eagerness in my voice. There is nothing in this world I want quite as much as having Felix Jamison as my husband.

His fingers toy with the ring for a moment, then he slowly lifts it out of the box. "Are you sure?"

"Oh my gosh, oh my gosh, oh my gosh," I say under my breath.

Then Felix drops to his knees in front of me and holds up the ring. "Will you marry me, Gracie?"

I nod. "Yes, yes, yes, yes, yes."

He reaches for my hand, which is trembling like a leaf in a fall breeze, and slides the ring onto my fourth finger.

I wouldn't have taken it to mean anything dire if the ring was too big or too small. We would have just gotten it sized and everything would have been fine.

We love each other! It's just a ring! It doesn't have to be a sign of anything good or bad!

But I won't pretend like there wasn't some part of me that didn't squeal, at least on the inside, when the ring was an absolutely perfect fit.

I launch myself off the bed and into Felix's arms, and he lifts me up, spinning me around until we both fall backward onto the bed with an audible oof.

Then we're kissing and laughing and kissing some more.

"I'm sorry if I ruined your proposal plans," I say in between kisses.

Felix shifts to the side, propping himself up on one elbow so he can look down at me. "I just wanted it to be special for you. But I was nervous about involving Parker or the rest of the team, so if you're happy, I'm happy."

I tug him down for another kiss. "I promise I'm happy. This was perfect."

He lifts a hand and runs it along my hair, his thumb sliding across my jaw and grazing over my bottom lip. Fire ignites deep in my chest and crackles along my skin, and I lean into his touch. "I can't believe you're going to be my wife," he says.

I could say the same thing to him, but I'd rather show him instead.

I take hold of the collar of his T-shirt and tug him toward me, catching his mouth with mine. His arm slips around my waist, and I deepen the kiss, my tongue sliding against his. Then he shifts, curving his big body around mine, and we lose ourselves in the taste and feel of each other.

We have kissed countless times before. We've held each other, sought comfort and solace, pleasure and joy.

But it feels different this time. This time, our kisses feel like more than just soft touches and gentle caresses and murmurs of affection and love.

This time, they feel like forever.

This man is all I have ever wanted.

A freaking hockey player.

My younger self never would have believed it. But I'm glad she grew up and accepted that sometimes, life is funny like that.

Best to just embrace it, *love it,* and laugh.

For bonus content, including a bonus epilogue featuring Felix and Gracie, visit www.jennyproctor.com

ACKNOWLEDGEMENTS

I'll be honest. I was totally terrified to write a hockey romance because up until I started drafting, I didn't know a lot about hockey! But when my critique partner suggested we write hockey players on the same team, (Go Appies!) I decided to jump in and go for it. And I'm so glad I did! I watched so many videos. I watched games and player interviews. I even watched a twenty minute clip on how to train goalies so I get a sense of what Felix went through! Mostly, I just wanted to get the language right, to get a real sense of what motivates hockey players to dedicate their lives to such an intense and rigorous sport. If I made mistakes, I hope you'll forgive me! I take my research seriously, but I know it can never rival living and breathing a sport in real life. I did my best, but the only thing I claim to be an expert in is ROMANCE. Hopefully any hockey errors didn't detract from THAT part of the story!

As always, it takes a village to get a book ready to go. Kiki. You know how much I love you. Best critique partner ever. Thank you for pushing me. To the women of Sweater Weather, you all are freaking amazing. I loved working with you. Writing with you! Harvest Hollow will be in my heart forever. To my family, thanks for hanging with me. And Josh—you keep me believing that men like Felix really do exist...because YOU do, and that's all the proof I need. Thanks for loving me so well.

ABOUT THE AUTHOR

Jenny Proctor grew up in the mountains of North Carolina, a place she still believes is one of the loveliest on earth. She lives a few hours south of the mountains now, in the Lowcountry of South Carolina. Mild winters and of course, the beach, are lovely compromises for having had to leave the mountains.

Jenny works full-time as an author of romantic comedy. She and her husband, Josh, have six children, and almost as many pets. They love to hike as a family and take long walks through the neighborhood. But Jenny also loves curling up with a good book, watching movies, and eating food that, when she's lucky, she doesn't have to cook herself. You can learn more about Jenny and her books at www.jennyproctor.com.

Printed in Great Britain
by Amazon

34760156R00184